ERIKA,

HAPPY 21st!, BRING YOURSELF
BACK TO AGE 7-10, SHARING YOUR
LIFE WITH DEBORAH. REMEMBER
THE LOVE THAT SISTERS SHARE AND
CHERISH IT FOREVER.

REMEMBER THE FUN OF FAMILY &
CHILDHOOD FRIENDS. THINK OF THE
COMING FUN WITH YOUR CHILD.

HOLD ALL OF IT IN YOUR HEART, FOR
IT IS THOSE MEMORIES THAT WILL
STAY WITH YOU FOREVER.

ENJOY "THE SNOW ANGEL"

John R Crawford

The Snow Angel

The Snow Angel

JL Crawford

Library of Congress Control Number: 2013908366
ISBN: Hardcover   978-1-4836-3734-1
                 Softcover   978-1-4836-3733-4
                 Ebook   978-1-4836-3735-8

Rev. date: 05/21/2013

To order additional copies of this book, contact:
Xlibris Corporation
1-888-795-4274
www.Xlibris.com
Orders@Xlibris.com
135120

Dedication

To the 'real' *Helena*, the source of all of my inspiration, whether in snowy winter, flower-ful spring, summer's warmth, or autumn's glory. An "angel" in every sense of the word!

To *Ruth Gander*, aka Lorraine Gunder. My teacher for but one year, my supporter for half a century, my friend for a lifetime. No one better epitomizes the term "teacher." No teacher has had a greater impact on so many students. She is 'the best of all time!'

Chapter 1

I N A DISTANT land that lay between two rugged mountain ranges, there lived the people of Ashburn. The seasons were kind to the gentle people who lived in the spacious valley between the formidable peaks of Daedalus and Colossus, the names of the two behemoths that reigned supreme over all who lived in, visited, or simply traveled through the quaint farming village. All of the seasons that is, except for winter.

The people of Ashburn had learned long ago to expect the worst and hope for the best, as one never knew what the uncertain, moody temperament of Mother Nature might wield in any given year. Two years before, Daedalus and Colossus had unleashed the most devastating storms on record, pummeling Ashburn with more than seventeen feet of snow in just five storms, which seemed to follow right on the heels of one another month after month.

Just this past winter season the storms came again, dropping almost four feet of snow in only two days. Even now, when spring should be producing tender plants, grasses, and flowers, there was still more than two feet of snow remaining on the ground. In shaded areas, the snow drifted to over five feet. Roads into and out of Ashburn were still blocked and residents feared the pass between Daedalus and Colossus might not open until mid-summer.

It seemed that everyone in Ashburn had grown to despise the snow and didn't care if they ever saw it again. All except the prettiest little girl in Ashburn, who was called Helena. Just ten years old, going on twenty-one, young Helena and her eight-year old sister, Barbara, lived at the home of their grandma and grandpa, Walter and Helen Broadhurst. Ten-year old Helena was her grandma's namesake and proudly made it known to all who asked if they were related.

Helena and Barbara lived with their grandparents because two years previously, their parents had been tragically taken from them while trying to deliver food to residents trapped on the other side of the mountain range. A horrible and unexpected avalanche had trapped six citizens of Ashburn; their bodies not recovered until the following spring. Helena and her sister were sent to live with their grandparents, on their mother's side, who they adored as much as any child could. Stout of heart, proud, and full of youthful vigor, Helena and Barbara called upon each other to 'live the life their parents would have wanted them to.'

Two sisters could not have been more different. Barbara, though younger, was the extrovert, always out and about, meeting new people in the small village. Her brilliant shock of red hair was known throughout Ashburn, as was her proclivity to have an answer for everything, most of which turned out to be right! Even her teachers wondered how this little sprite of a child could know so much at such a young age. Perhaps because grandma-Helen made her two little munchkins bury their noses in books every night, and for a half day on Saturday. Sunday was given to reading their Bibles, which each little girl cherished more than anything else.

The blond-haired Helena, with locks that hung well past her shoulder blades, was the quieter and more reserved of the two, friendly to everyone as well, but tended to keep to herself and to her many animal friends. As only an adorable little girl can do, Helena was seen skipping here and there, smelling the spring flowers, flitting about, engrossed in her own little world. People often heard her speaking, even when no one else was around, but all who knew her thought the introspective little girl was just carrying on with make-believe friends. As shocking was Barbara's red hair, Helena's golden locks were brilliant with light, wisps of it always blowing in her face though she seemed not to care a bit. Helena and Barbara were indeed, the little angels of Ashburn!

Like most of the grown-ups of Ashburn, Barbara had grown to dislike the snow. She still harbored a greater hurt for the loss of her parents than did Helena, but perhaps only because of her age. Helena told Barbara many, many times, to always remember what daddy used to tell us, "Girls, don't belabor the past, what's done is done and you can't change it. You must always look forward, for tomorrow will be a brighter day." Nonetheless, when the snow of this past winter came, Barbara was more melancholy than ever before.

Just the opposite, Helena adored the snow, whether just a flurry or three feet! For Helena, the more the merrier! Tall for her age, skinny as a bean pole, Helena could make her way through even four feet of snow, her long blond hair dragging along the top of a snow bank sometimes the only thing seen by passerby. There was a time when Helena and Barbara played for hours and hours in the snow, only coming in when their delicate hands were frozen inside their ice-encrusted mittens, their noses frozen to a bright red, and shivering so hard that the only sure cure was a steaming cup of hot chocolate—with marshmallow! Now, Helena was content in playing in the snow by herself.

Helena loved to go outside early each morning and look at the new tracks in the snow left behind by the forest animals that lurked just inside the woods edge. She could identify the tracks of rabbits, foxes, squirrels, deer, raccoons, and all manner of birds. Once, she even saw tracks of a mountain lion not far from the barn, and quickly told her father. She would follow the bunny tracks to the very spot in the bushes against the fence row where she knew they lived. The bunnies would see Helena looking at them through twigs and leaves, and would even sit still while she reached in and gently stroked their soft fur. Squirrels looked down upon her from above, barking at her in hopes she would climb the highest branches and pet them too!

This particular morning, Helena had arisen early once more for an even more special reason. She knew that their neighbor, Mr. Cranford, always walked his two beautiful dogs early in the morning, so pent up were they with unbridled energy. They were the two most beautiful dogs Helena had ever seen, and while they barked and emitted a high-pitched scream to most strangers, they loved it when Helena would play with them. They had the softest fur coats Helena had ever felt, and against the brilliant white snow, their black and brown coats and white faces presented the most striking contrast.

Her boots clasped tightly round her legs, her mittens freshly-warmed from the heater felt snug on her hands, and with her cap pulled down well past her ears, she was barely recognizable, save for her golden hair flowing down her back. Closing the door quietly behind her so as not to wake the house, Helena jumped the full four steps from the porch, landing right into the deepest snow bank. Laughing and giggling all the while, she brushed the snow from her coat and headed toward the farm next door.

In the distance, she could see Mr. Cranford out in the field, leaning against the fence, watching his two loyal pets run and romp in the snow, blasting their way through drift after drift. Their coats were so thick and lustrous, they would be warm through and through, even after hours of playing. Mr. Cranford said they were called Shiba Inu's, whatever that meant, and that they came from Japan. He had told Helena that they were from the mountains of Japan, and were sometimes called 'snow dogs,' for their love of cold weather and the snow. Helena didn't really care anything about that; she just loved playing with Samson and Duchess, as they were called.

Helena bounded through the snow in leaps, falling more than once head over heels into a snow bank, each time rousing herself while covered in white powder. As she neared Mr. Cranford's fence, she yelled out, "Samson, Duchess, c'mere guys, let's play!" Mr. Cranford waved at

Helena and turned to go inside, safe in the knowledge that Helena would watch over them, aware of just how much they loved her. Hearing her voice, Samson and Duchess raced each other to see which one could reach Helena first and lick the snow off her face. Samson was a bit bigger than Duchess and could jump higher, so he had a bit of an edge. Certain he was far enough ahead, he turned to see how close Duchess was, but was miffed when he didn't see her at all. Looking at Helena, Samson saw her too, wondering what had happened to Duchess.

Concerned, Samson retraced his tracks step by step, looking for his sister. Finally, more than seventy feet from him, he found Duchess buried in a four-foot snow drift, too short were her legs to get out all by herself. Pawing the snow in front of and all around her, Samson told her all the while, "You silly goof-ball, you should have followed in my tracks. You're too short to get through this deep stuff." Duchess looked up at her brother, blasted a huge ball of powdery snow in his face and took off running and jumping towards Helena. With snow in his eyes, Samson leaped up and raced after her, embarrassed that he had fallen for that trick. Alas, it was too late, for Duchess was already sitting at Helena's side when Samson got there, and sure enough, Duchess got to lick the snow off of Helena's face. Seeing his disappointment, Helena reached over and gave Samson a big hug and kiss, and licked a snow flake off his cute nose!

The three of them played for what seemed like hours, until Helena heard a voice she just, she, she, arrgggghhh! She just didn't know what to think. It was Mr. Cranford's son, Johnny, and boy was he a pest. Of course, all 11-year old boys are pests-maybe ALL boys are pests. He was always teasing Helena, calling her skinny legs and tangle hair, grabbing her book bag on the way to school. Oh, what a bother he was. In school, he was always writing nonsense notes, slipping them into the pocket of her dress. He sat behind her in school and was always pulling her hair. Helena thought that maybe he had a crush on her, but no way did she want to have anything to do with him! He was calling Samson and Duchess to come in for their breakfast and Helena knew that meant she wouldn't see them again until tomorrow. Pulling them as close to her as she could, she gave them each the best and biggest hugs she could, kissing their soft faces and told each, "I love you guys, we'll play some more tomorrow!"

After they had run off, Helena made her way back home. Happy for having played with Samson and Duchess, she was still a bit sad, for spring was nearing and very soon there would be no more snow in which to play. As she walked toward home, Helena spoke as though someone were near. Truth be known, she was talking to the snow. It mattered not that the snow couldn't understand what she was saying, and of course the snow couldn't talk back to her, but Helena loved the snow so much, she just chatted on and on. As she plowed her way through drift after drift, the powdery snow actually swirled round her, rising and falling on non-existent light breezes. Snowflakes covered her face and cap and each time she clapped her mittens together great puffs of flakes flew in her face. With flakes on her nose, she tried to reach them with her tongue, laughing and giggling all the way home.

Just as she reached the bottom of the steps, her grandma opened the porch door, broom in hand, which meant only one thing—chores to be done! Handing her the broom, her grandma asked, "Helena, whoever were you talking to just now? I don't see anyone about." Helena looked at her grandma and replied, "Oh, no one grandma, I was just talking to the snow!" Perplexed, her grandma turned and walked inside. Stopping short, she turned to Helena and said, "Dear girl, are you not feeling well today? Perhaps you have been outside too long. As soon as you are finished the sweeping, come in for your breakfast and some warm tea! Make sure all of that horrid snow is off these steps before you come in." Helena's grandma despised the snow more than anyone in Ashburn, never having gotten over the loss of her daughter and son-in-law. "Yes, grandma," Helena replied and started about her work.

As she started sweeping the snow from the porch, the snow again started rising and swirling round her as though she were in a whirlwind, but there was no wind at all. Helena loved the fine white powdery crystals and she danced inside the whirlwind as though she were in a snowstorm. A loud knocking startled her and looking in the window she saw her grandma watching her, a stern scowl on her face. Helena stopped her dancing and twirling and went back to sweeping the snow from the porch.

Snowflakes adorned her nose and eyelashes and if she stretched her tongue out all the way as far as she could, she could just feel the cool wetness of the flakes on her nose. She wondered why the snowflakes didn't melt when her tongue touched them, but sure enough, they stayed right in place. Sticking out her tongue, she shook her head as hard as she could so snowflakes on her cap and eyelashes would fall to her tongue. They were so cold and refreshing, but again, they did not melt.

Helena looked inside the window to be certain her grandma was not watching and, turning her back to the door, said out loud, "Snowflakes, why do you not melt on the tip of my tongue," as though she would receive a reply. She swept and she swept until the porch and steps were clear, having forgotten all about the snowflakes on her nose and tongue. Readying herself to go in for breakfast, she heard the tiniest little voice say, "Don't let us go inside, you must leave us outside in the cold air." Startled, she turned to see who had sneaked up behind her to poke fun. Looking under the porch, she called out, "Johnny Cranford, are you under there? Come out right this instant, if you are! That was not funny!" Peering into the darkness under the porch, Helena half-expected Johnny to jump out at her, but no one was there.

She was certain that she had heard someone speaking, and someone most definitely told her to not let them go inside. What on earth was that all about! Was her grandma correct and was Helena as simple as her grandma sometimes thought her to be? Finding no sign of Johnny Cranford about, Helena climbed the steps to the house, but as she reached for the door handle, the same, tiny voice called out, "No, don't bring us inside, we will melt for sure!" Spinning round and round, Helena quietly asked, "Who's there? Who is speaking to me? Come out, come out, I will not hurt you."

And there, on the end of her nose, jumping up and down, were three glistening snowflakes! In their tiny little voices, Helena heard them say in unison, "It is we, dear Helena, friend of the snow, who speak to you. If you bring us inside, we will surely melt away. You must leave us outside so we may play with you again tomorrow!" Helena shook her head and watched the three flakes float gently away, landing next to her on the porch railing. Bending closely, Helena asked, "Why did you not melt on my nose, or on my tongue all the while you have been there?" The biggest snowflake of the three moved closer, its entire being sparkling in the sun like the most brilliant diamond. In a deep man's snowflake voice, he said, "Helena, though your nose is warm enough to melt us, and surely your tongue as well, we do not melt where we are wanted, where we are liked. It is only the places that do not want or like snowflakes that we melt away!"

Unable to believe what she was hearing, Helena mumbled, "You can speak? You can understand what I say? How is it that . . ." Interrupting her, the snowflake replied, "Yes, of course we can hear and understand you, Helena, and speak to you as well. We are just one more part of nature, and the great Mother Nature has endowed us with the ability to speak in all languages where we come to rest. If the winds of tomorrow blow us to another country, we will speak to the people of those lands, just as we speak to you, but we only speak to those special lovers of snowflakes, and not everyone loves snow." As though apologizing, Helena said, "Oh, I know and I am so sorry that not everyone loves the snow as much as I. There are many people here in Ashburn who feel that way, including, I fear, most of my family, but it is only because they are sad."

Stopping her, the snowflake said, "Yes, Helena, we know what sadness the snow has brought you and your family, but you must know that was a different snow, of a different time. We are the snow of today and will only be around as long as Mother Nature provides the cold air we need to live. Soon, we will melt into the ground or into the river, serving the greater purpose for which we were created. Next year a new snow will come, but remember, with the snow of this season, no harm has befallen anyone. Helena, it is not always the snow that is the cause of accidents. People must respect the snow as they do the rain, the wind, and the ice."

Still in utter disbelief that she was actually talking with snowflakes, Helena put out her hand and gently blew the snowflake into her palm, saying, "Oh, snowflake, I do not blame the snow for our loss, though others still do. My mother and father loved the snow and played with Barbara and me for hours and hours, teaching us how to have the most fun ever. I know that Barbara still loves to play in the snow and she will again soon. And Samson and Duchess, have you seen how they love to romp and run and carry on, as though they were born for snow!" Even that pest, Johnny Cranford, loves the snow. He has the fasted sled in Ashburn, but one day, I just know I will beat him in the big race!"

Laughing at her infectious amazement, the snowflake told her, "Helena, we know of your love for the snow and that is why we have chosen you with whom to speak, for we knew that you would listen and believe in us." "I do, I do," Helena interrupted. Silencing her, the snowflake said, "You need only remember that snow will always remain where snow is loved and wanted by all. We cannot stay somewhere for the love of a single, young girl though, or even a couple of people, for when we visit, we blanket the landscape and all must want us to stay. Did you ever wonder why snow melts in one place, but not in another right next to the patch that is bare? In time, people grow tired of the snow, wanting spring to bloom, which is the time when we melt into water and help feed the flowers and pastures and gardens of spring and summer. Soon, people forget it was the snow that furthered Mother Nature's gift of food and fauna."

Realizing for the first time just how important the snow really was, Helena exclaimed, "Oh, snowflake, I don't want you to ever go away. I want you to stay here forever and ever!" With that, she launched herself off of the porch, landing squarely into a huge drift of snow. With both hands, she tossed handful after handful of snow into the air, the wind gently blowing sparkling gems all around her, and she heard them all calling her name, proclaiming, "Helena loves snow! Snow loves Helena!" Giddy with laughter, she made her way back to the porch and asked, "How long will you be here, snowflake? Where will you go when you leave here? Will I see you again next winter?"

The snowflake rose with the breeze and landed softly on Helena's nose. Though not as bright as the twinkle in her eye, he glistened and shined as he spoke to her, explaining, "It is not up to us to decide how long we stay; that decision belongs to Mother Nature, though she has seen fit to keep us here longer than even we had thought. From here, some of us will ride the wind towards the river and help to fill it with fresh water so that your grandpa and others can grow their crops. Other flakes will melt where they lay, allowing the earth to drink of our moisture, bringing forth the green grasses of spring and the pretty flowers that you like to pick and wear in your golden locks. In the end, all snowflakes will turn to water, which will be used to nourish all lands, to provide drink for all peoples and animals, to return the leaves onto the trees, and to continue the cycle that Mother Nature nurtures for all time."

Though she understood what the snowflake was telling her, Helena was saddened for the pending loss of her new friend. Still hopeful though, she asked, "And you will then return next year, and the next, and the next?" "Not I, dear friend of the snow, and not us, my other flakes here, for we will melt into water and serve the greater purpose. Though no two snowflakes are alike, billions and billions more will return next year and thereafter, and we will all appear the same so, as long as you believe in snow, Helena, and speak to the snow each year, you will always have friends in snow, and the snow will be good to you. You must remember though, Mother Nature, in all her infinite wisdom, will not send snow where snow is not welcome by the majority of the people."

"Barbara has told me of the lands to the south and the west, where Mother Nature brings only one season, summer, and it is hot all year round. Does she not bring snow and cold weather there for the will of the people? Do they not want snow, snowflake?" "Your sister is wise for her young years, Helena, and correct she is about the lands of the south and west. Long ago, elders went south and west to find temperatures more suited to their years, and settled in those areas. So vociferous were they that snow would never fall there that, in time, Mother Nature just stopped bringing cold and snow to those lands. In one such place however, called Flagstaff, the people decided that they missed the snow so badly, they implored Mother Nature and the higher power to bring them snow, and in the middle of what is otherwise a desert, cold weather and snow come each season to Flagstaff."

"Wow, what a wonderful story, snowflake," Helena said. "You and Mother Nature have taught me so much. I must share this with Barbara, and grandma and grandpa . . . but probably not with that pesky Johnny Cranford. Please tell me you'll stay around long enough for me to win the big sled race!" The snowflake replied, "We'll not only stay around long enough, we'll help you win the big race!"

All of a sudden, the snowflake and his friends arose in a blast of wind brought forth by the porch door being flung open frantically. Startled, Helena turned just in time to hear her grandma shout, "Helena, what on earth are you doing still out here? I told you to come in and get your breakfast. Surely, you have finished sweeping by now! Whatever has gotten into you, child? And, don't tell me you have been talking to the snow again, young lady, or I'll have your gramps send for the doctor." Without thinking clearly, Helena replied, "Well, yes, grandma, I have been talking to the snow, and you'll never believe what I, I . . . I mean, I was talking while sweeping away the snow, grandma. Of course, I cannot speak to the snow. I was just carrying on with myself as I always do." Rushing inside, she declared, "Oh, grandma, thank you so much for making scrambled eggs and tomatoes; it's my all-time favorite!"

Hiding her head in her plate of food, Helena giggled and giggled, still amazed that she had actually spoken with a snowflake. She knew though, she could never share this story with grandma; maybe with grandpa, because even if he didn't believe her, he would still give her the biggest hug and a kiss and say something like, "Helena, is there any sweeter little girl in the whole world than you!" That's what was great about gramps, he just loved you for who you were, even if you were crazy! Oh, but I must tell Barbara, for she will believe me, and maybe I can get the snowflake to talk with her, too! She'll see just how smart I am, and best of all, when I beat bratty Johnny Cranford in the big sled race, I'll tell Barbara how the snowflakes helped me do it!

After spending the first half of the day reading, with grandma regularly checking in on them, Barbara and Helena had the rest of the day to themselves. Helena had been anxious all day, just waiting to tell Barbara about the snowflakes and all she had learned. Barbara had sensed something in her older sister and as soon as they were outside, said, "Okay Helena, spill the beans. What have you been so anxious to tell me? Do you have a secret to tell me? Did you kiss Johnny Cranford when you were at his farm this morning?"

Aghast, Helena cried out, "Ewwwwwww, oh yuck, whatever made you think I would do that! I would sooner kiss a cow-pie than kiss yucky Johnny Cranford! I would rather hit him smack in the face with a snowball than kiss him!" "Then what is it, Helena?" Barbara asked. "You have been squirming around all morning, like the cat that ate the canary. I just know you have something really, really secret to tell me. So, tell me!" Her hands clasping her sister's, Helena looked her smack in the eyes and said, "Okay, but you have to promise, promise, promise to never tell grandma, and maybe not even gramps, unless I tell them first. And you better never, ever tell bratty Johnny Cranford! Do you promise, do you, do you? Cross your heart and hope to die?"

Fifteen minutes later, Helena had explained everything to Barbara about the snowflakes, her conversation with them, why they melted and sometimes didn't, why some lands got snow and others did not, and above all else, why the snow was so important to the rivers and the lands everywhere, and to people and animals. Barbara had sat with her mouth agape the entire time, first wondering whether her sister hadn't hit her head on a rock diving into a snow bank, or if what she was hearing wasn't the most incredible story! She couldn't help but remind Helena that it was the snow that had taken their parents, but Helena was prepared for this.

Holding her sister's hands tightly in her grasp, Helena looked her in the eyes and told her, "Barbara, dear sister, you must not think ill of or blame the snow for mother and father's passing, for it wasn't the snow as much as it was the avalanche. The snowflake told me that Mother Nature drops snow where Mother Nature sees fit, but the mountains always get more snow because they are colder. Too much snow in one place becomes too heavy for the ground under it to hold it. When mother and father climbed the mountains, they always told us how beautiful the snow was up on the peaks, but that it was deeper and more dangerous, too. The snowflake told me that the avalanche was going to happen because it was ready to happen. No one caused the avalanche, certainly not mother or father; they were just in the wrong place at the wrong time. It wasn't the fault of the snow. You must love the snow for its ultimate purpose, and never forget all the fun we used to have, and can once again."

Barbara hugged her older sister tightly, tears streaming down her face, thanking her for helping her get over the loss of their parents. The two sisters had always shared everything and each of them knew after this, they always would. Still somewhat reticent about talking snowflakes, Barbara asked, "Do you think the snowflakes will talk to me?" "Only if they think you believe in them, and you must convince them that you love snow, for they don't want to be around anyone who doesn't want them," she informed her. "I'll do my best to let the snowflakes know that you really do love snow. Do you think you could really love snow again, Barbara?" Stronger for what Helena had told her of the real purpose of snow, Barbara replied, "I never stopped loving snow, I was just angry with the snow for mother and father. I've always known that snow melted into water and helped feed the lands and rivers, but I guess I just needed something to be mad at. I do want to love the snow, Helena; do you think they'll believe me?" Hugging her sister and best friend, Helena said, "Let's get our coats, and boots, and mittens, and caps on and go outside and find out!"

Running down the stairs and flying through the kitchen, laughing and giggling only as young girls can do, they flew open the kitchen door as their grandparents looked on in surprise. In wonderment, grandma asked, "What do you suppose has gotten into them?" Quite wise for his years, with still a bit of mischievousness in him, Walter smiled slyly, telling her, "Beats me, but from the looks, I'd say that whatever spell Helena has been under of late, young Barbara just got it, too!" Grandma looked at him and said, "Well, it's a good thing they're still too young for falling in love!" Walter wiped a hand across his brow and a loud, "Phew!" was heard, followed by, "I don't even want to think about those days, dear!"

Out the door, Helena took a running leap off the top step, flew through the air and landed face first into four feet of snow, disappearing deeply into the soft powder, her laughter boisterous, though muffled by the snow. Surfacing from the depths, her face and coat covered in crystals,

JL CRAWFORD

she caught sight of Barbara torpedoing into a three-foot bank of snow just to her right. Not as fast as Helena, she hadn't flown as far through the air, but had picked out the next best landing site, and Helena heard her uncontrollable laughter as she came up with a mouthful of snow, her face barely discernible for the white snow mask she wore. In unison, both girls screamed out, "Wasn't that just the best of all time?" And snowflakes swirled round them both; which twinkled brighter, their eyes or the flakes, was anyone's guess.

Chapter 2

HELENA WAS FIRST to pull herself out of the drift, her eyes searching for an unspoiled patch of snow, one without tracks of any sort as though the snow had just fallen. Finding the perfect spot, and knowing not what possessed her, she spread her arms and legs in the shape of a five-pointed star, and allowed herself to fall straight back into the snow! Consumed with childlike excitement and energy, she flapped her arms repeatedly to her side, while opening and closing her legs rapidly together, laughing all the while. Hearing her sister's laughter, Barbara came over and squawked, "Helena, what on earth are you doing? Have you gone mad?" Helena just laughed and said, "I don't know, it just feels good, and it's fun! You should try it, too!" Under her sister's spell of laughter, Barbara found an untouched spot next to her, glanced over to be sure she did it the right way, spread her arms and legs, and allowed the soft snow to buffet her as she fell backwards onto the white carpet.

Having thrown caution to the wind, trusting that the soft snow would comfort the drop, Barbara, too, laughed and laughed as she realized what great fun it was to trust oneself to the snow. Mimicking her sister, she flapped her arms and legs together until the two of them had belly aches. The snow above them was swirling like a snow tornado, crystallized diamonds reflecting their rainbow of colors, and millions of tiny voices could be heard. Helena looked to Barbara and shushed her, saying, "Listen Barbara, I think the snow is talking to us." Both girls fell silent and the air was filled with, "Helena and Barbara love snow! Snow loves Helena and Barbara!"

In utter amazement, Barbara could barely get the words out of her mouth, "Oh, Helena, it's true what you say. The snow is speaking to us. Can I speak with them, too?" Before Helena could answer, Barbara heard a soft voice just on the end of her nose say, "Hi Barbara, I'm a snowflake, you can speak with me!" One on her eye lash said, "Me, too!" Yet another snowflake, this one on the end of one fiery lock of her hair said, "Yeah, me too!" Stunned, all Barbara could say was, "I, I, I don't know what to say! I've never spoken to a snowflake before!" And Barbara laughed at herself, along with Helena and millions of snowflakes!

The two girls lay on their backs for hours, talking about who knows what young girls can dream of, until they realized that the snowflakes were settling down into the snow. Wondrous, Helena asked, "Where is everyone going? Do you not wish to stay and talk more?" A wise snowflake chimed up, "Girls, of course we wish to stay and talk more, but darkness is setting in and we must prepare for tomorrow's journey of the wind. We must sleep tonight for tomorrow we may travels hundreds of miles or, we may melt into water tomorrow, though we gladly accept the fate that Mother Nature has determined for us. If you are up early, before the winds pick up, perhaps we shall have more great times before we travel on." As though they were twins, both girls replied, "Oh, yes, we will. We'll be up with the sun! Good night snowflakes, good night!"

As the snowflakes arose into the sky to find their nightly resting place, they watched Helena and Barbara rise from their snow beds and the wise snowflake remarked to the others, "Look below us, all, where our two new friends lay speaking with us. Look at the impression their shapes have left amongst our carpet of white. The shapes are that of angels, the very angels we see as we fly through the heavens. Can it be that these two new friends are but angels in disguise?" In unison, they "Ooohed" and "Ahhhed," until the wise snowflake said, "Yes, they are indeed, 'snow angels'! They have left their marks upon the snow, yet know not what they have done, what they are, or what they mean to us. We must let all snowflakes that visit here or fly near, know of the special land of Ashburn, where snow will always be welcome!"

After the girls had gone inside to warm up and get ready for supper, grandpa had climbed out onto the porch roof certain that too much snow had accumulated, wanting to sweep it off lest it cave in the porch. As he swept his eyes across the vast expanse of the farm, which, for the blanket of white looked more like a cotton farm in summer, he spied two unusual shapes in the snow. Wiping snowflakes gently off his glasses, he peered more closely at the holy shapes that lay before him. "Could it be?" he wondered to himself. "Could it be that angels have come to rest upon his farm?" Or, "Could it be that the almighty has returned their daughter and son-in-law to them, in the form of snow? The very evil that took them from their lives would now return them in angelic form?" As darkness obscured his view, he returned inside and was left to ponder this revelation. He had better not tell mother just yet.

Later that night, after the girls had gone to bed, gramps and grandma were sitting by the fire, each with a book, as they did most winter evenings. More often than not, Walter would fall asleep in his chair and the book would crash to the floor, awakening him with a start. Helen could always tell it wasn't far off by the increasing voracity of his snoring, something she had learned to live with over the fifty years they had been married. As she always did, she shook Walter awake and said, "Dear, why don't you turn out the lantern and go up to bed; you're just sleeping down here, no longer reading." Walter said, "Yes, dear," and rose from his chair, a sturdy one he had made himself, but which had seen better days. Starting to go up to bed, he turned and said, "Mother, I must show you something before we retire, it's a great mystery. Put your coat and boots on and come outside with me." "Oh, Walter," Helen cried, "Must we go outside in this cold, we'll both catch our death!" Walter turned and looked her in the face and said, "Dear, this is something you will want to see, I promise."

JL CRAWFORD

All bundled up against the cold, they walked out the back porch door. Walter had the lantern in one hand and held his arm tightly round Helen's waist as she made her way down the slippery porch steps. Safely on firm ground, Walter led her over to where the mysterious shapes were firmly ensconced in the snow. Holding the lantern high over his head so as to broadcast its bright light, Walter pointed to the angel-like shapes, saying to Helen, "Look dear, do you see what is there in the snow?" Helen was looking for 'something,' but she knew not what. Not seeing anything in the snow that might be a "mystery" she told Walter, "I see nothing unusual at all. What am I supposed to see, other than snow, which frankly, I am quite tired of!"

Walter angled the light so it would cast a brighter hue on the snow, telling her, "Dear, look *at* the snow itself, not as though you were looking for something in the snow." Just as she was about to tell him she had had enough of this nonsense, her mouth opened wide and her hand clasped to it tightly. She swiveled quickly round to face Walter and remarked, "Walter, are they what they appear to be? Are they impressions of angels? How did they get to be in our yard? Oh, Walter, do you suppose that angels came to visit us? How long have they been here?" "Mother, I don't know. I saw them just for the first time this afternoon, from the roof of the porch, but surely I would have seen them before, had they been there." Grasping his hands, her eyes tearing, Helen asked, "Walter, do you think it is a sign from heaven? Do you think that Eleanor and Samuel have come to visit us, and this is how they have let us know?" "I don't know for certain dear, but we must be watchful for more signs," Walter told her.

The next morning, Helena and Barbara rose early. Helena wanted to be certain not to miss the chance to play with Samson and Duchess and Barbara wanted to talk with the snowflakes again. She was almost certain that she had dreamed all of it, but when Helena said, "Remember, you must love the snow and want the snow or the snowflakes will not talk to you." Barbara shouted, "So, it was true! I didn't just dream it after all. I really did talk to snowflakes, didn't I Helena?" "Shhh!" her sister silenced her. "Grandma will think us simple for talking to the snow; we must be quiet and tell no one."

Both girls dashed outside, jumping in leaps and bounds through the snow, laughing and carrying on as they made their way to Mr. Cranford's farm. They could see Samson and Duchess romping around in circles, jumping in the air to catch snow that blew round them. Each time they landed, their faces were covered in white powder. Duchess wagged her tail furiously in Samson's face to rid him of the snow and he returned the favor. Off again they went, headfirst into the next snow bank, repeating the process over and over again. As the girls neared the gate to the snow-covered pasture, Mr. Cranford waved to them and made his way inside once again. They had no sooner gotten inside the gate and yelled to Samson and Duchess when the two excited pooches burst upon them. Duchess leaped into Helena's arm, showering her with white crystals. Barbara laughed uncontrollably, until Samson leaped into her arms as well, knocking her backwards into the snow. Unable to stop laughing, she went to tears when Samson licked all of the snow from her face! Composing herself, Barbara asked, "Is this why you come over to play with them every morning! Are they always this silly?"

The girls played with Samson and Duchess for a full hour, only stopping to talk to the snow when great puffs flew into the air, usually brought forth by Samson and Duchess shaking furiously. The air was filled with tiny diamond-like flakes of snow, to whom Helena and Barbara would wave, shouting, "We love you snow!" From afar, anyone watching would have thought the two girls were having their own private snow squall. Unbeknownst to the girls, someone *was* watching from afar, though it mattered not to them for the fun they were having. Helena was certain that in short order, either Mr. Cranford or bratty-Johnny would call the dogs in for their breakfast, and their fun would be over until tomorrow. Sure enough, just as she had finished the thought, Mr. Cranford called for Samson and Duchess and the two beloved pooches ran off to eat their breakfast of beef scraps and dry cereal.

Their fun finished for the morning, Helena and Barbara made their way towards home. They were as happy as two children could be, their small hearts filled with the joy of just being children and not having a care in the world. When Helena spied a sizeable patch of virgin snow, she spread her arms and feet and, as she had done the day before, fell flat onto her back. Giggling, she flapped her arms and legs back and forth, making yet another beautiful snow angel. Not to be out done, Barbara found a bare spot close to her and fell backwards just the same. Their laughter could have been heard on the other side of Ashburn, had anyone wondered what great fun two little girls could have to warrant such expression.

As they neared the gate that separated the two farms, which lay at the bottom of a very steep hill, they heard an awful cackling sound that was half-laughing and half-crazed excitement. Turning to see what had made the sound, they were pummeled with snowballs and armloads of snow as Johnny Cranford and his friend, Petey Braun flew by on sleds. Covered in snow from the furious and unforeseen assault, the girls quickly scooped snow into their mittens and hurled snowballs back at the marauders, but they had flown by so fast, they were long gone. Barbara yelled, "Did you see how fast they were? They must have the fastest sleds in all of Ashburn!" Furious at the two little pests, Helena said, "Oh no, they don't. I'm going to beat that bratty Johnny Cranford once and for all . . . and the snow is going to help me!" Seeing the confused look on her sister's face, Helena responded, "That's right! Yesterday, the snow said they would help me win the big race next week," and they made their way toward home, planning as they went.

In the days ahead, after school was out each day, Helena and Barbara carried their sleds to the top of Wilkins Hill, the steepest hill in all of

Ashburn, for this was to be the site of the big sled race, held each year just before the snow finally melted. Gramps would wax their sled rails each day while they were at school, clean off all the mud and dirt, and oil the handle joints so the girls' sleds would be in tip-top shape. The girls had never ridden so fast in all their lives and had to hold on tight at every turn, for fear they would topple over or fly through the air. They were certain to practice their sledding only when Johnny or Petey were nowhere to be seen, for they didn't want the competition to know they were getting better. Little did they know, but they were actually faster than either Petey or Johnny, who had built up so much confidence in their own sledding abilities that they had stopped practicing all together; so they thought . . .

The sun was warmer each day as the day of the big race grew closer and the snow was rapidly melting. Helena was afraid the big race would be cancelled and she would have to live with Johnny Cranford being the champion sled-rider for another whole year. Saturday just could not get here soon enough. Each day after school, the girls continued to practice, and each day they talked to the snow, asking, "Why do you have to leave so soon? Is there going to be enough snow that the big race will still go on?" To each question, the snowflakes assured them, "Don't worry girls, we have a plan to make the race go on . . . and a plan to help you win, as well!" The girls knew that the snow would not let them down, for they loved the snow and the snow loved them.

Each day though, the snow melted more and more, and soon, large bare spots of dirt and grass were making themselves present up and down Wilkins Hill. The ground was still hard as ice, but there wasn't nearly as much soft white powder as was needed to blanket the course. On Thursday, in school, Johnny Cranford pulled Helena's hair and whispered in her ear, "Nah, nah, nah, if the race doesn't go on, I'll still be champ for another year!" Helena turned angrily and told him in no uncertain terms, "Oh, the race will go on Johnny Cranford and when it's over, there will

JL CRAWFORD

be a new sled champion of Ashburn!" She turned back around to see Mrs. Gunder staring at her, and was asked, "Helena is everything okay? Is there something you would like to share with the whole class?" Embarrassed, Helena replied, "Sorry, no, Mrs. Gunder. I was just helping Johnny with one of his many problems!" And all the other girls in the class giggled along with Helena!

The next morning, as the girls were heading off to school, they were greeted at the back door by Mr. Cranford, with Samson and Duchess in tow. Mr. Cranford asked if their grandpa was home, to which the girls replied in unison, "Yes, Mr. Cranford, he is just finishing his breakfast." He asked them to watch the two pups while he went inside and moments later, gramps came out the door with his coat and hat and boots on, walking hurriedly towards Mr. Cranford's farm. Mr. Cranford thanked the girls for watching Samson and Duchess and had to almost run to catch up with grandpa. "What do you suppose could be wrong?" asked Barbara, to which Helena replied, "I don't know, but it must be very important. Grandpa didn't even finish his muffins and jam." The girls made their way to school, stopping to take a look at the deteriorating conditions at Wilkins Hill. Rounding the bend, they spied Johnny Cranford and Petey Braun coming down Wilkins Hill on their sleds. The girls darted behind a big tree out of sight of the boys, just as they raced past them. "So," Helena said, "That's why they have been late for school each morning this week. They've been practicing in the morning. They're getting used to the bare spots so they'll have an edge tomorrow. Ooooooooooh! They make me so furious!" she wailed. They could just barely hear Johnny and Petey laughing and cackling, and heard Johnny say, "Those two stupid girls think they can beat us, hah!"

As they walked to school, the girls petitioned each flake of snow they stirred, asking them again, "Are you still going to be here tomorrow? How will we beat those two boys when they know all the bare spots and best places to sled over?" Each snowflake they spoke with implored them,

"Don't worry girls, those boys do not love snow as you do. They want the snow just for their own needs, but will they care about the snow when summer is here, as you two will? We have a plan to make the race go on, and an even better plan to help you win. You have to trust us, all the way up to the start of the race, and all the way through, for we will be there for you!"

The entire school day, Johnny Cranford was an unbearable nuisance, teasing Helena about the race the next day, saying, "Don't worry Helena, after I win I'll let you ride the fastest sled in Ashburn—my sled!" In Barbara's class, Petey Braun was every bit as unbearable, but when Barbara turned and asked him, "Petey, do you know why the variable quotient of the wind factor versus the angle and impediment of the sled rails will drastically segue the outcome of the race?" Petey turned around dumb-faced and didn't say a word the rest of the day. Barbara and all the other girls giggled all day long!

In Mr. Cranford's pasture, he and grandpa stared befuddled at the two mysterious shapes that presented themselves in the snow. Mr. Cranford had seen them just this morning and sought Walter's help in making sense of them. Walter told him about the two very identical shapes in his yard, proclaiming not to know exactly what they were, what they meant, or how they could have come to be. Mr. Cranford was quick to point out that they were clearly the shape of angels, to which Walter agreed, wholeheartedly. He recanted the notion held by he and Helen of a visit by angels, perhaps the spirit of Eleanor and Samuel, in the form of angels. Deeply spiritual, as was almost everyone of Ashburn, Mr. Cranford shared his belief that the earth was indeed, visited by angels on occasion, but asked, "Why did they make their mark in my pasture, and not in yours again?" Walter scratched his head, thoroughly dumbfounded, saying he did not know. After comparing them to the shapes in Walter's yard, they both agreed that the shapes were made by the same two angels. When he told Helen of the discovery in Mr.

Cranford's yard, she was convinced that Eleanor and Samuel were trying to send them a message.

Saturday morning arrived cold and crisp. Fortunately, the night had been very cold so no more snow had melted, but Wilkins Hill was a sad looking course for the big sled race. Many citizens of Ashburn said the race should be called off, some saying, "No one can beat those two, Johnny and Petey, anyway; let's leave it until next year." Still others shouted, "No! The kids have been practicing all winter. We say let the race go on!" In the end, the race committee agreed with those who wanted the big race to go on, for it was one of the biggest events of the year. In town, merchants had set tables out front of their stores, selling their wares at low, low prices in support of the event, promising the best deals of the year. Children and mothers had baked every sweet treat imaginable, from cookies and brownies and cakes to muffins, sweet rolls, and everyone's favorite—key lime pie! One inspired youngster, clearly brought up on peanut butter and jelly sandwiches, begged his mother to let him make something of his own creation, and was born for all to behold, the world's first 'triple-decker' peanut butter and jelly sandwich! Children with appetites large enough to try it became a mess of peanut butter and jelly from head to toe, and there were more sticky finger prints all over Ashburn than at any time ever before. Grown-ups demanded the recipe and it even became a menu item at Mrs. Kendall's boarding house!

The sled racers had no time for all of the food excitement though, for they were busy looking over the course, getting ready for their individual races. The races were set up by age group, so the little ones were only competing against kids of their own age. The kids under eight all received trophies, regardless of winning or not, along with coupons to try a free triple-decker peanut butter and jelly sandwich, which also won the prize for "best new creation!" Those who could eat the whole sandwich received a slice of ice cold key lime pie, and those who could not, got a free helping of stomach relaxer.

When the under-eight year olds had finished racing, and the remains of uneaten peanut butter and jelly sandwiches had been removed from the course, it was time for the serious racing to start. Eight and nine-year olds would race against each other, as would ten and eleven-year olds, and twelve and thirteen-year olds. Kids older than that were deemed too big to be in the race and helped man the course, retrieved little kids who sailed off into the trees, and picked up scattered sandwiches. As bad as the course appeared, they would be lucky to get in any racing after the last group anyway. With so many kids racing, they paired them off into heats and the winners of each heat would advance forward, with the last two in each age group racing for the championship.

Barbara was the first racer in her heat to advance to the final, having defeated two boys and one girl to advance. She would be facing Petey Braun for the championship. He had beaten three boys, and all by a considerable margin. She told Helena that the course was in terrible condition, but each time she had neared a bare spot, snow appeared from out of nowhere just in time to provide purchase for her sled rails. She feared she would stop dead in her tracks and be thrown head over heels, but not once did it happen. Helena told her, "Barbara, it must surely be the snow helping us as they promised they would. Keep believing in and loving the snow and you will win. I know you can!" Sure enough, in the head-to-head battle between them, Barbara bested Petey by almost ten-seconds! At one point, Petey had been set to race ahead of Barbara when a swirl of snow engulfed him and he veered off into a snow bank built up to contain racers from flying off the side of Wilkins Hill. Recovering quickly, but still with a face full of snow that he just couldn't shake off, he blindly tried to make his way to the finish line, but was far too late. When Barbara last saw Petey, he was crying to his mama on his way home.

Helena had beaten two girls and only one boy on her way to the final race, but one of the girls had been age champion since she was five years old and was thought to be the champion again this year. As she suspected, she would face Johnny Cranford in the final. Johnny had beaten three boys, all bigger than he, and one was later found to be fifteen years old. Helena's chances did not look good. In fact, other than her grandparents and Barbara, the whole town just naturally thought Johnny Cranford would win one more championship. In all of his years of racing, he had never lost to anyone. Gramps was busy cleaning all the dirt from her runners and oiling the handles so she could negotiate the turns. He put an extra layer of wax on the runners and told her, "Helena, it's as fast as I can make it for you, my angel. Do your best. We're all proud of you," and gave her a big hug. Grandma and Barbara waited at the finish line.

When the starting bell was rung, Helena and Johnny, sleds in their arms, raced as fast as they could to the top edge of Wilkins Hill. Each of them had done this hundreds of times before, in practice and in competition, but this was the biggest race of their lives, and never before had they ever raced against each other! Older by a year and faster, Johnny had a lead of ten feet when he reached the top edge and threw himself over the edge, landing with an audible 'whump' as his sled hit the snow with him squarely on top. Helena reached the precipice and threw herself over the edge as well. Lighter and a bit smaller, she landed more gracefully and as a result, was faster on the smooth surface. She quickly caught up with Johnny and, taking him by surprise, passed him around the first turn. The spectators who lined the hill could not believe what they were seeing. Was the undefeated champ of Ashburn going to suffer his first defeat?

Down the second straight-away, Helena flew over a hill and went airborne, landing hard on her stomach, enough to have the wind knocked out of her briefly. That was all that Johnny needed to fly past her as his runners found a patch of unmarred snow and went passed as though shot out of a cannon. At the bottom of the hill, it was apparent to all that after this mishap, Johnny Cranford would win another championship. Helena regained her composure and 'magically' found fresh patch after fresh patch of snow under her runners, quickly gaining ground on Johnny. Ironically, each time Johnny steered onto a fresh patch of snow it seemed as though it would disappear right out from under him. The sheer rate of speed at which he was flying though, allowed him to continue speeding downhill toward the finish line. The look of victory was in his eyes and on his face, for he had been here many, many times. He turned his head to see how far back Helena was, and with only fifteen yards to the finish line, and Helena still twenty-five yards back, the victory was sealed.

At the finish line, it was but a foregone conclusion. Most of those who had hoped for Helena to upset the champ, headed off to get some key lime pie and to try that new sandwich everyone was talking about. The hardcore enthusiasts though, would stick around to congratulate the long time champ. Having turned his head to measure his margin of victory, Johnny turned back to steer across the line. Raising one hand in victory, he had only fresh snow in front of him. The lone bare spot ahead did not faze him as he had sailed across and over all others. With only one hand on the handles though, he felt a sickening feeling in his stomach as he hit the bare spot. His sled, which had flown over all other bare spots, which remained slick from melting snow, was now halted in its tracks. Or was it? No, he realized, he was still sailing toward the finish line, as though he was flying! Victory was only a few feet away. He felt light as air. Ahhhh, the feeling of victory no doubt, but why was everyone so small looking and far below him? Looking beneath him, he realized he had no sled handles in his grasp, no sled beneath him at all! He was flying, but still he flew right across the finish line landing deep into a drift, but still well ahead of Helena—and victory was his once more!

Helena was only looking at the finish line, never saw the bare patch that Johnny had hit, but knew he was almost twice the distance from her, a distance she could not make up. Regardless, she would make her grandparents and Barbara proud for having made it to the championship and would congratulate Johnny for his victory. As she and her sled crossed the finish line, she watched as the townspeople lifted Johnny Cranford on their shoulders and carried him off to receive his trophy. Barbara and her grandparents hugged Helena and congratulated her for putting up such a gallant race, and they prepared to go home.

As they walked off, they saw the crowd moving their way. "Oh great," Helena thought, "Johnny Cranford is coming back to throw this in my face." Not wanting to give the little braggart is due, gramps stepped between them. As the crowd grew closer, the race judge stepped forward with Johnny Cranford next to him, proudly holding the trophy in his hand. Helena had decided she would shake his hand and congratulate him, but if he mouthed off, he would get a mouthful of snow, one filled with rocks! Preparing to hear his bragging, Helena staved herself. The race judge stepped forward, no doubt, Helena thought, to make a big to do over the undefeated champ, but the words she heard would stay with her forever.

Taking the trophy from the stunned Johnny Cranford, the judge handed it to Helena and said, "Helena, the race committee has made a decision regarding the outcome of the race. We have decided that Johnny did indeed, cross the finish line before you, but his sled did not. If you look at the hill, his sled remains where it stopped, but this is a sled-race, not a person-race. Helena, because you and your sled crossed the finish line first, the race committee proclaims you to be the winner of the race!" The townsfolk rushed to put Helena on their shoulders, but she declined. Instead, she raised her hand to stop them. Barbara said, "Helena, you're the champ! Let everyone know you're the best by riding into town on their shoulders." Warmed by the moment and the offer, Helena replied for all to hear, "Thank you for declaring me the champion of the race. It was well-fought by both, Johnny and I, but it's just a race. Today, I may be the champion racer, but every other day, I'm just a girl from Ashburn. I *would* like to try one of those triple-decker peanut butter and jelly sandwiches though, and of course, my favorite, key lime pie!" On the way to town, she saw Johnny Cranford walking as well. She looked over toward him and smiled. He winked at her and gave her a thumbs-up, for she would always be first in his heart, even if he had been beaten by a girl!

Chapter 3

WITHIN A WEEK of the big race, the snow had all melted, save for a few spots shielded from the sun's warmth. Spring had arrived and the earth was rapidly becoming the flowery arboretum that reflects the start of the cycle of life year after year. Helena and Barbara visited every remaining patch of snow they encountered, wishing the snowflakes well and thanking them for helping each girl win their race. Never before had two girls won a championship in the same year, and never, ever—two sisters! The 'angels of Ashburn' were celebrities! As much as the girls loved the snow, they also loved spring time, for what little girl doesn't love flowers! What girl of any age doesn't love flowers! Coming home from school each day, they would pick bunches of flowers for grandma, surprising her each time.

Helena's favorite flower was the buttercup, which she would always stick under Barbara's chin, or grandma's, or grandpa's, and giggle at the bright yellow reflection that presented itself. Grandma always had a small glass of water handy for Helena to place the buttercups in each day, for Helena just couldn't pass by them without picking a bunch. Putting a buttercup under her own chin, she would ask Barbara, "Is there something yellow under my chin? What could it be Barbara? Am I ill?" Growing tired of buttercup after buttercup, Barbara replied, "I think I'd rather walk home with Petey Braun than hear anymore about buttercups," to which Helena remarked, "Ewwww, you like Petey Braun?" Barbara quickly cut her off from any more teasing saying, "No, I do NOT like Petey, I've just had enough of buttercups!" Running on ahead of her, Helena turned, and with her thumbs in her ears and fingers wiggling, her tongue sticking out, she joked, "Barbara loves Petey, Barbara loves Petey, I'm going to tell everyone that Barbara loves Petey!" Furious, Barbara chased her all the way home, both girls laughing until they got to the back porch. Out of breath as they plopped onto the bottom step, Barbara said, "Helena, if you won't tell anyone that I think Petey Braun is cute, I won't tell anyone that you have a crush on Johnny Cranford!" Locking thumbs, looking each other squarely in the eye, they both said, "Deal!"

Before anyone knew it, spring had sprung and summer was now upon them. School was out and Helena and Barbara were able to play every day, after chores of course. Grandma still made them read each day, and on Saturday, too, and Sunday was still reserved for church and Bible reading. The season of work had begun for grandpa way back in the spring as he set about planting seed throughout the fifty-acre farm. Early summer had already brought a record crop of corn and grandma's garden was full of the fattest, juiciest tomatoes, sweet blueberries, and row after row of yellow and green squash, zucchini, cherry tomatoes, lettuce, and strawberries! Barbara and Helena helped pick the fruit and vegetables from the garden each day, and to no one's surprise, when they came into the house carrying pecks of berries, their mouths were always stained red and blue!

Grandpa and Mr. Cranford helped each other plant the seed in spring and bring in the crops in summer and into the fall. Johnny Cranford was now big enough to help with the summer harvest. Having just turned twelve, he was growing into a young man. Catching Helena peering through the drapes one day, no doubt watching Johnny work in the field, Barbara tickled her sister's waist, startling her, saying, "I see you looking at Johnny Cranford. He's got some muscles, doesn't he?" Embarrassed to no end and very red-faced, Helena responded, "I don't have any idea what you're talking about. I was watching Samson and Duchess play in the pasture." Sensing she had not fooled her wise sister, Helena asked, "Barbara, is he getting more handsome every day?" Barbara turned and skipped away, telling Helena, "I wouldn't know, I don't like yucky boys!"

In late July, Helena turned eleven and Barbara turned nine just three weeks later; each lucky to get a birthday party of their own and not having to share one for both. August had brought a sweltering heat, but the pond was still full and the creek by Wilkins Hill was still running fast and cool; the result of so much snow from last winter. Helena reminded Barbara of the fact, telling her, "See what the snow was teaching us about how it helps the earth by turning into water! Grandpa says the ground is moist and wonderful for his crops and grandma's garden is the best it has been in years!" Nodding her head in agreement, Barbara tucked herself under the cool water and sprang to the surface, splashing water everywhere. She said, "I know. Even grandma is happy about her garden, but Helena, I heard grandma tell gramps she hopes the snow doesn't come this year. She said she was saying prayers that the snow never comes again. Can she do that, Helena? Can she make the snow stay away?"

Consoling her sister, Helena told her what the snow had said to her when they first spoke. "Barbara, the snowflake told me that Mother Nature decides where she will send the snow; that one person or even a few people cannot determine where it will snow or not. So, no, grandma cannot will the snow to never come again." Interrupting her, Barbara said, "But what about the story you told me of that town called Flagstaff, where all the people wished for snow and Mother Nature now brings it?" Remembering, Helena replied, "You're right, Barbara, I had forgotten, but that happened because all of the people wanted snow and willed Mother Nature for it to come, not just one or a few people." Feeling a bit better, Barbara revealed to her sister, "I hope you're right, but I have heard grandma talking to people in town, asking them to pray for no snow. Could she be trying to get the whole town to pray for no snow? What if that happens?" "Barbara," Helena responded, "All we can do is pray *for* snow. The town will never get *us* to pray for no snow. We must be strong. I'm sure we can get Johnny and Petey and all the other children to pray for snow!"

The girls filled the remaining weeks of summer with play and little thought about the possibility of no snow, for never before had snow not come to Ashburn. School started again and at the same time, the air became cool with the arrival of autumn. Each child being a year older, the four friends were now in the same class with Mrs. Gunder. Johnny didn't seem to be as much of a pest as he had always been, promising not to pull Helena's hair, but telling her he would still write her sweet notes! Helena just rolled her eyes, but felt good at the same time and actually smiled when she gave it some thought. Barbara proclaimed Petey to still be a brat and a pest, but after all, he was still only nine and not nearly as mature as the nine-year old Barbara! Learning from Helena, Barbara made sure she sat behind Petey instead of the other way around, and every time he did something stupid, she gave him a little kick, but with a smile, of course! All the girls in class enjoyed making fun of Petey, but Barbara had felt the tiniest spark inside.

Grandpa and Mr. Cranford brought in the last harvest of the season, proclaiming this season to be the best in memory. Their cellars were full of food, the grain bins overflowed, and grandma had never canned so much food in her life. The dinner meal included green beans, potatoes, tomatoes, beets, carrots, squash and zucchini, and the delicious, warm bread that grandma baked daily; the wonderful aroma always filling the house. Grandpa had culled a steer and a hog early in the season and there was plenty of meat. The hunting season had brought them venison, pheasant, duck, and wild turkey, though the girls were never made aware of how it made its way to the table. With her stomach full to bursting one evening, grandma, quite uncharacteristically, pushed back her chair and announced to all, "I declare, we may have enough food to last us forever! What a wonderful season it has been!"

Helena and Barbara looked at each other intently, when Helena spoke out, "Yes, grandma, it has been a wonderful season indeed. I believe that we owe it all to the good Lord above, Mother Nature, and the wonderful snow she brought us this past winter, for the snow melted into the rivers, which made grandpa's fields moist and fertile. The ground snow melted where it lay and made your garden the best it has ever been as well. Do you remember all the flowers we had this spring? Barbara and I brought you flowers every day . . . all courtesy of the snow! I think we should all say prayers for even more snow this season, don't you grandma? Don't you, grandpa?" Barbara quickly chimed in, agreeing with Helena, adding, "You're so right, Helena. That is just what we learned in school from Mrs. Gunder, and she knows everything!" Seeing where this was going, grandpa stayed quiet, but did add, "Mrs. Gunder is a smart one, I'll give you that much."

Perplexed as to where this fusillade of support for snow was coming from, grandma replied to all of them, "Well, I don't know any such thing. The snow was not good to us two years ago when it took your parents from us, and each year it hurts more and more people, and your grandpa and I are getting too old to get around in it. If it were up to me, I'd see to it that Mother Nature just went on her way each winter, dropping the snow somewhere where it is wanted, but not in Ashburn. That is where my prayers will be directed. And I know a good many people in town who feel just the same." The girls fell quiet, certain that grandma was mustering support amongst the town folk to keep the snow from returning. Grandpa thought it best not to join in on either side, convinced that Mother Nature would do as she saw fit, but ended matters by saying, "Girls, mother, the good Lord will have the final say, not the people. Each of us may pray as we wish, just be sure we are thanking the Lord for the bounty that he has brought us this season, and for the love we share as a family. Girls, upstairs you go, be sure your homework is complete before you turn in." "Yes, grandpa," the girls replied in unison, and made their way upstairs. Grandma pushed her chair from the table and stood. Looking at Walter, she said firmly, "Dear, I believe you have some dishes to clean before you start reading!" The room suddenly felt a bit cooler than it had only moments before.

Mother Nature spared no expense in delivering her artistry to the fall leaves. Born from strong roots that had drunk of water throughout the summer, the trees lavished the countryside with the brightest colors ever. Never before had anyone remembered seeing such vibrant reds, yellows, and oranges and they seemed to last for weeks and weeks longer than ever before. Grandpa built a fire each night in the outside stone fire-pit and the family would roast marshmallows in the cool night air, enjoying the wonderful smells that only autumn can bring. During the day, on the way home from school, the girls collected all manner, shape, color, and size of leaves, which grandma showed them how to place between pages of books to preserve for years and years to come. Grandma replaced the cool cotton sheets of summer with warm, flannel sheets and downy-soft comforters. The cool nights of autumn made for deep sleep, not that children needed any help in that regard. Rare was the night that, their angelic eyes did not close tightly as soon as their heads touched the pillow. Rare was the night that, Helena and Barbara didn't dream for the snow to return.

Snow came to Ashburn each year in the first week of October, almost without fail. When the second week had come and gone and still no snow had fallen, there was still little, if any concern, for it was still autumn. All Hallows Eve was always celebrated in the snow, ensuring that children could not stay out too late; guaranteeing they could not get more candy and sweets than they needed, either! Yet, this year, there was still no snow. Making their way to the Cranford's farm on All Hallows Eve, Barbara, asked Helena, "Do you think grandma and her friends have prayed so hard that we shall never see snow again?" Comforting her sister, Helena replied, "I don't know, dear sister. All we can do is keep saying our prayers."

Thanksgiving was but one week away and the girls and boys of Ashburn were all talking about the snow, wondering why it hadn't yet snowed. Time off from school for the Thanksgiving holiday always meant sledding down Wilkins Hill. The temperature had certainly been cold enough, for all of the lakes and ponds were already frozen over. The streams, creeks, and the nearby Rapidon River were almost frozen. Sharp edges of ice bit from the banks, almost reaching each other from side to side. In another few days, the streams and creeks would be frozen solid; the Rapidon would take another few weeks. The more worried the girls were about the lack of snow, the more light-hearted grandma seemed to be. Grandpa told the girls not to worry for winter was still a month away from arriving and the worst snows of the year always came after the first of January. It had never before not snowed in all the years that grandpa had lived in Ashburn.

Helena and Barbara had everything to be thankful for when Thanksgiving Day arrived. They had already decided that they would not give the lack of snow any thought, and would certainly not allow it to ruin the special holiday. Tradition held that each person would tell all of the things that they were thankful for. Starting with Barbara because she was the youngest, they would all have the chance to say whatever their hearts wished, ending with grandpa. Barbara rose from her chair, pushed it back under the table as she was taught to do, and folded her arms behind her back. In a quiet voice, unlike her regular voice, she said, "Well, I am thankful for my family, each and every one of you, especially for grandma and grandpa for taking care of me and Helena and for loving us. I am thankful for all of the things that you teach us, including the difference between right and wrong. I am thankful that you just send us to our room without any dinner when we misbehave, and don't spank us like other kids parents do. I'm thankful for the wonderful dinners that grandma makes all the time, and for the horseback rides that grandpa takes me on . . . and I'm grateful that I'm all finished and can eat my dinner." Before she could take her seat though, grandma looked at her a little sternly, and said, "Did you forget some people?" Miffed, Barbara thought for a moment then, realizing her forgetfulness, she added, "Oh, yeah! I'm thankful for mother and father, even though they aren't here with us anymore, and for the best sister in the whole world, and most of all, to the Lord, Jesus, for watching over us!" When her grandma smiled at her, she knew it was time to be seated.

Helena smiled at Barbara as well, affectionately mussing her hair with her hand as she pushed away from the table. In her quiet voice, she thanked Jesus for looking after her mother and father and for delivering her and Barbara to grandma and grandpa, proclaiming them to be the 'best grandparents in the history of the world!' Walter and Helen looked at each other and smiled, and grandma wiped a tear away from her eye. Trying to be stoic and strong, grandpa still had a little quiver in his lips that Helena caught the slightest sign of. She said she was thankful for having the best and smartest sister that any girl could have, promising to be her best friend forever and ever. She told how thankful she was to have Samson and Duchess to play with each day, and how fortunate she was to have as many friends as she did. She thanked Jesus for all of the food they had, and fresh water and ice cold milk to drink! Preparing to sit, she stopped short, as though remembering something and said, "Oh, and I am so thankful that it is still only autumn, for we still have all of winter for it to snow and snow and snow!" She didn't dare look at grandma, who was giving her quite the frown.

Grandma rose slowly, clearly taken aback by Helena's underhanded attempt at asking for the Lord's help with snow. Looking straight ahead and at no one in particular, she started with an audible, "Hmmmpfff," followed by, "Well I can't say as I have THAT to be thankful for, but I am very thankful for the wonderful weather the Lord has seen fit to provide to this point, and of course for the wondrous bounty of the season. I'm also thankful for the best young ladies any grandparents could ask for!" As she started to sit, grandpa loudly cleared his throat, with a look of almost shock on his face. Grandma immediately had an embarrassing look on her face, which quickly turned to a half smirk. She rose once more and said apologetically, "I almost forgot, I'm also greatly thankful for my dear husband, Walter, but that goes without saying!"

Feeling just a bit slighted, but not seriously so, Walter replied, "Well, maybe all that I have to say will just 'go without saying.' Grandma quickly replied, "Oh, no it won't, Mr. Broadhurst, it's your turn to rise and give thanks!" Chuckling to himself for getting in a little dig, grandpa rose and in his deep voice said, "Lord, I am thankful to you for all that I have in my life. You have blessed me with a home which I can share with the woman of my dreams. It is a home which shelters the three loveliest ladies of Ashburn, if not even the whole world." Helena and Barbara looked at each other, embarrassed, giggling at being called "lovely," and looked at grandma. Her face was aglow and she looked lovingly into grandpa's eyes. She thought to herself, "That man always has had a way with words!" Grandpa said a few more thanks and ended with, "And Lord, I'm thankful for the most wonderful life a man could have, save for not having our beloved Eleanor and Samuel with us, but we are all blessed nonetheless." Everyone was quiet for a brief time, pensive in their own thoughts, until Barbara said, "I forgot to say how thankful I am that it's time to eat!"

The Thanksgiving break ended for the girls and school started once again, but they were glad for having time with their friends, even though typical afternoons had them engaged in snowball fights and sledding and ice skating. All of the ponds and lakes were frozen solid and many children did skate the afternoons away, but Helena and Barbara longed for snow, not just for the fun snowball fights and for sledding, but they longed to talk to the snowflakes and find out why they were so long in coming to Ashburn. The peaks of Daedalus and Colossus were deep in snow, but they were unreachable by the children. Even grownups had no desire to climb to the heights where snow lay as deep as five feet.

From the ground, the children could see snow swirling high about the mountain tops, sometimes blizzard-like and they were just certain that it would soon blow their way, but to no avail. Occasionally they got a few flurries, but before the girls could rush to speak with them, they had either melted or blown away.

Chapter 4

I T WAS NOW the third week in December and winter was officially about to arrive. Everyone was absolutely certain that winter would bring snow and more snow. It seemed that the only people worried about the snow were the children. Always inquisitive, Barbara asked one day, "Helena, is it just me, or do you think that no one wants snow to come except for the children? Do you know of any grownups that are sad the snow has not yet arrived?" Helena thought for a moment and said, "You might be right Barbara, I cannot think of any grownups that have really complained, except for Mr. Bainbridge." Mr. Bainbridge owned the local hardware store and always sold all of his snow shovels, sets of chains, new sleds and saucers, and all manner of snow-related items. This season, his store was chock full of things that in normal years he would already be sold out of. Barbara inquired, "Do you think grandma and grandpa will buy me that new shiny saucer I asked for? It's still in the window of Mr. Bainbridge's store, so maybe grandma has prayed so much for no snow that she doesn't see a reason to buy it. I was really hoping for a new saucer." Helena told her, "Don't worry, Christmas is still more than a week away and I think Mr. Bainbridge has a lot of those in his back room, but if it doesn't snow, you won't need one." "It's going to snow, Helena," Barbara offered back, "I just know it's going to!"

Watching the girls through the window, with the door cracked just enough to hear them grandma opened the door and stepped onto the porch. "Girls, have you finished your homework yet? With Christmas so close, you want to be certain that you're on your best behavior, lest

Santa Claus pass right over our house, just as the snow has seen fit to do." Barbara and Helena were too old to believe in Santa Claus, but they let grandma and grandpa think the opposite. Each evening, they could hear the wrapping of gifts downstairs, after they had gone up to bed, grandma and grandpa thinking they were fast asleep. Without peeking, they tried to guess what presents were being wrapped, but the next morning, there were no signs of wrapped presents, no string or bows, no pieces of paper lying about, nothing to indicate that any present-wrapping had occurred at all! Helena and Barbara both wondered what they could have done with all of those presents. The tree was up and decorated, though they would save the popcorn stringing for Christmas Eve, so Santa could eat fresh popcorn, after the milk and cookies, and brownies, and pie, and other treats grandma always left on the table for him. It was funny how each Christmas morning it was grandpa who would say, "Wow, I'm really stuffed, I must have eaten too much last night," and there just happened to be no treats left where grandma had put them!

'T was the night before Christmas and the girls and grandma and grandpa had finished a wonderful dinner of ham, sweet potatoes with marshmallow, green beans, squash, corn, and grandma's favorite wheat-bread muffins with jam and butter. Fresh out of the oven, grandpa told her to leave the oven door open so the delightful aroma could fill the house. Grandpa said grace as was the custom and everyone plowed into the food like they hadn't eaten in weeks. When everyone had pushed away from the table, hands on their full tummies, there was still a formidable amount of food remaining. Fresh from drinking her third glass of ice cold milk, a large white mustache adorning her face, Barbara pleaded with her grandparents, "Please grandma, gramps, can't we open just one present tonight?" Helena knew the question was coming, just as it had last year, for it was a custom at their house before their parents had passed, but not so at grandma and grandpa's house.

Before grandma could answer though, grandpa stood and said, "Just a moment mother, come look at this. I wanted to show you this earlier. It's in the kitchen." Bewildered, grandma rose and followed grandpa into the kitchen. Barbara looked curiously at Helena and asked, "What do you suppose that is all about? I still don't see a saucer under the tree; guess I'm not going to get a new one this year." In the kitchen, grandpa raised a quieting finger to his mouth just as grandma was about to ask why he brought her in there. "Mother," Walter said, "Before you tell them we don't open gifts on Christmas Eve, why don't we go ahead and change things this year. The girls are already despondent about having no snow to play in. Come on, mother, what do you say?" Grandma hugged him tightly and said, "Okay, you big softie!"

Back in the dining room, grandma and grandpa sat back down and grandma said, "Thank you for showing me that dear, it is indeed very unusual." Looking at each other, the girls blurted out, "What, what did he show you? What was so unusual grandma, gramps?" It was almost as though two voices came from a single body, so in unison were they; both thinking there was a wonderful surprise forthcoming. Grandma looked at each of them and said, "Oh, it was nothing at all, just something silly your grandpa wanted to show me. Now, what were we talking about before?" "Like you said yourself, grandma," Barbara started, "It was nothing at all," sadly turning away. Helena joined in and said, "Grandma, Barbara had asked if we couldn't open just one present on Christmas Eve." Grandma looked her squarely in the face and said, "Girls, we have traditions and it has never been our tradition to open a present on Christmas Eve." Caught completely by surprise, grandpa turned to look at grandma and was about to ask her, when she said, "But there isn't any reason why we can't start new traditions. So, your grandpa and I have decided that we will NOT open one present on Christmas Eve—we will open TWO presents on Christmas Eve!!!"

Each of the girls flew from their chairs, knocking them back over onto the floor. They raced to their grandparents, hugging and kissing them, saying, "Oh, thank you grandma, gramps, thank you, thank you, thank you" and they raced over to the tree, scurrying through package after package, squeezing all and trying to figure out what could be inside. Grandpa looked at grandma and gave her a quick wink and a large smile. He moved closer to her and planted a kiss on her cheek and said, "You're a wonderful woman, Helen." Grandma lowered her head demurely, put her arm round Walter's waist, pulled him closer and said, "Well, maybe, but what I really am is a lucky woman." He gave her a short kiss and as they looked into each other's eyes, two voices rang in their ears, "Grandma and grandpa, sitting in a tree, k-i-s-s-i-n-g, first comes love, then comes . . ." "Oh, alright, enough of that nonsense," grandma blurted out. "Let's see what we have to open!"

Barbara and Helena were so caught up in the unexpected excitement of opening not one gift, but two, they were beside themselves. Grandpa sat in his chair and watched them pour over gift after gift, trying to decide which they should open. Warmed through and through by the two wonderful little girls, he was a bit saddened for Eleanor and Samuel not being here. He remembered all the years they had enjoyed with Eleanor at Christmas, sad when she moved away after marrying Samuel, but glad when they came to visit for Christmas and even more so when Helena and Barbara had come along. With Helena and Barbara in the house at Christmas, it so reminded him of the years when Eleanor was growing up; Christmas being all the more special for children. "Walter? Walter? WALTER?" he heard, shaking him from his thoughts. "Yes? Yes, dear" he answered. Grandma said, "Helena is thanking you for your gift. Did you fall asleep?" "Oh, no, dear," he replied, "I was just remembering wonderful times." Helena was in his lap by then, giving him a big hug and kiss on the cheek, thanking him for the wonderful bird house he had made for her. She quickly jumped down from his lap, ran upstairs and came down just as quickly, her hands full of stuffing and cotton and other soft things to put inside the bird house. She asked grandpa, "Can we go hang it up right now grandpa, can we, can we?" She was just certain that there would be a family of birds living in it by morning, and grandpa said, "You bet we can sweetheart. It will give the birds more time to get used to it," and outside they went.

Barbara was tearing through the wrapping on her first gift just certain she knew what it was, while grandma looked on with adoring eyes. The look in Barbara's eyes was nothing short of utter fascination. She would tear a piece of wrapping off, close her eyes, squeeze the gift and try to think what it was. Another piece of paper would fly off in another direction and she would squeeze it again. This happened three or four times before she squealed in joy, tore off the last vestige of wrapping and beheld the rag doll that she had hoped it would be. She ran over and threw her tiny frame into grandma's lap, hugging and kissing her, trying to speak in between hugs and kisses. Just as Helena and grandpa walked into the room, they heard her say, "Oh, grandma, it's just like my doll from last year, just the same. Now they each have a friend to play with. They are going to be so happy when I'm at school, for they will never, ever be alone again." She jumped off her grandma's lap and raced upstairs. In what could not have been more than thirty-seconds, she brought her other doll over to grandma along with her new doll, placed them side by side and introduced them to each other.

The new doll was a boy to go along with the girl doll grandma had made her last year. Grandma said, "I thought it might be nice for your little girl doll to have a brother to play with. I made him just a bit bigger so you could pretend that he was the older brother and could watch over her." Oh, thank you so much, grandma he's just wonderful," Barbara screamed. Holding them in each hand, she turned to look at grandma and said, "I think he's going to be her boyfriend, not her brother, and just like the story we're reading in school, I'm going to call them Romeo and

Juliet!" She pressed the two dolls together, danced round the room, and in her squeaky nine-year old voice mocked, "Oh, Romeo, Romeo, kiss me Romeo!" Grandpa looked over at grandma, rolled his eyes, shook his head, and said, "Oh brother, and she is only nine-years old!" Helena just giggled away at both of them.

A few minutes later, Helena opened her second present, a beautiful dress that grandma had made for her. Holding it up against her, she twirled round and round in circles until she was almost dizzy. Falling against her grandma, plopping down into her lap, she hugged her tight and said, "Thank you so much grandma, it is just lovely. Can I wear it to church service tomorrow?" "Well of course you can, Helena. In fact, I was hoping you would want to!" Helena gave her grandma a kiss on the cheek, only to be interrupted by yet another nine-year old scream. Barbara had torn the paper off what she knew was a book, but never in her wildest dreams did she think grandpa would let her read the book about planets and stars and the whole universe! "Oh grandpa," she cried out, "I have seen this book high up on your shelf so many times and I have wondered and wondered about all of the amazing things it would teach me. I thought you would not think me old enough or smart enough to understand it all, but you do, you do think I'm smart enough to understand it." Yes," grandpa replied, "I do think you're smart enough Barbara. You have been getting such good grades in school, your grandma and I think we have a great many books you may be able to start reading, and very soon. Let's see how you do with this one."

She threw her arms round his neck and kissed his cheek. "Oh grandpa, grandma, I love you both so much. I'm going up to start reading right now. That Petey Braun thinks he knows everything about the planets and the universe; I'll show him!" Picking up her two rag dolls, she marched toward the stairs saying, "Come along Romeo and Juliet, doth we not have some reading to do?" Helena just grinned then smiled at the innocence of her little sister, while grandma and grandpa beamed from ear to ear. Helena gave each of them a big hug and another kiss and thanked them profusely for allowing them to open gifts on Christmas Eve, telling them how much it reminded her of Christmas Eve with her mother and father. She went upstairs and found Barbara in the chair in their room, Romeo on one side and Juliet on the other. She had just started to read, "Chapter One, The Making of the Universe, oh, you guys, you're really going to love this book!" Helena smiled and made her way to the other side of the room.

Saying her prayers before climbing into bed, Helena thanked Jesus for her wonderful grandparents and her goofy, fun little sister. She asked Jesus to be certain he provided good weather for Santa Claus to make his journey, realizing how silly that was as she was saying it, and ended saying, "And please, Jesus, can you talk to Mother Nature about bringing snow to Ashburn. Most people really, really, really want and like the snow. Thank you Jesus, we'll see you in church tomorrow." She climbed into bed and while she should have had visions of sugar plums dancing in her head, instead, she dreamed of soft, white snow drifts, bright powdery crystals, and of talking with snowflakes."

Chapter 5

CHRISTMAS MORNING BROUGHT a wonderful surprise to the girls, one more wonderful than even Santa Claus himself could deliver. Helena was just starting to rouse from her pleasant sleep when a blood-curdling shriek pierced through her. So loud was it that grandpa and grandma burst into their room, afraid that something terrible had happened. They found Barbara at the window, the sash torn wide. She had pulled open the window and was yelling "Snow, snow, Helena, it has snowed, it has snowed!" She scooped a small handful of powdery crystals into her hands and tossed them onto Helena, who was still laying in bed, still in disbelief. Grandma raced to the window to behold the sight she could not have wished for in all her dreams. She turned to face them saying, "Oh, well, it's just a dusting, nothing at all to be concerned about. It will probably melt before church service is over. Girls, let's get up and get dressed, we have to get some breakfast before we go to church, and then we'll come back and see what Santa has brought everyone." Grandma and grandpa left to get dressed and Barbara turned to Helena, excitedly saying, "Oh, Helena, I prayed and prayed for snow, but I wouldn't let grandma hear me. Do you think this is the start of much more to come?" Helena was just looking at the snow for the first time. Turning to hold her sister's shoulders, she replied, "Oh, Barbara, I, too, have prayed each night for snow, including last night. I was hoping for much more, but maybe this is just the start. Let us get dressed and maybe we can talk to the snow and find out!"

The girls dressed hurriedly, though Helena stopped to look at herself in the dress grandma had made for her. Seeing her look in the mirror, Barbara said, "Helena, you are so beautiful. I hope I grow up to be as beautiful as you are. Do you think grandma will make me a dress like that one day?" Hugging her tightly, Helena responded, "You nut, you are already gorgeous, and you're only nine years old! You'll be much more beautiful than I will ever be. If you like, I'll let you have this dress when I outgrow it soon." "Oh, will you Helena? Will you really?" Barbara asked excitedly. "I would love to have that dress!" "Of course I will let you have this dress, silly. Sisters share everything, forever and ever! Now, let's hurry and go outside and talk to the snow where grandma won't hear us."

They raced downstairs as grandma was making breakfast, right past the Christmas tree that was now loaded with more gifts than the night before. Grandpa was slicing some bacon when he saw a flash of yellow and red fly by, instantaneously recognizing the two girls by their golden and auburn locks. He looked adoringly at grandma and said, "Those two little angels remind me of just the way Eleanor was when she was their age, but who would ever think that a little snow could best a tree full of presents!" He heard grandma issue a quiet, "Hmmpf," followed by, "We're just lucky that it's only a dusting. I certainly haven't prayed for any snow." Grandpa placed the bacon in the hot pan and told grandma, "Keep a watch on the bacon dear, I'll make sure the steps are clear of any snow."

Barbara and Helena had gone round the side of the house, wanting to be certain that grandma didn't look out the window and catch them talking to the snow. It was bad enough that she thought Helena might be daft, but best that she not think it of both of them. If she thought for a moment that Helena had made Barbara talk to the snow as well, she just might very well call Doc Smithers. Helena was quick to tell Barbara that they should whisper when they talked to the snow this morning. The two girls were beside themselves with excitement. They each had scooped up a mitten-full of powder and tossed it high in the air. As the snow fell around them and on them, they danced and twirled as though under a confetti storm. Giggling all the while, they sang, "We love you snow, we love you snow! Please talk to us." As the snow swirled round them, landing softly on their noses, in their hair, on their outstretched tongues, the girls' hearts were alive anew. Snowflakes didn't melt on their tongues and Helena quickly told Barbara, "See, Barbara, they are not melting because they know they are wanted here."

Grandpa had come out onto the porch and was quietly sweeping the light snow off the steps wanting to be sure that grandma would not slip when they left for church. Unaware of his presence, Helena and Barbara were whispering away, just around the side of the house, but not so far away that, grandpa couldn't hear them. He was curious indeed about who they might be talking to and why they were whispering, but he wasn't one to listen in on other people's conversations. After all, what could two adorable angels like his grandchildren be up to? Certainly, nothing troublesome. He went on with the sweeping, but soon heard a voice that did not belong to either Helena or Barbara. This was a lower voice, a male voice. He wondered whether Johnny Cranford or Petey Braun hadn't come by to wish them a merry Christmas, but this voice did not sound like either young man.

One of the snowflakes had landed on Helena's outstretched mitten. Barbara moved closely and told him, "Snowflake, you must speak in your quietest voice so that grandma does not hear you." "Yes," Helena chimed in, "Pray tell, where has the snow been this season? Why are you so late in arriving? Is this the only snow we are to see this year? Will we see more of you?" "Dear girls," the snowflake started, "I must first ask whether you two are the 'snow angels' that we have been told to look for in this part of the land?" Unsure of what he was referring to, Helena replied, "Oh, snowflake, we know not of what you speak. We are not angels, but we have loved the snow all of our lives. Just this season passed we talked with the snow everyday and the snow helped Barbara and me win the big

JL CRAWFORD

sled race. We made great friends with billions and billions of snowflakes and they promised they would return year after year, but only where the snow was loved and wanted. Snowflake, we love the snow, as do all of the children of Ashburn and many grownups, but not all we fear, love and want the snow." Despite the softness of their whispering, Grandpa could clearly make out what the girls were saying, but he wondered who on earth they could be speaking to in this way.

The snowflake listened to all that Helena and Barbara had to say, their stories of the past winter season, the big race, the days afterwards before all the snow had melted, but neither girl knew anything of the 'snow angels.' When they had finished speaking, the snowflake told them of an old snowflake from the season passed, one that had not melted into the ground or the river. The old snowflake had been blown round and round by Mother Nature's winds, circling the globe until he landed back in the coldest place on earth, from where all snow is created.

This snowflake had story after story to tell, having landed in many, many lands and spoken with many, many snow lovers. Not certain where Mother Nature would send him next, he wanted all snowflakes to know of the land of the 'snow angels,' a land, he said, was the most beloved of snow. To all who would listen to him, the old snowflake said, "You have never been loved and wanted more than by the people of the land of the 'snow angels.' Go and find this land and it will be the land where you should serve the greater purpose, for it is the land more than any other, where snow is loved and wanted the most!" But, when asked where they might find this land, the old snowflake could not tell them for sure.

Before any snowflake left the land where snow is created, they all inquired of the old snowflake, "How can we find the land of the snow angels? How did you come to find this special land, old snowflake? What is it that we should look for?" The old snowflake could only tell them what he remembered and how he came to believe that this special land was the land of snow angels. Barbara and Helena were mesmerized by the story the snowflake was telling them, wondering how one land could be more special than another, and what could a 'snow angel' possibly even be. When the snowflake asked them once again, "Is it possible that you girls might be snow angels?" they replied, somewhat shocked, "I don't see how we can be angels of any sort, snowflake, for we are still alive." Helena added, "Our grandpa calls us his little angels, but I think that's just a special name he has for us."

Swirling above them now, the snowflake said sadly, "Special girls, little angels, we have been told to look for the land of the snow angels. We landed here last night, hoping that this might be the place, for it is close to the high mountain peaks the old snowflake said it was near. Unfortunately, many snowflakes here are telling us that too many people of this land do not want us here. We can hear the prayers that are said about snow and this land has too many prayers for snow to pass it by, for us to believe that this could be the land of the snow angels. Some of us will stay here and melt into the river and the ground, but most of us will blow away during the night, continuing our search for a land where we are wanted and loved."

Grandpa had run into the house and gotten pencil and paper, failing to answer grandma's inquiry as to what he had been doing outside. Having heard more than his ears could believe, he slowly rounded the corner of the house, pretending to not know that Helena and Barbara were even there. Startled by their grandpa, the girls could only blurt out, "Oh, hi grandpa, we were just coming in for breakfast. We've been playing in the snow." The snow was in a furious frenzy, swirling round and round, up and down and sideways. Grandpa told Helena and Barbara, "Girls, you probably should go inside and get your breakfast so we won't be late for church. I'm sure you'll want to say a few more prayers for more snow, especially on this most holy of days! Tell grandmother that I'll be right along." Barbara turned to go inside, but Helena looked closely at grandpa, wondering what he meant by suggesting they say a few prayers for snow while at church this morning. Had he heard them talking to the snow? Had he heard the snow talking to them? Was grandpa a lover of snow? Grandpa put his arm on her shoulder, turned her in the direction of the house and gave her a big wink, saying, "Go on now. I have a few things to say . . . I mean, I have a few things to do. I'll be right along." Helena threw her arms round her grandpa, kissed him on the cheek, and told him, "You're the best, grandpa. I love you so much!"

Grandpa waited until he heard the porch door close. The snow had stopped swirling and had settled on the ground. Uncertain of how he should approach things, grandpa just started speaking, talking to no one in particular, but hoping the snow would listen to him as it did to the girls. "I'm not sure whether anyone can hear me, but I think I know of a place where 'snow angels' live." He waited and waited, but nothing was heard. A little snow had started swirling round his boots, which he thought odd for there was no wind to speak of. Curious, he continued, "I have seen what can only be described as 'snow angels' in this very land which we call Ashburn. If someone were looking for 'snow angels,' not that anyone I know of might be, they need not search any further than this very property and one farm over." Again, he waited to see if the snow might speak to him, or if this wasn't a great game the girls hadn't conjured up, but he heard nothing. Out of nowhere, the snow swirled in great circles, rising up from the ground, as though he were in a personal snow storm, blowing furiously, covering grandpa from head to toe in powdery crystals.

Inside, grandma asked insistently, "Wherever did your grandfather go? He said he was going to sweep the steps and bring you two in for breakfast. Did either of you see him?" Helena was first to reply, telling her, "Oh, yes, grandma. Barbara and I were just playing with the snow and grandpa called us in. He said to tell you he had a couple of things to do and would be right along. He promised we would not be late for church!" "That's right, grandma," Barbara chimed in. He said we should

THE SNOW ANGEL

59

probably say a few more prayers this morning for . . ." Helena's hand clamped tightly against Barbara's mouth like it had been shot from a cannon. "What Barbara was going to say was that we should say a few more prayers for continued wonderful weather, because grandpa knows how much you like nice weather, grandma. He'll be along in a minute." Grandma looked questioningly at Helena and Barbara, retorting, "Sounds to me like a bunch of malarkey going on around here."

Outside, still in a cyclone of snow, grandpa could have passed for a live snowman, so covered was he in snow. As the snow finally settled, grandpa blew a few flakes away from his mouth, saying, "Am I to assume that somebody heard what I said and might want to hear a little more?" On the very end of his nose, a large, bright, and very shiny snowflake jumped in the air two or three times, finally catching grandpa's attention. Sparkling like the most brilliant diamond, the snowflake asked Walter, "Sir, would you be a believer in snow and a lover of snow as the two young girls appear to be?" Grandpa, replied, "The two little angels you speak of are my grand-daughters, and they are indeed, lovers of and believers in snow. Yes, I too, am a believer in snow and a lover of snow, though my dear wife of more than fifty years does not share the same love, I am sorry to say, though she is the love of my life. There was a time when she loved the snow as much as I, but a recent loss to our family took the love of snow away from her."

"Kind sir," the snowflake started, "We are the snow of this season, created only a very short time ago. We know nothing of snows passed, except of a land where there are 'snow angels;' told to us by an old snowflake. It was a land he discovered in his travels of last season, and survived the winter long to tell all new snowflakes about. You see, sir, we wish to travel and land where we are wanted and loved, where we might serve the greater purpose, turning to water and furthering Mother Nature's cycle of life." Interrupting, grandpa said, "I know of Mother Nature's cycle of life, for I am a farmer, have been for all of my years, even

JL CRAWFORD

as a boy to my father. This season passed was the best growing season I have ever known, and it was born from two winter seasons of heavy snow. I believe the ground is still rich, fertile, and moist enough to give us another great bounty in the coming season, even if the snow does not come this winter. I understand and appreciate the value of snow and am thankful everyday to our Lord, as well as to Mother Nature for their benevolence."

"Then tell us, farmer and grandfather, what you know about 'snow angels,' for we must fly away to another place, if we are to find that special land. What do you know of snow angels?" Walter told them of the shapes he discovered in his yard and Mr. Cranford's last winter, even drawing a picture of them on the paper he had brought outside. He told them of their mysterious appearance and how they had outlasted all of the other snow, remaining for almost two weeks after all of the other snow had melted in Ashburn. Interested in what grandpa was telling him, the snowflake said, "The old snowflake described a shape to us. He said it was truly angelic, just like the angels we fly near when we are in the heavens. This drawing you have shown us looks very much like what he tried to describe to us. Perhaps this could be the land of the 'snow angels,' but if so, why are so many prayers against snow said in this land? Why would snow angels leave their mark in a land where snow is neither loved, nor wanted?" Bowing his head apologetically, grandpa said, "I do not know the answer to that question, snowflake. I know that many people of this land are tired of snow for the pain that it brought us in years past. I know that even my dear wife shares that sentiment, though she has been a lover of snow her whole life. It is our belief that the snow angels we saw here were made by our dear, departed Eleanor and Samuel, taken from us two years ago, in the heaviest of snows, along with four others from our town. We believe they came to visit us and left their mark in the snow, for us to know of their visit. We do believe in angels, snowflake."

Floating up in the air, the snowflake said to grandpa, "Sir, your story has great credence and could very well be the explanation for the old snowflake's story. All of the snowflakes around have heard what you told me and will decide for themselves if this is the land where they should serve the greater purpose, or fly away to another land. I must tell your story to those snowflakes that do not know of you. I cannot answer whether more snow will come to your land, for that is Mother Nature's decision. I wish your land a great bounty and all grace in Mother Nature's care." In a huge swirl, the snowflake flew away with millions of other snowflakes, but grandpa remained covered in crystals, almost from head to toe.

He made his way toward the house, brushing himself off as he opened the door. "Walter!" grandma shouted. "What on earth have you been doing? Have you been playing in the snow? You're covered from head to toe!" Not even aware of how much snow was still on him grandpa shook his self right in the middle of the kitchen, creating an instantaneous snowstorm. Snow swirled around grandma and grandpa, Barbara and Helena. The girls laughed and giggled, screaming, "Hello, snow, hello, snow!" Grandma opened the kitchen window and the snow flew outside like it had been sucked out through a giant straw. All of the snow that had been on grandpa disappeared right out the window! Grandma was aghast! How could that have happened? The girls laughed so hard, Barbara fell off her chair and Helena had to hold her tummy to keep from bursting.

Grandma quickly closed the window, tossed grandpa's plate of food on the table in front of him and said, "One of us doesn't have time to play in the snow; I must get ready for church," and stormed out of the kitchen. Grandpa sat in his chair and started to eat his cold eggs and bacon, when Helena giggled almost uncontrollably, pointing past him. Grandpa turned and looked in the direction where she was pointing, and all three of them burst out in laughter. The snow that had flown out the kitchen window was swirling just outside the window, as though putting on a dance for the three of them. Grandpa and the girls all waved at the snow and were greeted with the shiniest, brightest light show they had ever witnessed. Then, to their greatest delight, the snow flew upwards in a funnel, swirled round and round, and flew straight at the kitchen window, forming the words—***Snow Loves You!*** Grandpa and the girls all waved back and yelled, "We love the snow!" The snow flew away just as grandma came back into the kitchen. Firmly, she looked at all three of them, with no clue of what had transpired. Looking at grandpa, she said, "Well, I think it's about time we headed off to church. Walter, I believe you have some more dishes and cleaning up to do when we get home." "Yes, dear," Grandpa replied, as he gave Helena and Barbara a gigantic wink!

As they rode in the wagon to church, Helena and Barbara waved to all the snow that swirled round them. Grandma kept asking, "What is causing all of this snow to blow as it does? There is no wind about. Walter, perhaps you should slow the pace." "Mother," grandpa replied, "If we go any slower, the ants will get to church before we do and we'll be late for service!" Hearing Barbara and Helena chuckle in the back of the wagon, grandma turned sharply admonishing them with a stern frown. The girls quickly straightened up, but as soon as grandma turned back around, they scooped up handfuls of powdery snow and threw them in the air. Snowflakes landed everywhere, including on the back of grandma's coat and on her Sunday hat, but she was never the wiser! She had no idea why those girls could just giggle and giggle so.

Chapter 6

GRANDPA SECURED THE wagon near the front of the church and helped grandma down from her seat. Barbara and Helena had already jumped mightily from the back of the wagon and were making snowballs, readying themselves to torment Johnny and Petey who were just arriving with their parents. No sooner had the two boys jumped down from their wagons when they were assaulted by a barrage of snowballs from Helena and Barbara, pummeled from head to toe. They recovered and hastily made snowballs for the return attack, only to see Barbara and Helena wrap their arms round Reverend Hastings at the front door of the church. They were giggling so hard, they could barely muster "Merry Christmas, Reverend!" Mr. Cranford and Mr. Braun were quick to berate their sons, telling them, "Boys, you don't throw snowballs at girls," only to hear, "But dad, they started it."

Grandma and grandpa were just climbing the church steps, ready to greet Reverend Hastings when grandma heard the girls say in unison, "Reverend Hastings, we have been praying and praying for snow for so long. Last night we prayed extra hard and look what Jesus brought us! Isn't a snowy-white Christmas just the best ever, isn't it Reverend Hastings?" He was just telling the girls how Jesus hears everyone's prayers and tries his best to answer all of them when grandma interrupted, saying, "Well, I said prayers for no snow; He must not have been listening to me." "Now mother," grandpa quickly jumped in to save Reverend Hastings from her wrath, "The good Lord can't bring snow to those who pray for it and not bring snow for those who pray against it, when they live in the same house. You know as well as I do that Mother Nature has a say in the matter as well."

Surprised by his revelation, grandma responded, "Walter, since when did you become the provider of grand providence!" and marched into church, stopping short and turning to say, "Merry Christmas, Reverend Hastings, the Lord has indeed brought us a grand and glorious Christmas Day!" "Aye, indeed he has Helen, and a merry Christmas to you and these little angels. You and Walter are doing a fine job with these two—you're doing Eleanor and Samuel proud, you are!" Grandma planted a kiss on the Reverend's cheek, and teary-eyed, said, "Thank you, Reverend it's very kind of you to say." As grandma and the girls started inside the church, Reverend Hastings added, "It won't be long before we'll have these two fine ladies walking down the . . ." "Placing his hand firmly on Reverend Hastings' shoulder, grandpa chimed in, "Hold on right there Reverend, let's not go getting too far ahead of ourselves, shall we?" and they looked each other in the face and laughed heartily, one grandfather to another.

Throughout the service, Helena and Barbara watched Johnny and Petey and Johnny and Petey watched Helena and Barbara. The boys were furious at having been bested in a snowball fight they were never even a part of, making faces that Helena and Barbara knew meant they would be out for revenge—at their first opportunity. Only concerned just a little, the girls couldn't stop from giggling all through service, much to the chagrin of grandma who must have shushed them not less than ten times each! Reverend Hastings greeted the congregation with the heartiest "Merry Christmas to all and welcome to the church of the Lord!" He implored everyone to turn to his neighbors beside, in front, and in back of them and wish them a very merry Christmas as well. Barbara looked at Helena and said, "It's a good thing the boys aren't close, they would never wish us a merry Christmas after the pounding we put on them!" and they giggled even more.

As Reverend Hastings told the story of the birth of Christ, he reminded them of that cold and snowy day in the manger in Bethlehem, a day that had much more snow than today. He was convinced that Jesus had instructed Mother Nature to deliver even the smallest amount of snow to Ashburn so that the story of Christ's birth would be felt even more deeply. As he neared the end of his sermon, he raised his hands above his head and looked skyward. The entire congregation was silent, knowing not what holy reverence he would disperse. Reverend Hastings, still looking toward the heavens said, "Lord above, as your servant and messenger, I ask little of you. No man, woman, nor child here asks much of you either, for you are responsible for bringing each of us all that is good in our lives. However, dear Lord, we have a hole in our hearts in this village. We have a great want for something which we have no power to resolve of our own making." Everyone listening to his words could only imagine what he was going to ask for; each and every individual no doubt filling in the blank with his or her own wish, want, or desire. "Dear Jesus," Reverend Hastings continued, "On this day of your birth, I ask that you think only of the children, just as you were but a babe in the manger. Lord, for the children of Ashburn, please work in consort with Mother Nature and deliver us the wonderful gift of snow that blankets our lands, provides enjoyment for children and adults of all ages, and which nourishes our fields and rivers and streams! In your most holy name, we pray."

Every child in church was absolutely speechless, but not a single one could hold still either. Could Reverend Hastings really have asked Jesus himself to help bring snow? All of the children turned and looked at each other, round and round they turned, the sheer delight clearly reflected on all their faces. It just had to snow now! They would soon get the greatest snow of all time! The big sled race would be held for sure. Johnny Cranford and Petey Braun were strutting like peacocks, each mouthing, "Oh yeah, the champ is coming back!" Many of the grownups were also smiling, but a good many, lead by no one more upset than grandma herself, had powerful-looking frowns shown clearly on their faces. Barbara and Helena looked at grandma then, turned to grandpa who raised a finger to his mouth that suggested they not say a single word right now. Grandpa broke the silence, saying, "Well, that was a different Christmas sermon to be sure. Perhaps we best get home and open all those gifts that Santa brought last night!" Moving toward the aisle, grandma mumbled, "Yes, we best be getting home. If someone has His way, we're in for the biggest snow of all time! Come along children, Walter, let's be on our way."

On the way out, Reverend Hastings was saying good-bye to everyone, shaking hands, hugging the kids who thanked him profusely, getting some cold stares from the grownups that didn't appreciate his closing prayer. The girls hugged him tight, but said nothing, and Walter shook his hand, offering Christmas greetings once more, but nothing else. When Reverend Hastings placed his hand on grandma's shoulder to wish her a merry Christmas, she ducked right under it without looking his way. He had just gotten out the words "Merry Chr . . ." when grandma turned to him and replied, "Perhaps we'll see you next week Reverend, if we're not all snowed in!" She turned gruffly and made her way to the wagon. Grandpa looked at Reverend Hastings and gave him a sharp wink that told him not to worry, she would get over it. Grandma loved Reverend Hastings, as did everyone in Ashburn.

Barbara and Helena had been thinking about what Johnny and Petey might do when they got out of church, certain they had been planning a counter-attack. Before they went into the church, they had hidden four snowballs under the church steps. As soon as they got to the bottom step, the girls reached under and snared the artillery they would have at the ready in case of attack. They hadn't gotten another twenty feet when Johnny and Petey burst from both sides of the church, each with a snowball in his hands, yelling, "Ah ha! We've got you surrounded whiny girls! Did you think you could get away with that wimpy attack when we weren't even ready?" They were looking at each other, laughing, as they got ready to seek their revenge. They didn't even see Barbara and Helena reach into their pockets and pull out, not one, but two snowballs each! The girls moved away from each other, creating a smaller target for the boys' single opportunity, their hands behind their back. Still upset with Reverend Hastings, grandma let her emotions get the most of her and wasn't about to let those boys pummel her girls. She bent over to scoop some snow, prepared to come to their defense, not knowing that the girls already had two snowballs.

About that time, Petey launched his attack on Barbara. Throwing errantly, his snowball smacked grandma right in the bottom as she bent over to make a snowball! Surprised to no end, and even more embarrassed at the prospect of having a big white splotch on her dark coat, in the most inappropriate of places, she sought out the culprit. As soon as his snowball had found its unintended target, Petey Braun had run behind the church, well out of sight of grandma and the wrath he knew would surely come. Barbara had thrown one snowball at him as he ran and hit him squarely in the back before he had gotten around the corner of the church. Reverend Hastings had seen the whole thing and was laughing at Barbara's well-thrown hit on Petey, and yelled, "Great throw!" Grandma hadn't seen Barbara's snowball hit Petey and, shocked by it all, had dropped the snow she had scooped up. When she saw Reverend Hastings laughing and heard him say, "Great throw!" she assumed he was laughing at her and was making fun of her having been hit in the bottom by someone's snowball. Seeing that Barbara still had one snowball and no target in sight, she went to Barbara and asked, "May I borrow that?" Not waiting for Barbara to answer, she grabbed the snowball, reared back, took aim and let it fly—right in the direction of Reverend Hastings!

Realizing all that had happened, grandpa was just about to tell grandma it wasn't Reverend Hastings who had thrown the snowball and he wasn't laughing at her, but the words never got the chance to come out of his mouth before the snowball let loose from her hand. Reverend Hastings was laughing so hard still from Barbara's hit on Petey, he wasn't paying attention to anything else. Grandma's snowball could have been fired out of a rifle barrel, straight and true and fast it was. Just as he started to collect himself, he opened his eyes, wet with tears from laughing so hard, and then he saw it. Whatever it was, it was coming at him at a million miles per hour! His mouth was wide open in disbelief. The whole world came to a standstill.

Grandpa had watched the trajectory of grandma's throw and knew it was headed for the bulls-eye! It appeared as though it was moving in slow motion. Grandpa heard himself yell, "Duck, Reverend," but wasn't sure if the words ever came out. At the last split-second, Reverend Hastings' legs dropped from under him. Grandma's snowball blasted with all fury right smack into his monastic hat, knocking it clean off his head and inside the open church door! Not a sound was to be heard, inside or out. Johnny and Helena hadn't even thrown their snowballs yet, in fact, they each dropped them to the ground and fled to their parents' wagons. Realizing what had just happened, recognizing that some greater power had perhaps spared his life, Reverend Hastings, who was sitting on the top step, burst into uncontrollable laughter! Soon, everyone else did as well, except grandma, who stood there with her hands on her hips, looking to see if she could get off another throw.

Laughing just as hard as everyone else, grandpa pulled himself together and came to grandma's side. He quickly told her that it wasn't Reverend Hastings who had thrown the snowball that hit her, but was from out of nowhere. Sure he fibbed a little and didn't say who had really thrown it, for she wasn't the intended target anyway. He told her also that Reverend Hastings wasn't laughing at her, despite the bright white splotch on her backside, but that he was laughing at Barbara's hit on Petey Braun! Almost too embarrassed to speak, her face flushed the brightest red almost immediately. She clasped her hands to her face, not wanting anyone to see her, especially Reverend Hastings; she was at a loss of words. She turned to go to the wagon, telling grandpa, "Oh Walter, I'm so embarrassed; I could have knocked him senseless. I'll never be able to look him in the eyes again." The hand she felt on her shoulder did not have a glove on it though, as she knew Walter's did. Fearfully, she opened her eyes, only to be face to face with Reverend Hastings, who was wearing a huge smile.

"Helen Broadhurst," the Reverend said in his heavy Irish brogue, "Do no worry, my sweet friend, for we all make simple mistakes. Certainly, I've made more than me share of them. Even I have to go to confession—almost weekly . . . but don't tell anyone I told ya so!" Speaking more loudly now, he said, "What I really want to know, Mrs. Broadhurst, is, will you promise to be the starting pitcher on the church baseball team next year? With that fastball of yours, we'll win every game!" And he bent over and laughed and laughed and laughed, and so did grandma and everyone else. Collecting himself, he added, "I better go inside and check on my hat. The Bishop will make me do double penance for sure!" And he laughed all the way inside.

Johnny had climbed into his parent's wagon and was starting off, as was Petey Braun, sitting with his back to the church. Helena and Barbara had just climbed into the back of their wagon and were waiting for grandpa and grandma. Grandma told Walter to go ahead and get in, that she would get in on her side by herself. This was certainly odd, Walter thought, for grandma always expected him to be the consummate gentleman, helping her in and out of the wagon. As he started to climb into the wagon, he noticed grandma at the back of the wagon, bent over. When she straightened up, he saw in her hands the two snowballs that Helena had held, but not thrown at Johnny Cranford. Grandpa saw the look in her eyes that he had seen just a short time before she let one loose at Reverend Hastings. "Oh, no," he thought, "She's not going to do what I think she is, is she?"

JL CRAWFORD

In a rapid motion he didn't know she was even capable of, grandma let loose two speeding fastballs, one headed for Johnny Cranford and one for Petey Braun. Wondering what grandpa was looking at, Helena and Barbara had turned simultaneously, just in time to see grandma launch the assault. When each snowball was but seconds from its intended target, grandma called out, "Oh Petey, oh Johnny!" Each boy turned to see who was calling their name and as they did, they were both caught flush in the chest with white powdery explosions! The snowballs burst into a million snowflakes, splattering each boy's face. Grandma was on the ground laughing like grandpa had never before seen her laugh. Johnny and Billy were so stunned that they couldn't utter even the first words. Each boy's parents burst into laughter as well, with each dad saying, "I told you not to throw snowballs at girls. I hope you learned your lesson!" From the ground, grandma added, "If I ever catch you throwing snowballs at my precious angels again, you'll have to deal with Helen Broadhurst's fearsome fastball!" Grandpa almost fell out of the wagon he laughed so hard. Helena and Barbara jumped out of the wagon, picked grandma up from the ground, and started to brush the snow off her coat when she stopped them, saying, "Don't brush the snow off of me . . . this is one grandma that really does love the snow!" She hugged them both and they got into the wagon for the ride home. Opening Christmas presents was going to be the best time ever!

Indeed it was, too. No sooner had the girls gotten home than they ran inside and plopped down in front of the tree, each holding a present to open. Of course, they waited for grandma and grandpa to come in and get settled. Grandpa started a fire and grandma asked who wanted a steaming cup of hot chocolate! To no one's surprise, **everyone** did, and they all wanted some of grandma's fresh-baked Christmas cookies as well. Before anyone knew it, all of the presents had been opened and the girls were "Oohing" and "Ahhing," showing each other what they had received, and thanking Santa Claus and grandma and grandpa all around. Grandpa was giving grandma a great big hug and a kiss for making him a thick sweater, asking her, "Whenever did you find time to make this? I never saw you knitting anything!" Grandma just gave him that look that said, "I do lots of things that no one ever knows anything about," which got her one more, big hug! She thanked grandpa for making her a wonderful corner cabinet with glass doors and "more shelves than I have things to put in it!" She was always telling Walter that the china and crystal should be on display for everyone to see, not hidden away in cupboards, and now, finally, she could show it off. She was already taking dishes from the kitchen and putting them inside the new cabinet in the dining room.

Helena was looking at Barbara, who seemed a bit forlorn, at least not nearly as happy as she should be, despite having received more gifts than anyone! She was just asking Barbara what was bothering her when grandpa stood and asked, "By the by, who was making all that noise last night? What were you girls doing in your room?" Completely miffed at what he was talking about, as was grandma, the girls blurted out, "Nothing grandpa, we were sleeping. We didn't hear a thing!" Looking at them in a disbelieving way, grandpa said, "How could you not have heard that racket! There was banging and clanging enough to wake the dead, and it was coming from the chimney. By the time I got my coat on and went out to look, there was nothing to be found, and the noise had stopped. I was going to look again this morning, but I plum forgot. I guess I better go see if I can see what it was all about." Barbara jumped to her feet and said, "Well, since there aren't any more presents to open, and since there must not really be a Santa Claus, I might as well go with you, grandpa." Grandma quickly jumped in, saying, "No more presents? Didn't you get enough young lady?" Realizing how she had made them feel, Barbara quickly replied, "Oh, grandma, grandpa, I didn't mean it that way. It's just that I only wanted one thing more than anything else, and I only asked Santa Claus, and since I didn't get it, well, that just proves there is no Santa Claus." She hung her head down low and got up to get her coat, wearing the saddest little girl face the world had ever seen. Grandpa turned to go outside and told her, "Well, maybe a little fresh air will take your mind off of it," and outside they went.

Grandma looked over at Helena who seemed a bit sad for her little sister, telling her, "It's true grandma, the only thing she really wanted was a new saucer, and she made me promise not to tell you or grandpa." Grandma came over and took Helena's hand and said, "You don't ever question the power of the good Lord, Helena, and little children should never question the spirit of Santa Claus. Come with me over towards the window and let's see if they can figure out what made all that noise." Helena looked questioningly at her grandmother, but didn't say anything. Seeing her look closely at her face for any expression, grandma held Helena's hand and gave her a big wink, telling her, "Let's just have a look-see outside," a smile forming on her face. Outside, grandpa was looking all around for any sign of anything out of place, but looked at Barbara and, opening his arms wide, he gave her a 'you got me' look. Barbara had been following him, right on his heels, not really interested, so grandpa said, "Why don't you go around that side of the house and look and I'll go around the other side. If we don't find anything, we'll go back in and have another cup of hot chocolate." "Okay grandpa," Barbara mumbled quietly and turned in the opposite direction, moping as she went along. As soon as she got out of sight, grandpa high-tailed it around the corner of the house where he could watch her come around the far side, but not see him. He saw grandma and Helena looking out the window, grandma knowingly and Helena wondering what it was all about.

Barbara had not gotten five feet around the corner of the house when was heard the loudest scream known to man—a scream of utter joy and happiness! "Grandpa," Barbara yelled, "Grandpa, come look at what is here. Oh, it must be, it must be!" Grandpa came running, acting though he was out of breath, saying, "What Barbara, what is it?" She was standing over a large, round-shaped item, wrapped in Christmas paper and all scuffed along the edges. Grandma threw open the window and called out, "Barbara, whatever is the matter? Are you all right? What has happened?" Barbara was furiously tearing at the paper, the biggest smile on her face. She was nearly out of breath with excitement. Grandpa was telling her, "Wait, be careful. We don't know what that could be," but Barbara blurted out excitedly, "Oh, yes, I know what it is grandpa. It just has to be what I asked Santa for! It just has to be my new saucer!"

Playing along, grandpa asked, "Well what on earth is it doing outside? Why didn't Santa leave it inside with all of the other presents?" Barbara didn't hear a word grandpa was saying, as she tore off the last of the paper. In fact, she was spell-bound, or so it seemed. Grandma called out to her, "Barbara, what is it, angel? What was in all of that paper?" When Barbara didn't reply, Helena called out, "Barbara, are you okay? What is wrong?" Barbara spun around to face them, her mouth wide open, barely able to utter a sound, finally managing to get out a quiet, "There *is* a Santa Claus, Helena! Oh, grandma, grandpa, you must see what it says!" The three of them answered in unison, "What does what say?" "Here, on my brand new saucer. It's in the finest engraving, too. It says, "Merry Christmas, Barbara, my precious angel, Love, S.C.!"

She fell to her knees, hugging her new saucer. Grandpa looked at grandma and Helena, who were both giving him that all-knowing look, for who else used that phrase for Barbara and Helena? No one, but grandpa! Feigning bewilderment, grandpa rubbed his chin whiskers and, looking towards Barbara said, "I'll bet that's what all the racket was last night. Why, that saucer won't fit down the chimney, not even close. I'll bet Santa was having a dickens of a time and that's why it's all scuffed up, too. I guess he must have dropped it off the roof when his sleigh took off to the Cranford's farm!" Helena and grandma both agreed with grandpa, saying, "Yep, that's the only explanation I can think of!" After a wonderful Christmas dinner and even more hot chocolate, the two tired girls made their way to bed, each stopping to give their grandparents the biggest hug ever. Barbara jumped onto grandpa's lap and gave him a big kiss on his whiskery-cheek and told him quietly, so no one else could hear, "Good night, Santa Claus!" Grandpa, tearfully hugged her and said, "Good night, my precious angel!"

Chapter 7

BEFORE THE GIRLS knew it, the Christmas holiday was over and they were back in school; not a single snowflake having fallen since Christmas Day. Barbara got to use her new saucer just twice before the last of the snow melted away and Helena did not get a single chance to go sledding, for the snow wasn't nearly enough to allow for it. They got to ice skate with all of their friends, but the girls could feel the animosity for them by Johnny and Petey; the two of them just dreading the likelihood that Barbara and Helena would be sled champs for another whole year—without even getting a chance to race for the trophy! On the way home from school one day, all of the children were talking about the snow, wondering where it was, why it wasn't snowing and snowing and snowing like it usually did. Helena and Barbara didn't dare tell anyone that they had talked to the snow and had been told that the snow would not come where it was not wanted or loved. Who on earth would believe them?

Helena thought about a way to bring the subject up and asked, "Do you think that all of the prayers said by so many people against snow might be the reason? After all, if Reverend Hastings needed to say a prayer for snow to come, couldn't the prayers of a lot of people keep the snow from coming to Ashburn?" She waited to see who might have something to say about it, watching Barbara to make sure she didn't reveal their little secret. Mary Thomas chimed in, offering, "I know that my father has been saying prayers against snow, and my grams, too! They all said they were tired of snow and didn't care if they ever saw it again, as long as they lived!" Willie Pearson added, "My mom has been having a bunch of ladies over to the house for tea and they just sit around saying bad things about snow. My dad says they're just a bunch of cackling hens!" That got a laugh from everyone, and even Johnny Cranford pitched in, saying, "My grandmother and grandfather told my dad that all of their friends, maybe all of the grandparents in Ashburn, have been saying prayers for no snow!" "Well, not my grandpa or grandma," Barbara quickly retorted, "At least not my grandma anymore."

Helena silenced everyone saying, "Well, it sure sounds like a lot of people are praying for no snow. It might only be the children who want snow, and maybe our prayers aren't enough!" Petey Braun added, "I don't ever pray for snow, because I never had to before; it always snows. Maybe there aren't enough people praying *for* snow to counter those who are praying for no snow!" Shocked that Petey Braun could deduce something as brilliant as that, Barbara looked at him and said, "Well, Petey Braun, however did you become so brilliant? All of my brains must be rubbing off on you!" That got an even bigger laugh from everyone, except for Petey Braun. Convinced, that a lack of prayers for snow was not enough to counter all of the prayers for no snow, Helena told everyone, "We must be certain to pray for snow every night. Pray like you have never prayed before, and be sure to tell everyone else that they must actually pray for snow. It's not enough to just hope and think that the snow will come." With a plan for bringing snow to Ashburn all set in their minds, the children all went home.

It was the last day of January and still, not the first snowflake had fallen since Christmas Day. It was still plenty cold and the children could ice skate to their hearts content, but they all wanted to go sledding, make snowmen, build snow forts, have snowball battles, and just run and jump in the soft, fluffy whiteness. Sleds that had had been prepped for races, even those just for fun, sat rusting away in sheds. Barbara's new saucer didn't even have one scratch on it yet. In most years, her saucer would already have a hundred dents and dings by this time, and her rump would have been sore from too many uneven landings on rocks and stumps and the like. Wilkins Hill was as green as spring time, perhaps as green as the children were blue.

Everyone figured that February would surely bring the snow, for February was the snowiest month of all. The peaks of Daedalus and Colossus were covered in snow, but it was way too high for any of the children to venture to such heights; even the grownups didn't go that high unless they had to. Why had the snow come across the mountains and snowed on just the tops, everyone wondered. Towards the end of February, the skies darkened like they hadn't in months and months. Grandpa said that even if it started as rain, it would have to come down as snow because it was so cold out. Convinced it was going to snow, the girls went out to the barn and waxed their sleds; Barbara shined her saucer with a special oil that grandpa mixed up for her. By the time they went to bed however, not the first flake had fallen. Each girl had knelt down to say prayers before jumping into bed, and each of them had prayed and prayed their hardest for snow. When she gave them each a kiss goodnight, grandma said she, too, was going to pray her hardest for snow, and she would be certain that grandpa did as well.

The girls even promised each other they would dream of snow—nothing else. They locked fingers with each other and said, "Deal!" To their greatest surprise, when they awoke the next morning, grandma had just opened their door and said, "Well, the power of prayer must work! Look out the window!" Sure enough, the farm was covered in snow, if only about an inch or so, but that was enough for sleds and saucers! "Oh, grandma," the girls yelled, "Can we just go out for a little bit? Can we, can we?" Grandma looked at them lovingly and said, "Go ahead, but only until I fix your breakfast then back inside you come! You still have to get ready for school, although it might be okay just this one time to be a little late!" Grandma had never seen two children get dressed as she did that morning. Even grandpa asked, as they flew by him on their way out the door, "Did you see that lightning that just shot through here?" Grandma and grandpa watched the girls through the window. Grandpa had his arm around grandma's waist, and giving her a little tug towards him said, "Kind of reminds me of watching Eleanor when she was their age, doesn't it"? Giving him a squeeze back, grandma looked up at him and said, "Yes, yes, it does, Walter. We're mighty lucky to have these two sweet little girls!" Grandpa planted a kiss on grandma's head and replied, "My two precious angels!"

At school, all the talk was about snow, snow, snow. At lunch time, Mrs. Gunder announced, "Well, since no one seems to be able to think about anything but snow, class is dismissed!" The children poured out of the little school building, all of them making their way towards home so they could change into their play clothes. Wilkins Hill was about to be inundated with more kids than it had seen the whole year! Helena and Barbara were in and out of the house in such a flash, grandma didn't even know it was them. Grandpa only saw them for the two seconds it took for them to grab a sled and saucer and fly back out the door. "Nice seeing you," he said, though certain it had fallen on deaf ears. On their way to Wilkins Hill, Helena slowed for a moment. Looking at Barbara, she said, "We haven't even spoken to the snow today, Barbara. Do you think they will think it rude of us?" Comprehending their oversight, Barbara agreed, "Oh, yes, Helena, we must! How could I have forgotten it this morning?" They put down their sled and saucer and bent down on their knees. Each girl picked up a handful of snow and threw it into the air, crying out, "We love you snow, we love you so much! Thank you for coming to Ashburn!"

The snow flew above them, round and round and settled down on their heads and outstretched hands. Two big flakes landed on each of their noses, tickling them to the point of laughter. Helena was first to say, "Oh, snowflakes, where have you been? We have missed you so much and we have been waiting and waiting and waiting. All of the children are so glad that you have returned. Will more snow be coming?" Barbara was bursting with excitement as well, adding, "Yes, snowflakes, all of the children have been waiting and waiting. I got a new saucer for Christmas and the big sled race is nearing, and . . ." "Whoa, slow down girls," the plump snowflake said. "We don't have answers to all of your questions. In fact, we were on our way to another land when nightfall came upon us and we decided to settle here for the night. We know not how long we may stay, whether we may melt in this very land, or move on to the rivers, for we do what Mother Nature directs us to do. We have reason to believe that we may be the last snow of the season for the air over the land where we are created is getting warmer and warmer." "Oh, snowflake," Helena pleaded, "Certainly you can't be the last of the snow for the entire season. We have not even had a chance to enjoy you, and as Barbara said, the big sled race must go on to see who the new champions will be."

Another snowflake stirred in the air, twinkling like a star in the moon light. She told the girls that they were hoping to reach the land of the snow angels, relating the story they, too, had been told by the elder snowflake, back in the land where snow begins its journey. She said that all of the snowflakes on this journey were determined to find the land that had been immortalized as the land of the snow angels! Helena asked if she could say something about the snow angels matter, looking quite curious about the whole thing. She asked, "Snowflakes, what are these 'snow angels' we hear all the snowflakes talking about? Can we help you find them? If we do, will you stay here in our land and proclaim Ashburn the land of the 'snow angels?' And, will snow come here every year, forever and ever?" The plump snowflake, who seemed to be in charge of things, told the girls they were more than welcome to help look for the snow angels, but reminded them that time was running short. "Can you tell us what we are looking for?" Barbara asked. "Are these angels in the sky? Are they made of snow?"

The plump snowflake told them, "I'm sorry girls, but even we do not know exactly what we are looking for. We were told by the elder snowflake that we would know the snow angels as soon as we laid eyes on them. He was certain of that. He said further that, if any snowflakes made it back to the land where snow is created, we should tell the story to as many new snowflakes as are made each season, and tell them where this special land is." Helena and Barbara were beside themselves, but promised the snowflakes they would do their best to look for any sign of snow angels and would report to them early tomorrow morning, before the winds picked up and possibly sent the snow away. Barbara pleaded one last time before they started to Wilkins Hill, "Snowflakes, can't you at least stay until school is over for the week; it's only two more days, and then all of the children can play with you for two more days? Please, snowflakes, can you?" The snowflake reminded them that where and when they go was not up to them; that Mother Nature would decide that for herself, and the snow settled down on the ground around their feet, reminding them, "You better start playing while we are still here, for tomorrow may find us in another land."

Helena and Barbara ran off to Wilkins Hill, telling all the children there to play, play, play, for this might be the last snow of the season! "Who says?" Petey Braun chimed in. "What do you dumb girls know about the snow? I say we have the big sled race today or tomorrow and we'll see who the real champs are!" "Yeah, me too," yelled Johnny Cranford as he barreled right past them down Wilkins Hill, almost running over their toes. "Watch out for the new champs!" he yelled as he flew by them, cackling as only he could do. From out of nowhere, a large white blast of snow hit him square in the back of his cap. Had he been looking back, he would have caught it right in the mouth. "Hey," he screamed as he skidded to a stop. "Who threw that snowball?" "Yeah, who threw that?" Petey offered, as he bent down to get a handful of snow. Just as he did, a big burst of snow exploded on his butt, knocking him to the ground, face-first. He came up with a mouthful of snow, sputtering and spitting snow, ready for a fight, as Johnny moved toward him in support.

Stunned by the torrent of snowballs from out of nowhere, Barbara and Helena both raised their hands, saying, "It wasn't us, we're standing here holding our sled and saucer. Look, there isn't even any snow on our mittens!" Perplexed, the boys looked all around. Children were going up and down Wilkins Hill, no one seeming to pay the boys any mind. Completely clueless, Johnny called out to no one in particular, but for all to hear, "That better not happen again, or there will be heck to pay, you hear me!" "Yeah, that goes for me too," Petey followed, puffing out his chest, but scaring no one. Helena and Barbara just looked at both of them and laughed as the boys made their way to the top of Wilkins Hill once more. They were half way up when the snow swirled around the girls' feet, furiously rising up to eye level. The plump snowflake was laughing so hard, he could barely speak, but between laughs he managed to say, "Wow, that was pretty funny! What do you call those big blasts of snow?" Helena looked at him quizzically, saying, "We call them 'snowballs,' snowflake. Did you have something to do with that?" "Well, of course we did, girls. When snowflakes get too big for their britches, we all gang up on them and drop them into a river. When those two little braggarts started to make wise, we thought we would gang up and do something to stop them, too!" As the snowflakes flew off to land on Wilkins Hill, Barbara and Helena could hear them laughing and laughing.

Helena was so taken by the funny snowflakes she looked at Barbara, dropped her sled off to the side, spread her arms and legs, and dropped backwards to the ground, landing in a burst of snow on either side of her. Giggling all the while, she waved her arms and legs furiously back and forth to her sides and outward, oblivious to the importance of her actions. Seeing her sister having so much fun, Barbara did the same, and they each laughed over and over. Looking down on them from the top of Wilkins Hill, Johnny and Petey yelled out, "That's a good way to practice sledding, you dumb girls! Are you both, crazy or something?" Their cackling laughter could be heard all across the valley as they flew down Wilkins Hill, though Helena and Barbara paid them no mind. Other children though, looking to see what they were doing, looked on in amazement, wondering how something like laying down in the snow could be so funny. Soon enough, two other girls and one boy plopped down flat on their backs into the snow, watching the snow explode out from under them. Before long, they were all three, copying Barbara and Helena, flapping their arms and legs from side to side, laughing and laughing!

Further down the hill, two smaller children were in tears, having flipped off their sleds, when they heard laughter from up above and down below. Looking up and down Wilkins Hill, the two youngsters were amazed to see older children lying on their backs in the snow, flapping their arms and legs and enjoying it so much! "It beats crying," one boy said to the other. "Yeah," the other said, "Let's try it!" Moments later, laughter was heard the full length of Wilkins Hill. Within minutes, every kid on Wilkins Hill was making snow angels, though none had the first clue regarding the importance of things to come! Every kid, except for Johnny Cranford and Petey Braun. They looked up and down the sled course, yelling in unison, "You're all a bunch of dummies! We're gonna be the new sled champs!" Cackling as they went, they made their way to Johnny's house because his dad had promised to make his sled the fastest it had ever been!

By the time all of the children had made their way home from sledding, Wilkins Hill was covered in not less than a hundred snow angels! Johnny and Petey reached the barn where Johnny's dad was working, just as his dad was going toward the house. "Oh, hello boys," Mr. Cranford said. "It's almost dark, but maybe I still have some time to work on that sled. Petey, you better make your way home before your folks get worried about you." "Okay, Mr. Cranford," Petey replied, but stopped to ask, "Can I leave my sled with you and see what you can do with mine?" "Well, sure thing," Mr. Cranford said, "You can pick it up after school tomorrow." "Thanks, sir," Petey responded. Looking at Johnny, he said, "See you in school tomorrow, Johnny."

As he made his way through the Cranford's pasture towards home, Petey remembered all the laughter that had come from Wilkins Hill. Thinking about what all the kids had been doing, Petey looked around to be certain no one was watching, especially Johnny. Hoping he was doing it just right, Petey spread his arms and legs and, trusting what he had seen, fell backwards into the soft snow with a pronounced 'floof,' as snow blew out from both sides. Waving his arms and legs furiously from side to side, he couldn't keep from laughing. In the barn, Johnny thought he heard someone laughing and poked his head outside, but darkness had fallen and he couldn't see his friend and buddy, Petey Braun, acting like a dumb girl! It probably was a good thing, for Petey would never have lived it down. In the Broadhurst's yard, Helena and Barbara were doing the very same thing, laughing away!

The next morning, Friday, the girls awoke to a bright, sunny day. Looking outside her window, Helena told Barbara, "Oh, I hope the sun isn't too warm today. There's so little snow that I don't want it to melt. Remember what the snowflakes said about maybe this being the last snow of the season." "We should be sure to speak to the snow this morning on the way to school," Barbara replied. "Maybe we can talk it into staying through the weekend. I really haven't gotten to use my new saucer very much." The girls rushed through the breakfast grandma had made for them, grabbed their book bags, threw their coats on and flew out the door like lightning bolts! Grandpa just stared in amazement, before saying, "I never saw them that interested in school before." Grandma said, "I remember running out the door each morning like that . . . when I was interested in catching up with a certain handsome boy on my way to school!" Smiling, grandpa looked at her and said, "That certain boy

JL CRAWFORD

remembers those days full well, my sweet, but let's pray they don't have, I mean, *we* don't have boy problems, not just yet!" Grandma smiled at Walter and quietly said, "Someday soon, dear; you'd better get ready!" Grandpa sighed and rolled his eyes.

Helena and Barbara ran around the side of the house and skidded to a halt. In front of them, big swirls of snow were rising up from the ground, catching the wind and blowing away from them. "Wait," both girls yelled simultaneously, "Don't go yet, we need to talk to you. We want to tell you how much we love you and let you know how much you are wanted here in Ashburn!" From out of the snow swirl the plump snowflake from yesterday twirled in front of them. "We're not going anywhere yet, girls, but word has come to us from where we were yesterday, of a possible visit from 'snow angels;' we must go there immediately!" "We'll go with you snowflake," Helena replied, "For it's on our way to school." Millions upon millions of snowflakes arose from the ground, just like the desert sandstorms the girls had seen pictures of in books. The snow blew in the direction of Wilkins Hill as the girls tried to keep up. No sooner than the snow had arisen high above the ground though, it stopped blowing eastward and spun in gigantic circles around their farm, round and round it went.

"What do you suppose is the matter?" Barbara called out to Helena. Helena was calling out to the snowflakes as though they were lost, "Wilkins Hill is that way," pointing in an easterly direction. Suddenly, as though regaining their direction, the snowflakes turned eastward, crossed the big pasture and moved across the Cranford's farm towards Wilkins Hill. The girls were running as fast as they could, but the snow was too fast for them in the wind. Half-way across the Cranford's farm, the snow stopped again, hundreds of feet up in the sky, swirling and twirling like a hoop skirt at a barn dance. "Why are they stopping again?" yelled Barbara, almost out of breath. Out of answers, Helena replied, "I don't know, but let's catch up and get over to Wilkins Hill!" Just then, the snowflakes started flying eastward once more, befuddling the girls even more. Ten minutes later and completely out of breath the girls leaned against the fence at the base of Wilkins Hill. High above them, it seemed as though every snowflake in the whole world was flying around Wilkins Hill. It was the biggest snow storm the girls had ever seen, but it wasn't settling onto the ground, just flying round and round as though it was lost and didn't know where to land.

More children stopped to look at the furious snow storm as they made their way to school. Even Johnny and Petey couldn't believe their eyes, for the sun was out and there were no snow clouds to be seen. Johnny finally said, "Wow! If all that snow lands on Wilkins Hill we'll be sure to have the big race!" Helena and Barbara yelled out, "We love you snow, we love you. We want you to stay here in Ashburn!" Dumbfounded, Petey looked at them and said, "You stupid girls, the snow can't hear you. It's just gonna go where the winds blows it." "He's right," Johnny said more delicately, "We better get to school before Mrs. Gunder keeps us after for being late, then we won't get to play at all!" "No, you're wrong!" Barbara blurted out. "We can talk to the snow and the snow hears us and speaks to us, too; you'll see!" "What do you expect from a stupid nine-year old?" Petey scolded her. "I know I am, but what are you?" Barbara mimicked, "you're only nine-years old too, and not very smart at all!" Helena silenced the two of them saying, "What Barbara means is that we can talk to the snow in our prayers, like everyone has been doing every night, right guys? It was all of our prayers that brought this snow to us, so maybe through prayer the snow does hear us." She quickly hushed Barbara who was about to launch into another snow-filled tirade, telling her, "Come on, Barbara, we better get to school."

The other kids had already set off towards school and Johnny and Petey were well ahead of them as well. When the girls were out of sight of everyone else, the snow flew down towards them, engulfing them so thickly that the girls could not see two feet in front of them. "What are you doing snowflakes?" Helena called out to them. "Yeah, what's going on snowflakes?" Barbara joined in. There must have been a hundred snowflakes talking at the same time, all of them so excited that the girls couldn't understand a single word. Finally, Barbara screamed, "Have you all gone mad? Why won't you answer us?" Just then, the plump snowflake landed squarely on her nose, shining as brightly as he ever had. Stopping to catch his breath, he finally said, "No, girls, we have not gone mad, but we believe we have found the land of the 'snow angels!' We have found the land that loves snow more than any other, but we must return to the land where snow is created and let the elder snowflake know what we have found."

Fearful of the snow's departure, Helena and Barbara pleaded with the snow not to leave, "But snowflake, where is this land? Is it far from here? Can we come and visit and play in the land of the 'snow angels'? Please do not go to another land, for we will be certain to tell everyone in Ashburn to love the snow and to want the snow just as we do. May we follow you to this other land?" The plump snowflake and many others were laughing, wrapping points of their star shapes around their middle, as though they had arms wrapped around their tummies. "Yes, of course you may come with us," said the plump snowflake. "Follow us to the top of this big hill!" Not understanding what the snowflakes were talking about, Helena and Barbara looked at each other in total confusion, but followed them to the top of Wilkins Hill, nonetheless.

Once at the top, with almost all of the snow swirling around them, the plump snowflake landed on Helena's nose. Turning his back to her he pointed downward across the vast expanse of Wilkins Hill. "Look," he cried out. "Look at the many, many 'snow angels' that have come to visit this land! Hundreds upon hundreds have come to visit since we were here yesterday. They must have come during the night, and left their mark so we would know where to land and stay. And not just here, either. We saw them at the farm where you live and where that loud-mouthed boy lives, at the farm next door. This truly must be the land of the 'snow angels'!"

Realizing what the snowflakes thought were 'snow angels' for just the first time, Helena inquired, "Those shapes in the snow? Are those snow angels?" "Well, yes," the plump snowflake replied giddily, "What else could they be? They are the perfect shapes of angels, and we should know for we see angels flying high in the heavens every journey we make!" Barbara burst in and just got out, "You don't really think those are act . . ." when Helena placed her hand tightly across her sister's mouth and answered, "You are SO right, snowflake. What else could they be? They are the perfect shape of angels!" Looking Barbara straight in the eye and giving her a quick wink, she asked, "Aren't they, Barbara? Aren't those exactly what Mr. Snowflake thinks they are?" Catching on to her sister, Barbara quickly added, "Of course they are! Those are definitely 'snow angels.' Oh, Mr. Snowflake, you are so smart. Does that mean that Ashburn must truly be the land of the 'snow angels' that you have been seeking?"

All of the snowflakes were swirling furiously, up and down, round and round, across Wilkins Hill and beyond, dipping down, over, and around the hundreds of snow angels that were carved into the snow. "See for yourself," the plump snowflake answered happily. "I am convinced that we have found the land the elder snowflake told us about before we left the land of snow creation. Now, we must return there and let all snowflakes know where to find this great land where snow is loved and wanted. The weather is warming quickly and I fear that we may not make it back before we all melt and serve the greater purpose." "Oh, snowflake, you must make it back to your land of creation," Helena implored them. "You must let all snowflakes know that Ashburn is the land that loves and wants snow more than any other. Please tell Mother Nature, too, and we will be certain to pray to Jesus to tell Mother Nature about our love for snow, as well." "Yes," Barbara added. "We will be certain to tell all the people of our land to say prayers for snow, and to welcome the snow each season with all our hearts! But, Mr. Snowflake, are all of you going to leave to return to the land of snow creation? Can't some of you stay for at least one more day?"

Telling them what they didn't want to hear, the plump snowflake said, "Dear girl, as we have said and you well know, we do not decide our fate, whether day to day or for the whole season long. Mother Nature sends us where she will and it is she who decides where we land and where we melt. I am certain that many of us will stay here and melt into the ground and the rivers and streams, for that is our ultimate purpose. At least one of us must make it back to the land where we were created, so many of us must make the journey in order for at least one to make it back. We must leave immediately for the sun is high and the wind is picking up, but I hope that we see you next season. Not all people in all lands love the snow as you two girls do, and as do the children of this land you call Ashburn. We will tell all snowflakes and Mother Nature as well, that this is the land where snow should come every year, but we must go now." With that, there arose a flurry of snow so great that the sun was completely obscured, the sky appeared almost as dark as night. With a great swirling motion, the snow arose high into the heavens and started blowing eastward with the wind. The girls waved frantically, screaming at the top of their lungs, "We love you snow! Please come back next year!"

Happy as they had been in months, Helena and Barbara set off for school, when a last furious swirl of snow blew down around them, shining and sparkling like never before. The girls were certain that they could hear laughing and giggling from amidst the snow storm, and just as quickly as it had descended upon them, up it flew again, and off towards the heavens. Knowing how late they were going to be getting to school anyway, the girls threw caution to the wind, stopping at every fresh patch of snow they encountered, making brand new 'snow angels' all the way to school, laughing and having the best time ever! "Oh, Barbara," Helena proclaimed, "Did you ever think that this silly game we played in our yard would ever be important enough to bring snow to Ashburn? Before all of this snow is gone, we must get all of the children to make more 'snow angels'—everywhere there is snow! And, we must tell them that they are making 'snow angels'!"

Arriving at school very late, with their backsides covered completely in snow, Mrs. Gunder looked at them in complete shock. Knowing what good girls they were, and of their village nickname 'the angels of Ashburn,' Mrs. Gunder gave them both a stern look and asked, "I suppose you're going to tell me that the 'angels of Ashburn' got caught in a snow storm?" Helena and Barbara looked at each other, smiling uncontrollably, about to burst into laughter. Helena responded, "Sorry for being late, Mrs. Gunder. We're not the 'angels of Ashburn,' we're just girls from Ashburn." Barbara added, "Well, maybe the 'snow angels' of Ashburn!" and they burst out laughing, as did all of the other children. Getting control of the class, Mrs. Gunder replied, "Well snow angels, I'll look forward to seeing you for two hours after school is over." Johnny and Petey laughed the hardest then!

At home, grandpa was half way across his farm, headed towards his neighbor when he saw Buddy Cranford, Johnny's father, walking towards him. Greeting each other good morning, they both said in unison, "They're back! They've come again!" Shocked at the chorus they had each expressed, Walter was first to add, "That's right, two more of them in my yard this time; in a different place, but two more of them." Buddy quickly countered, "I only have one this time, but sure enough, this one's the same size as before! What do you make of it Walter?" Not having given it much thought since the last episode, Walter replied, "I don't know for certain, Buddy, but one thing is for sure, the last two times we have had snow, these angels have come to visit. The way the kids play in the snow, it sure reminds Helen and me of Eleanor and Samuel. I can't explain it any more than you, but we're going to keep believing that these angel impressions are the spirit of Eleanor and Samuel, and Helen and I are going to keep praying for snow over and over!" Shaking his good friend and neighbor's hand tightly, Buddy said, "That's good enough for me Walter. I'll tell the missus and we'll be certain to keep saying prayers for snow as well!"

Chapter 8

S URE ENOUGH, THE next morning awoke with little if any snow on the ground anywhere. The sun was already high when the girls rose and the temperature was warm enough that they didn't need coats when they went out. Grandma was just telling the girls how sorry she was that they didn't have any snow to play in when Helena jumped in, "It's okay, grandma, we had a wonderful time with the little snow we had. I just know that next year we will have lots and lots of snow to play in!" "Me, too," Barbara tooted. "I got to use my saucer just enough this season to be sure that next year I will appreciate it even more. This year was the absolute best time for snow—ever!" Not believing her ears, grandma walked over to them where they were seated at the table eating their breakfast and, touching her hand to each forehead said, "Hmmpf, you girls never cease to amaze me, but at least you're not carrying a fever!" The two girls looked at each other and just giggled, and grandpa gave them each a knowing wink!

Spring came early to Ashburn and with it came all of the flowers they had enjoyed last year. Grandma's garden came in just as overloaded as last year as well, as did the crops at their farm and Mr. Cranford's. Despite getting little rain, April proved to be a wonderful growing season. May arrived and with it came much higher temperatures than ever before remembered. Along with the scorching temperatures came a strong, dry wind. Talking to one another at the fence post one day, Walter asked Buddy, "When do you think we're going to get some rain?" "We should have had it all April," replied Buddy. "I guess it's a good thing we got a little bit of snow at the end of the season, or we may not have gotten in this first crop." "Well, it's not totally grown yet," Walter reminded him, "And the way this heat is beating down on us, I don't know if we'll get a second crop into the ground at all." Looking a bit worried, Buddy asked, "How is your food supply holding out? We still have a fair amount left from last season, but I don't know if we'll make it all the way through next winter if we don't get in a second crop." Walter grabbed his neighbor's arm and looked him in the face, replying, "I'm with you on that, Buddy. We're okay for now, but come next January, I'm not sure what we'll have left. What do you hear from any of the other folks?"

Mr. Cranford had a sullen look on his face when he told Walter, "From what I'm hearing, you and I may have more stock than anyone else in Ashburn. Some folks are saying they may not even make it into fall with what they have now, and if they don't get a second crop, things could be bad." "Well," Walter responded, "Like we always have before, we'll stick together even in the worst of times. If only we would have had as much snow this season as in years past." "That's something to think about, Walter," Buddy added, "Especially when folks are doing too much praying for no snow. Kind of gives new meaning to the saying, 'Ye reap what ye sow'!" "Yes sir," Walter added, "Except that we might not get the chance to 'sow' or to 'reap' anything at all!"

June brought the end of school and blistering heat to Ashburn. Temperatures were already reaching one hundred degrees and more. No one could ever remember temperatures that high in June before. Everyone wondered what July and worse, what August would bring. Grandpa's and Mr. Cranford's first crops were beginning to wither in the extreme heat. They were debating on whether they should bring them in early just to be sure they had any crop at all, for fear that the scorching temperatures would burn everything up. Grandma's garden, which had started off so strongly, was now a dry spate of parched ground having produced less than half what it had the previous year.

The family had already eaten all that it had yielded and were into the canned foods from last year. Nary, a single drop of rain fell in the entire month of June. The children were used to swimming in the ponds and creeks, but there was barely enough water in any of them to even get their feet wet. It was going to be a long summer, indeed. The merchants in town, who had been accustomed to buying fruits and vegetables from the local farmers, had shelves that were rapidly going bare. The families that bought most of their food from the stores were being hit the hardest. Even towns as far away as fifty miles were experiencing the same hardships, for the rivers that flowed through all the lands were dry as creek beds from the lack of melting snow.

July and August brought only more misery for everyone, along with record-breaking temperatures. No farmer dared put a second crop into the ground, for the ground was dry as autumn leaves. The corn had been cut at only three feet when it normally reached seven to eight feet. The apple and peach trees, which should have been bearing green fruit by now, had nothing at all. September and October would bring no apple or peach picking this year, which meant no pies, cobblers, candied apples, caramel apples, or dried peaches. The first rain of the entire summer finally fell in the last week of August. It rained for a full day; just enough to lower the temperatures into the low nineties, but the earth drank every drop before the next morning arrived. Grandpa had set out every barrel, watering can, cup, and container he could find in hopes of collecting enough rain water to pour in places where it was needed most.

Word came from Mr. Cranford that four wells had dried up in Ashburn, forcing all of the families to either move in with relatives or friends, or to move away. The newspapers were all printing stories about the great drought that was upon them. Grandma and grandpa told Helena and Barbara not to worry, for they had enough food to get them through winter and into next year's growing season. Hunting season would soon be along and they would have plenty of fresh meat as well, but not even

JL CRAWFORD

the first fish had been caught the entire summer, for lack of water in any pond, lake, creek, stream, or river.

September brought a new school year. Helena had turned twelve, Johnny Cranford had turned thirteen, and Barbara and Petey had each turned ten. The four of them had played throughout the summer, but hadn't had nearly the fun they had enjoyed the summer before. All of them were tanned as could be from the relentless sun, but Petey had sustained a terrible burn early on, thinking that splashing around in only one-foot of water in Cragun's Creek would be enough to prevent it from happening. That got a lot of teasing from Barbara all summer long until he recovered.

In school, the main topic was the weather, despite having other subjects to teach. Mrs. Gunder began the year by giving everyone a weather lesson, reminding the children of the importance of the four seasons to the entire cycle of life. In particular, she told the children of the role that different forms of weather played in the cycle of life, especially snow. Kathy Clements told everyone that her father was glad they had had so little snow last year, and was hoping for the very same thing this year. Her father was quite well-to-do, since he was the town banker, and they could buy whatever they needed, even if they had to go across the mountains to another town. Her father had told her one day, "If we get too much snow dear, the customers cannot come into the bank. We don't like the snow," and that was enough for Kathy, even though she liked playing in it.

Before Helena could respond, which she was all too ready to do, Johnny stood up from his chair, turned to face her and, red-faced, said, "What about the people who grow all of the food that you eat, even if you can go somewhere else and buy it? Don't you know that the snow melts into the ground and helps make the ground wet and moist so crops can grow? And more snow melts into the creeks and rivers that flow throughout the whole country, which helps other lands and other farms in other places. Where do you think all of the food comes from?" Defiantly, he turned back around and plopped into his seat, almost angry enough to burst. He turned slightly enough to see Helena staring at him, and just as he was about to mouth the words, "What?" he received a big smile from Helena, along with two thumbs-up!

With a look of pride on her face, Mrs. Gunder thanked Johnny for providing a brief lesson on the benefits of snow. To help everyone fully understand the importance of snow in the whole cycle of life, she assigned them all the task of writing a composition about snow. They were to write about all of the benefits of snow to them, personally, whether they thought well of snow, or poorly. On Monday, they would go over everyone's paper and have a great big discussion. She told them to be sure to ask their parents, grandparents, siblings, and neighbors to be sure they could write the best composition.

The second week of September finally brought some relief from the high temperatures of summer. The nights were getting a bit cooler and the days had finally dropped into the seventies. Clouds appeared overhead, but moved on to the east. Even if it rained for two weeks straight, grandpa said they would still not get in a second crop. He reminded the girls and grandma, that they had better say their prayers for a good snow this season, telling them in a straight forward manner, "If we have another summer like this one, with not enough snow before it, we'll not make it through the year." Helena and Barbara had never seen grandpa that serious.

Not only did it not rain for two weeks straight, it didn't rain a single day for the next two weeks either, and before anyone knew it, October had arrived. All of the fields in Ashburn and the surrounding area were as dry as grandpa could ever recall. When the wind blew, dust and dirt covered everything in sight, choking anyone who dared walk outside. After arriving at school each morning and back home each afternoon, Helena and Barbara had to shake their clothes out before even going inside. Grandma threatened to brush them off with her straw broom, so filthy were they each afternoon. Grandpa had to keep the livestock in the barn all day and told grandma that their supply of winter hay was already running low reminding her that winter had not even arrived.

In school each day, all of the children had stories of hardship to tell, everyone except for Kathy Clements, of course. Mrs. Gunder made it a point each morning to bring biscuits, sweet rolls, molasses, and some bacon, sausage, or jerky; so certain was she that some children did not have enough food at home to get breakfast each morning. When the same children started arriving early each day, quickly gobbling down what she had brought in, she was convinced, but said nothing to any of them, except, "Oh, please, help your selves. I must have made too much food this morning and I don't want it to go bad!" Finally, one morning when there were more kids to feed than she had food for, she said to herself that she had had enough and was going to do something about this. At the very end of the school day, she handed sealed notes to Helena, Johnny Cranford, Kathy Clements, Paula Winters, Jeremy Wright, and Gerald Clemmer, telling them to deliver the notes to their parents as soon as they got home. Barbara looked at Helena and Johnny and immediately said, "Oh, you guys are in such big trouble. What did you do?" All of the children were equally stunned, each of them wondering what they had done to warrant having a note sent to their parents! Thinking quickly, Helena responded, "Maybe *you* are the one in trouble, Barbara. Maybe that's why she gave *me* the note to give to grandma and gramps!" That stopped Barbara's snickering almost immediately, but every other student went home with a worried look on their face.

Once home, Helena handed grandma the note from Mrs. Gunder. Grandpa was just walking in the door when grandma said, "Walter, before you go back out, you best take a minute here." Showing him the envelope from school, she added, "It seems we may have a little problem to deal with." Looking at Barbara and Helena, she said, "Girls, you better have a seat. Before I open this, is there anything you want to tell your grandfather and me?" Helena and Barbara were utterly speechless, but Barbara quickly blurted out, "All I did was hold Petey's hand outside the schoolhouse. Helena's the one who has been kissing Johnny Cranford!" "Barbara! You dirty, rotten, little snitch! You promised you wouldn't tell. I'm never telling you another secret as long as I live—never, ever!" Both girls were pleading their case to grandma and grandpa as grandma was reading the note from Mrs. Gunder. Grandpa had his head down, his face in his hands, and seemed to be chuckling, though quietly so the girls couldn't hear him, or so he thought. Barbara said, "I'll bet that's why Johnny Cranford got sent home with a note, too!" Furious with her sister, Helena gave her the look of the devil, but could only muster a, "Ooooohhhhhh, you!" She turned to face her grandparents, waiting to find out what fate was to befall each of them.

Grandma whispered something to grandpa and his face went from his customary red to pale white. He slowly rubbed his chin; the sound of his rough palms against his whiskery face making an audible sound that all of them could hear. He looked from grandma to Helena and then to Barbara without saying a word. He slowly stood, and moving closer to where the girls each sat, he knelt down to face them, his hands resting on his bent knees. Looking each of them in the face, he said, "Girls, this is a very serious problem, one I was hoping would not come so soon. I was hoping it would never come, but I guess I knew one day, sooner or later, Mother Nature would have her way." Helena quickly jumped up, confessing, "Grandpa, I swear, it was just the littlest kiss of all time, and only once did we ever kiss." Barbara was right on her heels, adding, "Me, too, grandpa. I mean, I didn't kiss Petey, I just held his hand, but only for a second. I think he had boogers on it or something and it was yucky! I swear, it was just that one time!" Grandma had turned her head away, but soon the girls could hear her chuckling, which then turned into a raucous laughter. Even grandpa couldn't hold back any longer, and he too, was laughing so hard that the girls thought he would burst his buttons!

Helena and Barbara had no idea what was going on. Seeing the note from Mrs. Gunder on the floor, Helena picked it up and quickly read it to herself. The more she read, the redder her face became as though she was going to boil over. When she finished reading the note she threw it down on the floor, looked Barbara square in the face and screamed, "You little creep! That note is not about us. We're not in trouble at all. You and your big mouth have us in big trouble now when we weren't in any trouble at all. Ohhhhhhhh, I'll never tell you another secret!" Barbara was so stunned, tears started streaming down her face and as loudly as grandma and grandpa were laughing, Barbara was crying even louder. Helena looked at the three of them, not knowing who to yell at next, or what to do. Looking helplessly at the situation, she soon broke into laughter as well. Still bawling, Barbara finally managed a weak, "Will someone please tell me why everyone is laughing except for me? What on earth is so funny that it's making me cry?" Helena handed her the note and the three of them watched her face turn from anger and confusion to one of sudden realization. She looked from her grandparents to Helena and back again. Excitedly now, she yelled, "You mean, we aren't in any trouble? It wasn't us, I mean, not me, not Helena, we didn't, I mean . . . I don't know what I mean!" Jumping in, Helena told her, "What it means is that you blabbed away our little secrets and now we might just be in trouble, when we were not before you opened your big mouth!"

Grandma and grandpa had collected themselves by this time and, looking at the girls, grandpa said, "When I said we had a serious problem, I was referring to the children and their families who do not have enough food to get by." Grandma jumped in and added, "But, that doesn't mean that we don't have a few things to talk about, young ladies. Are we crystal clear on that matter?" "Yes, grandma, yes, grandpa," both girls muttered quietly as mice, their heads facing straight down to the ground. Grandpa steered them back to the note from Mrs. Gunder, telling them, "Girls, the reason that your teacher sent the note to us and to the parents of the other children you told us about, is because we have the biggest farms, and we probably have the most food remaining from last season. Mr. Clements has more money in town than anyone and he can also make loans from the bank to help people. However, this is a very serious problem and Mrs. Gunder doesn't want any of the less fortunate children or their families to be embarrassed. Do you understand?"

Grandma added, "It is no one's fault that we did not have enough snow this past winter to produce a good enough crop. That is all the doing of Mother Nature, and other folks have smaller farms than we have, so no one is to blame, or to be looked down upon for this unfortunate time." Grandpa looked to be certain they were understanding all there was to know about the matter, finishing up by adding, "Mrs. Gunder has called a meeting of all of the families to whom she sent notes, along with the town council and church elders, and we're going to see if we can't pitch in as a community and help everyone."

"Oh, grandpa, grandma, what a wonderful idea that is," Helena called out. Barbara chimed in, "We can help too, can't we grandpa, grandma? Don't we have enough food that we can spare some? They can have all of the lima beans and brussels sprouts they want, and beets, and all the things we don't like!" Grandma stood up and moved closer to Barbara. She put her arm around her and beckoned Helena closer so she could hold her as well. Pulling them closely against her, tight against her bosom so they couldn't see, she then looked at grandpa and winked, offering, "Of course we have enough food to help as many people as we can. However, given what we have learned about you two hooligans, it's only fitting that we give away all of the foods that you girls like, and save the beets, and brussels sprouts, and lima beans for you!"

Barely able to contain herself, she looked at grandpa and said, "Walter, why don't you cook up that big piece of liver you've got stored away and

JL CRAWFORD

I'll make up some onions, cabbage, and beets to go with it. Oh, won't that make a tasty dinner!" Patting the girls on their rumps as she shooed them away, she said, "Now run along upstairs and get your homework done before dinner. Oh, and while you're at it, why don't you each write us a little composition that begins with—"All of the ways I can think of to be a nice, young lady . . ." I think something in the order of five hundred words should be appropriate, don't you, Walter?" Before grandpa could answer, the girls let out a mutual moan, crying, "Five hundred words?" As soon as grandpa started to say, "I was thinking something more in the way of . . . ," the girls dashed upstairs in a flash, calling behind them, "Okay, five hundred words, that's the deal!"

Helen went over to where Walter was standing and put her arm around him. Looking up at him she said, "Holding hands and kissing already, Walter. Are you sure you're going to be able to handle this?" Suddenly feeling weak, Walter looked down at her smiling face and said, "I heard about a job opening, three counties away from here. Maybe I'll look into it and see you in ten years or so!" Flushed, Helen shot back, "That's just fine with me, Mr. Broadhurst. There are plenty of men in Ashburn that have taken a liking to me and my cooking!" Grandpa held her close, knowing his plan had been bamboozled from the start, gave her a big kiss and told her, "And your biggest fan is standing right here, sweetie-pie!"

The next night, the parents who had received letters from Mrs. Gunder all met at the church, along with the town council and Reverend Hastings. A plan was formulated that would have Reverend Hastings make an announcement at church on the coming Sunday, about an overflowing church kitchen. He would let all citizens of Ashburn know that the church kitchen was just too full of canned goods, fresh fruits and vegetables, fresh and salted meats, and many other things that had been donated to the church recently. It would be open to any and all who wished to partake of the good Lord's abundance. In this way, any family taking advantage of the offer would not seem to be asking for handouts, or worse, begging. Reverend Hastings would tell everyone that it was important they took as much as their cabinets could hold, for otherwise, it might all spoil and that would not sit well with the Almighty. The families in attendance would bring over whatever they could spare, and each of them promised to bring at least a full wagon load. Reverend Hastings and Mrs. Gunder were ecstatic, thanking everyone for their generosity and community support.

When the plan was being discussed, Kathy Clements' father, Harold, the banker, stood and revealed to all, "Folks, I am not a farmer and I have no stores of food. I'm a widower as most of you know, and though my dear wife used to bake seven days a week, I'm afraid I don't have anything to bring." Mrs. Gunder responded immediately, saying, "Harold, for goodness sake, you are the town banker. Everyone knows the bank is a 'for-profit' operation and most banks give back large amounts of profits to the community where they are located." "Yes, Mrs. Gunder, I am certainly aware of that," he replied. "But what do you want me to do, give these families money? The bank charter does not allow me to do that."

With her hands on her hips, Mrs. Gunder looked at him like he had not the first bit of business sense. "Harold," she said, "First of all, you may call me Lorraine, since we're all friends and neighbors here. Second, why don't you use the monies that you have available and buy food and goods from Mr. Godsey's store. I'm sure he will appreciate the business very much and you can help supplement what everyone else is bringing!" Jim Godsey jumped up excitedly, offering, "What a wonderful idea, Lorraine! Harold, I'll sell you whatever you want at cost, plus a small handling fee. Whatever you want!" Everyone applauded the three of them for working out another great solution to this very important issue.

Mrs. Kendall said she and her staff of three cooks would bake pies, and cakes, and muffins, and breads, and as much as they could right up until Sunday morning! Reverend Hastings asked the town council if they had to do something formal to approve everything. They quickly convened, voted to approve the bank action, and adjourned just as quickly. Sam Quigley, the council chairperson added, "On behalf of the town council, we would like to commend and recognize this austere group of fine citizens for coming together voluntarily to address a serious community need and, more importantly, working together to construct a magnificent solution!" Closing, he offered, "Say, any of you folks who aren't on the council, you might want to consider it when the vote comes up in a few months!" That got a big laugh from everyone as they headed for home.

As they walked out of the church, Harold Clements approached Mrs. Gunder. Hemming and hawing like a teenage boy asking a girl to the big dance, he asked, "Ah, pardon me Mrs. Gunder, I mean, Lorraine. Say, if you aren't doing, I mean, if you don't have any, I mean, if you might like to, ah, ah . . ." Raising her hand to silence him, wearing a smile she just couldn't hold back, she replied, "Well, Harold Clements, if I didn't know any better, I'd think you were trying to ask me over! That would be very nice, one evening." Not hearing a word she said for his befuddled state, Harold responded, "Well, that's alright, I understand. I just thought that, well, you know, it might be, well, because, you know . . ." "Harold?" Mrs. Gunder interrupted. "Harold, I think I said that was a lovely idea. Yes, I would very much like to come over one evening!" "You would?" he asked, looking dumbfounded. "I mean you *would*! Yes, well, that's just wonderful! I'll make arrangements and we'll . . ." he started to say as they were walking down the steps, but he wasn't looking where he was going and completely missed the bottom step.

He went head first into the grass and came up sputtering with a mouthful of dry weeds. Mrs. Gunder rushed over to help him, downplaying his clumsiness saying, "That bottom step has been loose for years!" Trying to take away his embarrassment, she added, "Perhaps,

Harold, if it's not too much to ask, you could follow my wagon until I make the turn toward my house, since we do go the same way." Buffeted with new found courage, Harold offered, "I'll do better than that Lorraine; I'll follow you all the way to your house, ah, just to be safe, of course." They rode most of the way with wagons side by side until the road narrowed at her lane.

They had found many topics on which to converse during the twenty-minute ride to her home, which came as no surprise to Harold, for he found Lorraine to be a wealth of knowledge on many different topics and a wonderful conversationalist. When they made the turn onto her lane, he followed her wagon for another quarter of a smile 'til she turned into the gate. Harold jumped down and rushed ahead to open the gate for her, sweeping it open with a low bow, saying, "Your castle awaits, my lady!" Lorraine drove the wagon through the gate, stopped the horse just inside, and turned to watch as Harold closed it behind her. Harold had just fastened the rope over the post and was about to turn towards his own wagon, when he felt a warm hand on his. Startled, he turned to find Lorraine at the gate, smiling at him warmly. "Thank you dear sir, or should I say kind prince, for seeing me safely home through this rugged territory. Whatever would I have done without your chivalrous manner and more-than-capable assistance?" They both got a laugh at their silliness, but Lorraine pulled him a bit closer and gave Harold a quick buss on the cheek. "Thank you, Harold, for seeing me home like a proper gentleman," she told him. "And I do look forward to enjoying an evening together!"

Harold was overcome by her affection, red-faced and without words. He tried to utter a, "Uh, oh sure, you know, well," but finding no semblance of a sentence, he just waved and smiled at her, finally managing to say, "Ah, you bet, we'll do that soon. Good night, Lorraine!" He turned on his heels and floated off to his wagon, his feet never touching the ground. Lorraine called out to him, "Good night, Prince Harold, until we meet again!" Chuckling to herself, she drove her wagon into the barn, unhitched her horse, covered him with a warm blanket and strode into the house. As far down the road as Harold was by then, she could still hear him whistling a sweet tune, though she had no idea what it was. Funny, neither did Harold!

For the next couple of days, grandma and grandpa and all of the other involved parents and grown-ups collected and delivered food to the church; all of it under cover so no one outside the plan would be the wiser. Harold Clements bought more than one hundred dollars worth of food from Jim Godsey's store, which was probably twice what he would have sold in weeks. Reverend Hastings had to push chairs and tables out of one entire room to make space for all of the food and goods that were piling up. On Saturday afternoon and into the evening, Mrs. Kendall and her helpers brought over not fewer than seventy-five pies, twenty-five cakes, three dozen loaves of bread, and tray after tray of cookies, brownies, muffins, and more. Remembering the great popularity of the triple-decker peanut butter and jelly sandwiches, she also made up five dozen of the delicious treats! The whole church had such a wonderful aroma to it, Reverend Hastings wondered if would be able to keep anyone's attention during his sermon!

For those involved in the community effort Sunday arrived in a flash, so busy was everyone. As the townsfolk made their way into the church and were seating themselves, everyone stopped to sniff the air, for the church smelled like a bakery and a restaurant, and like home on Thanksgiving Day; filled with every smell imaginable. The church was filled with talk about where the smells were coming from. People were actually squirming in their seats and tummies could be heard grumbling throughout. Mouths watering as people turned their heads, searching for the source of the heavenly delights. More than once, people were overheard to say, "Wow, if heaven smells this good, I can't wait to knock at the pearly gates!"

As Reverend Hastings entered from the side where his chambers were located, the wonderful aroma almost knocked him over. Gathering himself before anyone saw his amazed look he strode up to the altar and took his place behind the pulpit. Raising his hands, he greeted the congregation warmly, offering, "Friends, neighbors, citizens, good people of Ashburn, children of our Lord, the church welcomes everyone this day, this very special day, for this day represents all of the greatness of our Savior, as well as the goodness and warmth of His disciples. On this day, the citizens of Ashburn have embodied all that Christ stands for, all that He asks of His followers, all that He would do, were He with us this day! And now, wonderful people of Ashburn, I ask that you bear with me through a short sermon, one that speaks of the glory and power of giving. When I am finished delivering His message, we shall all enjoy the heavenly smells that He hath brought forth this day!"

The Reverend's sermon lasted but a short fifteen minutes, less than half the usual time, but there wasn't a single person who could sit still for even that short time. Even Reverend Hastings occasionally turned his head in the direction of the rooms—yes, three full rooms, where everything had been brought, sorted, and laid out in an orderly fashion. More than once, he was seen breathing in deeply all of the delightful smells, sighing deeply before returning to his sermon. More than once, he lost his place completely, and was seen taking drinks of water from the glass below the dais over and over.

There wasn't a dry mouth in the place, when more often than not his sermons left nary a dry eye. Finally, when the last prayer was said by all, he bid them, "Go in peace and God be with you," but asked everyone to wait for one last moment, while he explained what everyone was clamoring to know. Stretching the truth only a little bit, looking aloft and silently asking for forgiveness, he informed everyone that through some mystical, if not heavenly miracle, having recently prayed to have the church's cabinets and cupboards filled in case of some inexplicable need, his prayers had been answered and food had been brought in by many, citizen and stranger alike—more than ever before! So much food and goods were coming in that he just had to ask anyone and everyone present to, "Please, take as much as you need. Take as much as you can carry! Oh, one thing more . . . be sure to save me one blueberry pie!"

His final word had barely escaped his mouth when the full congregation was on its feet and headed towards the rectory and the kitchen. Mr. Bainbridge had brought over enough boxes and sacks so that those in the greatest need could take as much as they wanted or needed. Reverend Hastings and Mrs. Gunder were quick to oversee things, wanting to be certain that those most in need got the most benefit, telling some who were hesitant to take large amounts, "Oh, please, go ahead. Help yourselves. You have three children. Please, please take more." They even helped many people load up their wagons, making doubly sure that the families she knew needed the most received more than they would have taken without further encouragement. Within one hour, the church was bare, except for the mess of crumbs all over the counters and floors, and one blueberry pie for Reverend Hastings!

Surveying the whole situation, standing with his hands on his hips, Sam Quigley, the council chairperson, asked for a moment. "Folks," he said, "I can't thank you all enough once again. This turned out to be quite the community effort and it appears that a whole lot of good, nice folks went away with hope to get through the rest of the winter. The town council is going to take notice of this effort and we're going to recognize someone, for sure!" Stepping up quick as he could, Harold Clements said, "Ah, Sam. You should know that this whole idea was brought to our attention by Mrs. Gunder, here. She noticed too many children not having anything to eat before they came to school each morning, and she got everyone together. I say she should be the one to get the recognition." Looking embarrassed, Mrs. Gunder lowered her head and said, "Oh, Harold. I just brought it up. Everyone here pitched in and came up with the idea and put it all together. I really think," but before she could finish, the whole room was shouting, "Here, here! Three cheers for Lorraine Gunder! Three cheers for Lorraine!" Sam Quigley waved his hands to silence them and said, "That's all I need to hear. I'll bring it up to the council for a vote. You know, Lorraine, I think we just might have a 'Lorraine Gunder Day' coming up in Ashburn!" Everyone cheered and patted her on the back, except Harold. He gave her a big hug!

Chapter 9

FINALLY, TO THE relief of everyone, the first snowfall arrived almost at the end of October. The Almanac said to expect up to two feet of snow, but of course, it had not been very accurate for the past year, so who knew what to think. It had started to snow just as grandpa was turning off the oil lamps and readying for bed. Barbara and Helena had gone upstairs earlier and were most likely fast asleep. Grandma had just closed her bedroom door and grandpa had just started up the stairs when the night time silence was rocked with shouting and laughter. Helena and Barbara were high-tailing it down the stairs so fast, grandpa had to turn and grab the banister to prevent being bowled over. Both girls were yelling and screaming, "Snow! Snow! Snow! Grandpa, grandma, it's snowing and it's really coming down," as they headed for the door. "Whoa," grandpa called after them. "Where do you think you're going?" In unison, the girls replied, "Well, outside, grandpa. Didn't you hear us? It's snowing!" "Yes, I heard you," grandpa responded. "And I think the rest of Ashburn heard you too! But, it's also only twenty degrees out and you don't have coats or shoes on, and, it's well past your bed time. The snow will be there when you wake up tomorrow and it's Saturday, so you'll have all day to play. Now, back upstairs you go, and slowly. Do you want to knock your old gramps down the stairs?" "Awww, gramps," the girls said, "You're not old, and no, we don't want to knock you over. Sorry, it's just that we haven't had any snow in soooooo long!" Shortly thereafter, the house was quiet, but two little girls were still up, sitting on their beds, watching the snow come down, and praying that the Almanac would be right!

Saturday morning broke early for the Broadhurst house. Grandpa figured the girls would be up at the crack of dawn, but he was wrong. They were up *before* the crack of dawn! He heard them trying to descend the stairs as quietly as they could, but they were kids, of course. Each of them could clearly be heard saying to the other, "Shhh, be quiet, you'll wake up grandma and grandpa," as they clomped loudly down the stairs. Grandma poked her head out the bedroom door, quickly asking, "Girls, do you both have on warm coats, boots, and mittens? If it's real cold, be sure to come back in and get a scarf, too! We don't want anyone catching their death!" "Yes, grandma," the girls echoed. "We just want to see how deep the snow is. It has covered everything," and out the door they scrambled. From the top step, Helena was all set to dive headfirst into a deep snow bank. Pulling up just before she was ready to launch herself, she looked out and, turning to Barbara said, "Well, if that doesn't beat all. There's barely any snow at all!" "You're right," Barbara countered. "I wonder where it all went. That stupid old Almanac said we were going to get two feet!" Helena suddenly grasped her sister's shoulders and turned to her face to face. "Let's ask the snow, Barbara! Certainly, they will know why we didn't get as much as we thought. I forgot all about talking to the snow!"

The girls flew down the steps and ran towards the barn, Helena telling Barbara, "We have to make sure grandma doesn't hear us talking to the snow. She'll send us straight to bed and call the doctor!" Safely out of sight, the girls bent down and each filled their mittens with snow and threw it high in the air. As the snowflakes swirled round them, they yelled, "We love you snow! Helena and Barbara love the snow!" Anxiously, they waited for the snowflakes to answer them. Snowflakes landed on each girl's nose, but not a sound was to be heard. Curious, they looked at each other and, thinking the same thought, bent down, scooped up another handful of snow and threw it high in the air again, once again yelling, "We love you snow!" Again, there was no reply. Barbara was first to ask,

JL CRAWFORD

near to tears, "Helena, why doesn't the snow talk to us? Doesn't the snow know that we love it more than anything?" Before she could answer, a small snowflake with the tiniest voice was heard to say, "Well, hello. Were you talking to the snow? How did you know that we could hear people speak and understand their words?"

"Oh, snowflake," Helena responded. "Of course we know that snowflakes can understand us and speak to us as well. We have been speaking to the snow for the past two seasons . . . though, last year, you barely visited us at all. But, you're back now, and this is the land where you are supposed to come to forever and ever. This is the land of the snow angels!" Barbara quickly added, "Yes, she's right! Didn't the snowflakes from last season return to the land where snow is created and tell the elder snowflake about Ashburn? They said they would when they left here, they promised!" The little snowflake seemed quite confused, not knowing anything about what the girls were telling her. "I'm afraid we don't know what you're talking about," she said. "You see, we left the land where we are created before any snow returned from last season, and we have been traveling for such a long time. What are these 'snow angels' that you speak of?" Helena and Barbara quickly turned their backs to the snowflakes, spread their arms and legs and flopped down backwards. "Ouch!" they both cried out, for there was just a dusting of snow on the ground. Nonetheless, they each flapped their arms and legs in and out vigorously and just as quickly as they had plopped down they popped up. Turning round to face the snowflakes, they said, pointing, "Look, snow angels!" The snowflakes all looked where the girls were pointing and, befuddled, said, "All I see is grass!"

Turning back around, the girls saw what the snowflakes were looking at. She was right; there were no snow angels as the snow of last season had seen. There was only bare grass that just barely resembled the shape of an angel. "Oh snowflakes," Helena pleaded. "Last season, the snow told us that they were searching for the land of the 'snow angels,' for that was the land where snow is loved and wanted. They told us of the greater purpose for which snow is created and how snow will only land and stay where it is loved and wanted." She told the snowflakes about the elder snowflake from two seasons past, who had returned to the land where snow was created and told all of last year's snowflakes that they should look for the land of the 'snow angels.' The snowflakes all listened very intently and all agreed that they would want to land and stay, and later melt in a land where snow was loved and wanted. In fact, they were the very first snow to leave their land, but there was no elder snowflake there telling them a story such as they were now hearing. Barbara had noticed some snow swirling around her boots and looked down to see what was causing it. As she did, a gust of wind tossed snow right into her face, even up her nose. Tickling her, she let out a loud sneeze.

"Whoa, what a ride that was!" everyone heard a voice call out. "Thought I was being blown to the north Atlantic!" Just then, a large snowflake, very much misshapen and rough around the edges landed on Barbara's nose. "Hey there, cutie," he said, "You wanna take me on that ride again?" "Shocked, Barbara replied, "Whatever are you talking about? Who are you?" Just then, the little snowflake with whom they had been speaking flew up and landed on Barbara's nose as well. She settled down next to the senior snowflake and explained to the girls. "Oh, sorry, allow me to introduce Floyd. He has been traveling with us since just after we left our home land. He said he was lost and . . . hey, wait a minute." She looked at Floyd and asked, "Didn't you say that you were from the snow of last season?" "You bet your cold little icicles, sweetie! How do you think I got so old and crusty? Yessirree Bob, I was hoping to catch on to some new snow from this season and maybe find me that place where there's s'pose to be some angels, or something like that!"

Her ears perking up dramatically, Helena cried out, "Angels! Did you say angels? What kind of angels, Floyd?" Just then Barbara let loose another big sneeze and snow flew everywhere. So much snow was swirling

JL CRAWFORD

that Helena didn't know where Floyd had blown to; not until she saw an odd-shaped flake fluttering down, calling out, "Wahoooeee, that's better'n the wildest blizzard, missy!" He landed this time on Helena's nose and she cupped her hands around her face, telling Barbara, "If you're going to sneeze again, please turn away. We need to talk to Floyd about the snow. He might know about the snow angels!" "What's that you say, missy, something about snow angels?" Floyd asked.

"Oh, yes," Helena responded fervently, "We were telling the other snowflakes about the snow from last season. They were sent to look for the land of the snow angels for that was believed to be the land where snow was loved and wanted by all. Before they left our land, the land of Ashburn, they knew that this was the land where all snow should come each year. They were going to try to get back to the land where snow is created so they could tell the elder snowflake that they had found the land of the snow angels! Oh, Floyd, am I rambling on? Do you understand what I am trying to tell you?" Trying his best to absorb all that she was saying, Floyd told her, "Whooooeeee, missy, that's sure some story! Seems too mis-conbobulated to be all made up. I seem to remember some old feller talking about angels, mebbe it was snow angels. I think he said he seen them on the ground when they was flying overhead and all the snowflakes agreed that they was angels what had laid down in the snow. Said more about how all the people in that land loved snow, or some fool nonsense like that."

Barbara was absolutely beside herself. Jumping up and down she was screaming, "No, no! It's not nonsense, it's the truth!" Winking at Helena, she went on tell them that the snowflakes were all convinced that snow angels, just like the angels they flew past high in the heavens, had landed in the land of Ashburn and had left their mark in the snow, in the shape of angels as a sign to the snow that this was where they should land and stay, and then melt. She went on to tell them that the snow angels had not visited yet this season, for there was no snow yet, on which to leave their mark. Helena quickly added, "But I'll just bet they come and visit tonight and tomorrow morning you'll see that this is the land of the snow angels and where all the snow should come each year!" "Well," the little snowflake replied, "I guess we probably should wait and see if they do come, for we wouldn't want to go to another land where we are not wanted." "Heck, no," cried Floyd. "I ain't got too many flyin' days left in me no how. I'd just as soon stay right here where I know people want me, and I'll melt away in peace and quiet!" Barbara leaned toward Helena and forcefully blew Floyd off her nose, up in the air and all around. Laughing, she said, "Oh, no you won't go melting anytime soon, mister. Not before we have bunches of fun!" Floyd could be heard laughing all the way down.

As the girls ate their breakfast they watched through the window as the snow flew round and round in circles, darted through the air in great big swirls, twinkling brightly and shining like silver stars. Grandma saw their mesmerized looks and inquired, "What on earth has you two in such a trance? It's just a little bit of snow blowing around in the wind. As soon as you finish your breakfast and your reading, you can go outside and play for the rest of the day." "Aw, grandma," Barbara whined, "Can't we read later? The snow might all be gone by the time we finish reading!" "Nonsense, young lady," grandma replied. "It's so cold out there that even that little bit of snow isn't going anywhere anytime soon; it certainly won't melt before you finish your reading." "But grandma, you don't understand. The snow told us that it might go to another land because they aren't sure if this . . ." Just then, Helena made a loud, throat-clearing noise that caught Barbara completely by surprise. Even Grandma turned to see what it was all about. "Oh sorry, grandma," Helena feigned coughing. "I had a bit of pancake stuck in my throat. I think Barbara meant to say that Mrs. **Gunder** told us the snow might blow to other lands because no one can say where the snow lands, only Mother Nature." Looking at Barbara, she asked, "Isn't that what you meant to say, Barbara?" Before Barbara could answer though, grandma jumped in, "I must say, there sure seems to be an awful lot of fool-hearty talk going on around this house of late. Every time there is even just a little bit of snow on the ground, you two girls act as though your brains are inside a full-blown snow storm. What is it about the snow that gets you all scrambled up?"

Grandpa tried to calm the air bit, adding, "Now mother, you remember very well how Eleanor used to get all giddy and silly every time it snowed. We wondered more times than I can count, whether we shouldn't call Doc Smithers and have him check to see if her head hadn't gotten all scrambled somehow. It's just the innocence of youth that has them all excited, not to mention the fact that we haven't seen any snow in almost a full year. It's better that they're crazy about snow than boys!" "Yeah, grandma," the girls chorused together, "We'd much rather play in the snow than have anything to do with boys!" No sooner had grandma stood to clear the breakfast plates though, Helena and Barbara looked at each other and winked! Grandpa just rolled his eyes, lowered his head and muttered, "Boy, oh boy, oh boy!" "What was that, Walter?" grandma asked. "Nothing, mother, nothing at all," he replied, as Barbara and Helena skipped off to do their reading, giggling as they went.

Outside, the snow couldn't decide what to think of the girls' story about the snow angels. Floyd told them what he had heard from some old snowflake long before this group of snowflakes had been created, how it seemed to match up exactly with what the girls were trying to tell them. After all, Floyd had told them, they did just fly over the two highest peaks of the entire journey and it was very close to there that the land of snow angels was supposed to be. So much of it seemed to make sense to everyone, but where were the snow angels? There was no sign of them. After considerable thought, the majority of the snowflakes decided they should move on with the wind, allowing Mother Nature to take them where she would. Floyd was very upset with them all and told them,

"Just go on with you, then. I'm too old and crusty to keep flyin' round ever place. I know where I'm wanted and I'm stayin' put right here. This is where I'm a gonna melt and serve the greater purpose. The least you others could do though, is to fly up to that window yonder and tell them sweet lil' angels good-bye before you up and leave 'em. After all, they're just tryin' to help every snowflake that flies over this way."

The snowflakes all rose up in a marvelous flurry of activity. Confusion swirled within their ranks, for no one knew what they should do. They acted like tumbleweeds in a windstorm, blowing aimlessly around, until the tiniest snowflake's voice could be heard above the storm, "Floyd is right, everyone. We may decide on our own to go elsewhere, but we should thank these two little girls for loving us and trying to help us, for they certainly do love snow." With that, billions of snowflakes flew high up into the sky, almost blotting out the sun entirely.

Inside, grandpa noticed the light diminish in the room where he was reading and, looking toward the window thought, "What the heck? Where did this snowstorm blow in from?" Peering out through the window, he saw that it was not a snowstorm at all, just a blur of snow outside the girls' bedroom window! "What could this be all about?" he wondered aloud. Deciding to find out for himself, he put his coat on, told grandma he was going outside to check on the animals in the barn, and quietly slipped around the corner of the house.

Upstairs in their room, the girls had been doing their reading, neither one of them really concentrating much for they couldn't wait to go out and play in the snow. They also sensed the darkening sky outside the window and both looked out to see what clouds were blocking the sun's rays which, moments before had been shining brilliantly inside their room. They both screamed, "It's snowing again," and rushed to the window. Helena threw open the window to see where this sudden and unexpected snowstorm was coming from. No sooner had she opened the window though, did all of the snow fly right into the room, blowing madly around them. Outside, peeking around the corner, grandpa laughed himself to pieces, knowing what was going on and thinking, "I sure hope mother doesn't go up to check on them right now!"

The girls were laughing hysterically, yelling, "What is going on? What are all of you snowflakes doing?" The snowflakes settled all over the two girls, making them look like snow-girls, so covered were they! Floyd landed on Helena's nose and said, "It seems that the snowflakes have something to tell you two." With that, Barbara and Helena plopped down onto the edge of Barbara's bed, which was closest to the open window, and Helena said, "Okay, snowflakes, we're listening. What do you have to tell us?" They were filled with anxious anticipation, just waiting to hear how the snow was going to stay all year and how more snow would see them in Ashburn and land here as well. It was going to be a wonderful year for snow!

Down in the kitchen, grandma had heard the ruckus coming from upstairs, wondering what the girls could be reading that would warrant such a scream as she had heard. Certain that Barbara was probably *playing* Romeo and Juliet, rather than *reading* the story, she was busy thinking up new chores she would have them do instead of going outside to play, as she silently made her way up the stairs. Just in case serious attention had to be brought to bear, she carried her broom along with her. She wasn't half way up the stairs when she heard a gruff voice, almost like an old man's voice. Looking behind her, down into the living room, she remembered that Walter had gone out to the barn. It wasn't his voice she heard. Then, she was certain she heard Helena ask someone a question.

She gently tip-toed her way up the stairs, remembering to by-step the stair that creaked the loudest, thinking to herself, "When will that man ever fix this step!" Just as she got to the top step, she heard the tiniest little voice speaking. She knew for sure that it wasn't either Helena's or Barbara's voice, but who else could be up here with the girls, she wondered. She edged closer to the door, careful not to make a sound and placed her ear as close to the open door as she dared.

The tiny little voice was just barely audible for grandma, who didn't have any hearing problems for her age, certainly not like grandpa. He could barely hear a thing it sometimes seemed. Funny though, he always heard when it was time for breakfast, or lunch, or dinner! The small little snowflake flew up and landed on Barbara's nose. She looked at Barbara and Helena, unsure how to start. Floyd looked over at her and said, "Well, go ahead, you know you have something to say. You best get on with it." Helena looked at Barbara, both of them sensing that what they were hoping to hear was not what the little snowflake was going to say. Barbara offered out, "Please, snowflake, tell us what you have to say."

Outside the room, grandma wondered crazily, "Who on earth is she talking to? Did she just ask a snowflake to tell her something?" The little snowflake lowered her head and, looking back and forth between them said, "We are going to leave this land and go elsewhere. Mother Nature is stirring up the wind and that means she has another place for us to go. We know nothing of the land of the snow angels, other than what you and Floyd have told us, and while we think this land could be a very nice place in which to serve the greater purpose, we must follow Mother Nature's wishes." Grandma could not believe what she was hearing, but she could also not see inside the room. "Who," she wondered, "Was doing all this talking about snow and snow angels and Mother Nature?" Her curiosity was growing by leaps and bounds. So caught up with wanting to hear more, she hadn't even noticed Walter come inside and sneak up the stairs behind her.

Just then, Floyd broke into the conversation, saying, "I told 'em girls. I told the others about the old snowflake I done heard before he melted away. I 'member clear as day now, I do. He said once we got passed them two highest peaks, the two with mighty scary names, we would come to the place where the angels visited. He said they seen where the angels

JL CRAWFORD

left their marks in the snow and that was the land where snow was loved and wanted, and where all future snows should look for to serve the greater purpose. I told 'em. Yessirreee Bob, I did, but seems as though they feel like they gotta go somewhere else. I told 'em I was stayin' put though. I like this land; it seems mighty friendly to me." Still unaware of his presence, grandpa watched the amazement building in grandma. She had leaned the broom against the wall and placed her hands on her hips. He could just imagine the look she must have on her face! He wondered just how long she would put up with all of this before she burst into the room, but he wasn't going to let her spoil anything at all. He had his hand so close to her apron sash that, as soon as she made ready to burst in, he would pull her right back.

Helena saw the tears building in Barbara's eyes, and felt them in her eyes as well. "Snowflakes," Helena started, "Thank you for coming to say good-bye to us and offering an explanation before you left. We would have been very upset and would not have understood why you left, but you must know that we are telling the truth. Just as Floyd said, the elder snowflake pronounced this to be the land of the snow angels. The snow of last season left here with the express purpose of going back to your land of snow creation and telling him that they had found the land of which he spoke. I suppose that none of that snow made it back before they found a place where they should serve the greater purpose, but Floyd was there, and he heard the elder snowflake. Please snowflakes, will you please believe us? We love the snow and we want the snow to land and stay here, and then to melt into our lands and in our rivers."

The little snowflake flew up into the air and stopped and twirled round, her twinkling points showing little tears, just as Barbara and Helena had large tears streaming down their cheeks. She said to them both, "I'm sorry, but we have decided that we must go and Mother Nature is calling us. Those who wish to stay in this land will find a place to land where the wind will not take them away, and those who wish to follow Mother Nature must be on our way. We simply do not have enough proof of snow angels to stay here, but thank you again for loving us and for playing with us! Perhaps the snows that follow us will elect to land here and serve the greater purpose, but we must go."

Grandma was absolutely flabbergasted! All this time, she just knew that the girls had been talking to the snow, thinking them both silly, if not crazed. Now though, she heard snow talking to them her very self. Was she crazy as well? Walter would never believe it in a million years. This was one story she would never tell Walter Broadhurst for he would think her mad as well, but it seemed to be gospel. She, Helen Broadhurst, was hearing it with her very own ears. She put her hand to her forehead to be certain she wasn't running a fever. Nope, cool as a cucumber! "Maybe, just maybe," she thought, "There was something she could do to help." All of a sudden, she felt so terrible about praying for no snow, but that had been last year, not this year. Maybe, if she had the chance to speak to the snow, they would listen to her. She inched her way closer to the door. She just had to have a look to see if everything she was hearing was really as it seemed.

Seeing that she had left her broom against the wall and didn't look as though she was going to break up the gathering, Walter let her move closer, sensing that she just wanted to get a better look. It was, after all, quite a sight to see the two girls covered in snow from head to toe, just like snowmen! Grandma had absolutely no idea the sight she was about to behold. As she peered around the door frame, finally catching sight of the girls, grandma could not believe her eyes. "Ahhhhhhhhhhhhhh," she screamed, seeing what she thought were two frozen children sitting on the bed. She just stood there aghast, as all of the snow arose in a frantic flurry of blinding shininess. She was suddenly caught up in the most horrific snowstorm she had ever seen! No sooner had the snowstorm started than it all flew out the open window, just like a tornado blowing through. One second it was there and the next, it was over. The girls, who just seconds before had been covered in snow, so much that grandma didn't know which girl was which, were now snow-free—not even wet from all the snow. How could that be? Why did it not melt in all that time it was on them?

Completely overcome, grandma fainted away, only to be caught by Walter who had rushed in behind her. Floyd, who had planned on staying anyway, remained on Helena's nose, but looked to be in complete shock! The tiny snowflake, whose name they found out was Aly, had stayed on Barbara's nose as well, for she had wanted to say one last thing before they left. Looking down her nose and seeing Floyd still there, Helena asked, "Why didn't you fly away with the rest of the snowflakes, Floyd? Weren't you scared like the others?" "Well, garshy sakes no, I weren't scared, missy," he replied. "I've flown all over the world; seen scarier things than an upset grandma before. Now, if she hadda carried that broom in with her, you betcha, I woulda skee-daddled outta here with the rest of 'em!" Helena laughed along with Barbara and grandpa and told him, "You know, Floyd, we're going to like having you around here!"

The tiny snowflake perked up just then, startling Barbara, who hadn't even realized she was still on the end of her nose, saying, "Well, I guess it's time for me to go, too. I wanted to be sure that your grandma was okay before I left. Oh, and by the way, my name is Aly. I'm sorry that we never got properly introduced yesterday. Floyd kind of steals the show whenever he's around. Before all the commotion started, I had wanted to wish you well and to let you know that we will be saying prayers that angels will come visit your land. When we see the angels in the heavens as we travel to new lands, we will ask them if they know of this land and as we encounter other snows, we will ask them what they know of snow angels."

Just barely coming around, grandma suddenly spoke out, "Snow angels? Did you just say something about snow angels?" Grandpa, too, chimed in, "Yes, please Aly, what did you mean when you said snow angels? Helen and I, and Buddy Cranford next door, we have all seen signs of snow angels!" Barbara and Helena looked at each other in amazement, Helena quizzing them, "Grandpa, grandma, you have seen signs of snow angels? Where? When? Why did you not tell us?" Grandpa told them all of the snow angels they had seen over the past two snowfalls, in the Broadhurst's yard and in Mr. Cranford's fields. He informed them how they had been certain that they had been signs of a visit by the children's parents, Eleanor and Samuel, visiting earth in the form of angels and leaving their imprint in the snow.

Knowing full well what the snow imprints actually were, Helena and Barbara looked at each other. Barbara was hoping her older sister had a good explanation for this, lest they learn the real truth and the snow would leave forever, realizing that there were no snow angels at all. Thinking quickly as she could, Helena said a silent Hail Mary, crossed herself in make-believe and said to all, "Grandpa, do you remember last season when you first spoke to the snow?" "What!" grandma screamed. "Walter Broadhurst, you have been talking to the snow as well?" With grandpa at a loss for words, Helena quickly picked up where she had left off, explaining, "Yes, grandma, grandpa learned of the snow's ability to speak to people in the lands where it falls, but only after he heard Barbara and I talking to the snow. He didn't tell us that he had actually spoken with the snow, but I know that he overheard us, and that's why he stayed outside one day, after Barbara and I had come inside. But, that's neither here nor there, because the very next day, when Barbara and I were speaking with the snow, the snow told us of all of the snow angels they had seen throughout Ashburn, not just the ones at our farm and Mr. Cranford's, but the hundreds of snow angels on Wilkins Hill, too!" She went on to tell them that it was that very last snow of the season that had seen the many snow angels and proclaimed Ashburn to be the land of snow angels, confirming the story of the elder snowflake.

"Whooooooooeeeeee!" yelled Floyd. "I knew this was a special place. Yesssiiiirrrrreeeeee Bob, soon as Barbara sent me on that first wind-blown ride I knew this were the place fer me. That's quite a story you got there, missy!" Lifting off from Barbara's nose, Aly twirled and sparkled once more for them, telling them, "Well, I must be on my way if I'm going to catch up with the others, but thank you again for loving the snow. I hope we find a land where people will want us as much as you seem to here in Ashburn," and off she flew out the open window. Barbara and Helena rushed to the window and waved good-bye, reminding her and all snowflakes in earshot, "We love you snow. Barbara and Helena love you!" Barbara turned to look at grandma and grandpa and, turning back to the open window yelled, "So do grandma and grandpa!"

Chapter 10

ELSEWHERE IN ASHBURN, Johnny and Petey had been hoping to get in a little sledding practice over at Wilkins Hill. Certain that this light snow was the start of bigger snows to come they were ready to get in as much practice as they could. Each boy knew for sure that, if they didn't beat those two girls this year, they would be the laughing stock for another whole year. They were convinced that was NOT going to happen. Looking down from the top of Wilkins Hill, they weren't too optimistic about how good the sledding was going to be. There weren't very many bare spots, there just wasn't very much snow altogether. Regardless, they needed all the practice they could get before the big race this year. They flew over the top edge five different times, each time landing on their bellies with a pronounced "whump!" Each time, their sleds ground into the turf beneath the shallow snow and held firm. Each time, the boys went head over heels through the air, landing hard. Each time, there was heard throughout the valley, words that young boys should not be using!

Disgusted, they walked back to their sleds and threw them as far down the hill as they could. Johnny looked at Petey and said, "I guess there just isn't enough snow this time for any good sledding. There must be some fun we can have with this snow. It's too dry for snowballs, or we could have pounded those girls like they did us at church." Petey piped up and said, "We could do what all those kids did last season. You know, fall backwards in the snow and kick our arms and legs out. All the kids were really laughing and having fun!" Johnny looked at Petey, like he was four years old and said, "Are you just a big sissy? That's for little kids to do. Tough guys like us don't do baby things like that!" "It's not a baby thing," Petey charged back. "I saw Helena and Barbara doing it too, and some older kids as well. They were all laughing. And the one I did in your field was . . ." "What!" Johnny interrupted him. "You did one of those already? In my yard? Hey, wait a minute, was that the night you dropped your sled off at my house for my dad to work on?" "Yeah," Petey joked. "It was really fun and made me laugh, too!" "Oh, brother!" Johnny exclaimed. "I can't believe what I'm hearing." Standing up to Johnny for probably the first time in his whole life, Petey said, "Before you think it's so stupid, maybe you should try it. I'm gonna do one right now!"

Petey spent the next few minutes gathering snow into a big pile, shuffling most of it around with his boots. He knew that he had to have a deep pile or he would hurt his backside when he fell backwards, and after having flown off his sled five times today already, his backside was already sore. Johnny just watched as his younger, much more immature friend piled up the snow. Finally, satisfied that it was deep enough to support his fall, he stood in front of the snow pile, spread his arms and legs, looked to see if Johnny was watching, and fell backwards into the soft powder. Braced by the snow, he landed with a soft plop. Snow flew out from under him from both sides, rose up in the air and landed back down on him. As he kicked and flapped his arms and legs, he couldn't help but let out the biggest laugh. Seeing him laughing so hard, Johnny could just barely stifle a chuckle. Petey got up, scuffed together another pile of snow and repeated the feat, laughing even harder the second time. "Well," Johnny said, "Maybe I'll try it one time, but it sure looks stupid. It looks like something those sissy girls do." Petey helped him scrape together a very big, deep pile of snow for Johnny was bigger than Petey and then watched as Johnny got ready. "Remember," Petey explained, "Just fall back and let the snow catch you. You have to trust the snow!" "Duhhhhh," Johnny threw back. "I'm no dummy. If you can do it, I sure can." Petey watched as Johnny stood in front of his snow pile, spread his arms and legs and let his self fall backwards. Johnny's face looked like the biggest scaredy-cat Petey had ever seen. As he fell backwards, all of two seconds, he let out a wail that could be heard a mile away!

Realizing that he was safe and hadn't been hurt after all, Johnny started flailing his arms and legs back and forth. Petey was laughing the hardest of all, having seen the look of fear in Johnny's eyes as he fell backwards. Seeing Petey laugh and realizing how fun it had been, Johnny started laughing as well. He couldn't believe just how much fun it had really been. He jumped to his feet and yelled to Petey, "Come on, let's do it again!" They repeated this fun all the way down Wilkins Hill. Each time, Johnny learned to trust the snow more and more, considering his self to be a 'pro' by the time they stopped. By the time they got to the bottom, Wilkins Hill had twenty-seven snow angels from top to bottom.

Johnny told Petey that he couldn't remember having had so much fun. As they collected their sleds and headed for home, Johnny told Petey, "You know, "I'll bet we do that better than anyone else; just like we're the best sledders in Ashburn!" Petey slowed down, turned and looked at his older friend and said, "Johnny, we don't have to be the best at everything we do. Can't we just have a good time at some things, without having to be the best?" Surprised at Petey's boldness, Johnny looked at his wise, little friend and replied, "Yeah, I guess you're right, Petey, maybe we should just worry about having fun," and then asked him seriously, "Say, you're not gonna tell anyone that I was afraid to do the first one, are you?" Petey told him, "Only if you promise not to be such a big, loudmouthed, blabber-mouth from here on!" Putting his arm on his friend's shoulder, Johnny said, "Deal!"

At home, Floyd had flown out the window because it was getting too warm inside. The girls showed him a nice cold spot on the side of the barn where the sun rarely ever shined, and he found some other snowflakes there as well, who had decided that they liked the land of

Ashburn. Barbara promised Floyd that she would come out and play with him, promising to fly him around and around and around. As it turned out, millions and millions of snowflakes had decided to stay in Ashburn, so Floyd had a lot of his friends to be with. He said they would find plenty of things to keep them occupied, but hoped that Barbara would come see him during the day . . . if he wasn't too busy chasing some of the girl snowflakes!

Grandpa and grandma had asked the girls to come inside and have a long talk about the snow. They wanted to know everything the girls knew so they could formulate a plan to be sure they got all the snow they needed. It didn't matter that other people may not like or want snow, grandma now realized more than ever how important it was to have snow every year, and the more the better. That really made Helena happy as she reminded everyone, "Isn't that what I have always said about snow, "the more the merrier!" Despite the millions of snowflakes that had remained, it appeared to be barely a dusting of snow on the ground. The wind might even blow most of this away if it got strong enough, for it was a very fine white powder. It was still far too cold out for the snow to melt into the ground, and the rivers and streams were still frozen. Grandpa said he hoped the sun might melt some of the ground snow, which would be a good start to the planting season.

The girls took turns telling their grandparents about talking to the snow; Helena telling them how she had come to find out the snow could talk while she was sweeping snow off the porch. Grandma remembered that day vividly, telling grandpa that she was all set to call Doc Smithers. Barbara recalled the time Helena told her about talking to the snow, telling all of them that, in no uncertain terms did she believe it could be true. Then, the next morning, when the two girls were playing and laughing in the snow it had come true—the snow did speak to them and they had the best time. Helena told her grandparents how the snow had helped the girls win the big sled race and they were incredulous!

"What?" grandpa asked, "How on earth did the snow help you two win that race?"

Barbara told them, "Remember when I was trailing Petey in my race and he all of a sudden got caught up in a big snow flurry and crashed into the snow bank? Then, when he got out of it and was coming after me at the bottom of the hill, he was still completely surrounded by snow and couldn't even shake it away? Do you remember that? It was the snowflakes that did that! They created a blizzard for Petey to sled through and he couldn't see where he was going!" Grandma and grandpa laughed and laughed so hard at that. Grandma said, "I wondered what was buzzing and swirling around that boy's head," and they all laughed again.

Helena told them about how the snow would magically appear under her sled runners whenever she approached a bare spot coming down Wilkins Hill. She didn't understand how it was happening at first, but once, when she looked over at Johnny and saw a beautiful stretch of snow disappear from under his sled to pure dirt, she knew what the snow was doing to help her. Still, Johnny had been going so fast, he was able to ride his sled right across those spots and she was certain as she could be that he was going to win the race. It wasn't until the very end when she happened to look up to see how much further she had to cross the finish line, that she saw Johnny flying through the air, his sled stuck in the ground behind him.

Coming down the final stretch, she had looked ahead of her to find the snowiest patches to sled across, but the entire area in front of the finish line was all snow, and it was then that she knew Johnny would win. Later, when the judge told everyone to look back and see where Johnny's sled was still laying on the ground, well before the finish line, she saw that it was sitting on a huge bare spot—all dirt and grass, no snow at all. Just then, she saw the snow swirling above her, twinkling and shining, reminding her that they had helped all along, just as they had promised. Grandma and grandpa were dumbfounded, but they could offer no other explanation for what the girls had told them.

Grandpa then told them of the time he first spoke to the snow, and grandma almost fell out of her chair. "What," she asked, her mouth wide open enough she could have put a whole apple in it. "Are you telling me that you have spoken with the snow as well? Am I the only sane one around here?" "Now, mother," grandpa replied, "You heard the snow yourself upstairs in the girls' bedroom, so you know it's true." Still in a state of almost shock, grandma said, "I'm not sure whether this is still all a dream and I just haven't woken up yet." Grandpa reached over toward her and grandma leaned toward him, thinking he was going to try and console her, but grandpa dropped his hand from near her waist and pinched her on the bottom.

"Walter Broadhurst, what has gotten into you?" grandma shrieked. As Barbara and Helena were trying their best not to burst out laughing, grandpa replied, "Are you awake now, dear?" Stuttering and stammering, grandma muttered, "Well, I guess I am, yes, but I just don't know about all this nonsense of talking snowflakes." "Mother," grandpa started to remind her, "The snow will only speak with those people who love and want the snow, just as the snow will only stay in the lands where people love and want snow to come and stay. Let me tell you of the first time the snow spoke with me and then we'll see if Floyd and his friends won't talk with you as well."

He went on to tell them about the time last Christmas when, after he heard Helena and Barbara talking to the snow, unbelieving he so was that he had to try himself. He mentioned the snow angels and no sooner had he done that then snowflakes started to talk to him. They told him the story of the elder snowflake having seen snow angels in a land near this one, telling them to land there and stay and serve the greater purpose for that was the land where snow was loved the most. They were all listening intently and that's when grandpa pulled from his pocket, the picture that he had drawn for them, one year ago; the picture of the snow angels that had visited their farm and Mr. Cranford's. Recanting his exact conversation with the snowflakes, grandpa said, "I showed them this drawing I made of the snow angels that landed in our yard. You remember seeing them, don't you mother? And Buddy Cranford found them in his pasture, too! I told the snowflakes that this was indeed, the land of snow angels, and how certain mother and I were, and Buddy Cranford, too, that angels were visiting our fair land and showing themselves in the form of snow." He told Helena and Barbara of their belief that Eleanor and Samuel were coming down to earth to visit the farm, trying, in their own heavenly way to show that they were watching over the girls from above.

Helena leaned her head back and issued forth a, "Oh, brother. What have I . . . . I mean, what a wonderful story that is grandpa." Looking at Barbara, she pointed toward the back door and said, "Barbara, come with me. Maybe we should call Floyd to come in and speak with grandma; come on, Barbara." She hurriedly went into the kitchen, the confused Barbara on her heels. "What's this all about, Helena" Barbara asked. Silencing her, Helena said, "Don't you see, Barbara, grandpa and grandma think the shapes in the snow are real angel impressions from heaven. The snow thinks they are snow angels, too. What will happen if everyone finds out that we made the shapes, along with other kids over at Wilkins Hill? The snowflakes may think we were trying to fool them, and grandma and grandpa might be heartbroken. Oh, brother, what a big mess we have created."

Just as they were about to go back in and tell their grandparents the whole truth about the shapes in the snow, the sky outside went from a bright, sunny, brilliance to darkly overcast, casting the kitchen immediately into shadows. This quickly brought the girls back from their thoughts of how to explain things to their grandparents, to a heightened sense of alarm. Barbara was first to say, "What's that all about?" as they went to the door to look outside. In the living room, grandma and grandpa, too, had gone to the window to see what storm front was rapidly approaching, grandpa saying, "Mercy, these storms keep popping up from nowhere at all!" Looking outside, grandma and grandpa could see nothing but snow; a wondrous snowstorm of unimaginable proportion.

In the kitchen, Helena and Barbara could barely see past the back porch, so heavy was the snow coming down and swirling around. Helena opened the back door just to step on the porch for a better look, when she was hit with a great burst of snowy powder, her face covered like she had been hit with a cream pie. Grandma had felt the blast of arctic air come in through the open door and had yelled out, "Helena, come inside, close that door. There's a huge storm approaching!" Just as she clamored back inside and slammed the door shut, covered with snow from head to toe, they heard, "Whoopee! I ain't seen that much snow since I come over those big mountains t'other day!"

Looking down her nose, Helena saw that Floyd had flown inside and landed on her upper lip. "Sorry, missy, had a bad landing. I was aiming for that cute li'l nose," he said as he jumped up onto her nose. Just then, grandma came into the kitchen, asking, "What's all the racket? Why on earth did you open that door?" Barbara quickly replied, "Well, grandma, we were going to get Floyd and ask him to come inside and talk to you, but the storm blew him in for us. Would you like to talk to the snow?" Before grandma could answer, Floyd said, "What storm? Ain't no snowstorm out there, just a great big ruckus. All of the snow what blew outta here yesterday is comin' back this a-way. I hear talk about some snow angels. Snowflakes are sayin' they come across bunches of snow angels over near that place where kids sled down the big hill." Helena looked at Floyd excitedly, "You mean Wilkins Hill? The snowflakes found snow angels? How could that be? Barbara and I haven't even been over . . . I mean, really? Snow angels?" "Yesssiiirrreeee, Bob! That's the talk I'm a-hearin'. I was just headed over that way to see for myself, along with all them other snowflakes you see swirlin' round out there. If you hadn't opened that door and blown me in here, I'd already be over there. Open up and lemme outta here, will ya?"

Grandma stood there in shocked disbelief, but she had the where-with-all to open the door. Floyd flew out the open door as fast as he could fly. Grandma was mumbling, "I'll be! Talking snowflakes and snow angels!" Looking around, she called out to all of them, "Well, come on; let's get a move on. If we're going to see snow angels for ourselves, we better get some coats and boots on!" Grandpa jumped up and said he would run out and hitch up the wagon while the girls and grandma got dressed.

Ten minutes later, the whole family was in the wagon and making haste for Wilkins Hill. In the back of the wagon, Helena and Barbara were whispering to each other, "How can this be? There isn't even enough snow to make snow angels!" Helena lowered her voice even more and told her sister, "I don't know, Barbara, but this might be just the chance we need to set the record straight. Don't say a word until we figure out what's going on!" Far ahead of them, they could see great swirls of snow, as though they were heading into a snowstorm that was approaching them. The sky was a dark grey, ominous-looking clouds of snow flying in great circles as though lost in a whirlwind. Grandma called out for anyone to answer, "What do you suppose the snow is doing? It looks like one big cloud of confusion to me; almost like they can't make up their mind what to do."

Arriving amidst the furious snowstorm, it was difficult trying to see anything. Shielding their faces with their hands for the fury of the blowing snow, Helena was first to call out, "We love you snow. Helena and Barbara, grandma and grandpa love the snow!" That seemed to calm things a bit as much of the snow landed on the ground, most of it landing in circles around the snow angel shapes that were clearly present. Able to see clearly for the first time, grandma, grandpa and the girls all looked at the vast expanse of Wilkins Hill. Sure enough, to everyone's surprise, up and down the length of Wilkins Hill were snow angel impressions set deep into the snow.

Helena was startled when Aly, the snowflake, landed on her nose. She was excitedly jumping up and down, so much so that she was tickling Helena's nose. Out of breath, she was trying to say, "Snow angels, snow angels," but it sure sounded like, "No ankles, no ankles!" Knowing what Aly was trying to say, Barbara looked over and said, "Slow down, Aly. Catch your breath and tell us again what you wish to say." Grandma looked over and asked, "Aly? I thought we were talking to Floyd! How many snowflakes do you girls know?" Just then, Floyd landed on grandma's nose and, to her total shock, said, "Well, hello good-lookin'. What's your name?" Just then, grandpa sidled over and answered, "Her name is Helen Broadhurst, as in Mrs. Walter Broadhurst. Do you understand that, Floyd?" "Oh, Walter," grandma countered, "It's just our friend, Floyd. He's just a snowflake!" "Ha," grandpa replied, "You mean just a flake!" He leaned toward grandma's face and, with a huge wind, blew Floyd fifty feet into the air! "Wheeeeeeee-haaaaaaaaa!" everyone heard Floyd calling out. "Everyone in that whole family is a big bag of wind!"

By this time, Aly had settled down and caught her breath. Helena asked her, "What were you trying to say, Aly?" Looking at all of them and speaking in her loudest voice for all of the snowflakes to hear, Aly told them about leaving yesterday, but only getting as far as Wilkins Hill as it got dark. The snowflakes that had arrived a bit earlier had seen what they thought could be snow angels and had flown back to tell as many others as possible. Upon arriving, it was too dark to make out the shapes, so they decided to spend the night and wait until morning. Sure enough, as soon as the sun was high enough to cast its rays over the top of Wilkins Hill, they saw laid out before them, twenty-seven snow angels!

Grandpa quickly pulled out the drawing he had made the Christmas past, the same one he had shown Aly earlier, and sure enough, it looked just like the snow angels on Wilkins Hill. He told her, "This is what the snow of last season said the elder snowflake told them about." Barbara quickly joined in, "Yeah, and before the last snow of the season this past year went away, they also came to Wilkins Hill and there were more than a hundred snow angels that had visited." "That's when they proclaimed Ashburn to be the land of snow angels," Helena added, "and said they were going back to the land of snow creation to tell everyone!"

The conversation seemed to excite all of the snowflakes, for there began another great swirling of snow up and down Wilkins Hill. Billions of snowflakes were twinkling, their bright points like a glistening light show; the sun reflecting off their shiny bodies. They swirled in great circles and loops all around the snow angels, over top of them then underneath, and around and around they went. The clatter they were making was almost deafening, but Aly and Floyd understood exactly what they were saying.

Aly, on Helena's nose, and Floyd, now on Barbara's nose, called out above the chatter, "Snowflakes of Ashburn! We, the first snow of the season, proclaim this land to be the land of the snow angels! All snowflakes that agree with us show your support by showing these wonderful people just how much you love them!" With that, hundreds of billions of snowflakes arose from the snow angels and performed the most beautiful snow waltz anyone had ever seen. Grandma and grandpa, Barbara and Helena just watched in total amazement, never before having witnessed such a lovely choreographed display by Mother Nature. Moments later, the snow flew straight up in the air like a giant funnel cloud, swirled round and round and round and then, pausing as though it was trying to decide their next move, flew downward in one huge snowstorm and completely enveloped grandma from head to toe! No other area of grass or tree or anything else had even the first flake of snow—every single snowflake was on grandma! She had become an instantaneous snow-woman!

"Walter," grandma's voice came out from under all the snow, "What am I supposed to do?" Just then there was a scuffle of snow about her face, or where her face should have been, and Floyd's voice was heard. Shaking her head just a bit to be able to open her eyes, grandma saw Floyd standing on the tip of her nose. "Hello, again cutie. We need to stop meeting like this!" "Yes, you DO," Walter was heard to say, but then Floyd, very eloquently, said for all to hear, "My good lady. It is apparent to all of the snowflakes present that, Mr. Broadhurst and these two, dear, precious angels love the snow and wish for the snow to come visit this land every year. However, we are not certain of your feelings about snow and we wish only to visit lands where snow is loved and wanted by all. Pray tell, dear, lovely woman, please tell all the snowflakes present how you feel about the snow!"

Looking from side to side, first to Walter, then to Helena and Barbara, grandma issued forth a great big shake of her entire body, sending snow flying in all directions. She jumped up and down like she was thirteen. Floyd was trying desperately to hold on with every ounce of strength in his little snowflake body. Dropping to her knees, scooping up handfuls of snow and throwing it high into the air, laughing as it fell down upon her head, her nose, and her outstretched tongue, grandma spread her arms apart, looked toward the sky and yelled for all to hear, "I LOVE the snow! Grandma LOVES the snow! Helen Broadhurst LOVES snow like never, ever before!" Grandpa came over and knelt beside her, Helena and Barbara knelt down on her other side, their arms wrapped tightly round her, and gave her the biggest, best hug of all time! The snow flew up in the air again, swirling round and round, and as it had done before, came swooping down and enveloped the four of them! From the top of grandpa's head, Floyd was heard to call out, "Yeeeeee haaaaaaa! I done told y'all this were the land of the snow angels! Yessssiiirrrrreeeee Bob, I done told ya!"

When they had shaken the snow from their coats, Aly once again found her way to Helena's nose. Asking for their attention she told them, "We have been talking amongst ourselves and we have decided, because we are a very small snow, we are going to stay here at this place where children like to play. When the sun gets too warm for us, we will move off to the rivers and streams and farms where we will melt into the waters and the earth, serving the greater purpose for which we were created. Hopefully, Mother Nature will keep the air cold for a while longer, so we can stay and be with you as long as possible!" "Oh, snowflake, oh, Aly," Helena started, "We DO love you so much. Thank you for staying to see if there were snow angels in Ashburn, and for agreeing to stay here to serve the greater purpose, for we need a lot of snow this season. How will other snows of the season know to come here if you do not go back to the land of snow creation and tell everyone of our land?"

Aly lowered her head, knowing she did not have the answer to Helena's question, but told her, "Sweet girl, it is not likely that we could travel all the way around the world and return to where we were created, for it is too difficult a journey to make with any certainty. Hopefully, a new snow will pass over the mountains while we are still here, see the snow angel shapes and decide this is where it will fall and stay, but we cannot be certain of that. But, because we hear the prayers of people that pertain to snow, you must be certain to tell all people of Ashburn to pray for snow. That's the best thing I can tell you!" Grandma stepped over immediately and offered, "I'm going to see Reverend Hastings about the matter this very afternoon. Come Walter, we have an appointment with the Reverend!"

The snow stayed on Wilkins Hill for almost three weeks before thinning and finally melting into the ground, some of it blowing over to the river, but no new snow fell in that time. The last of the snow angels had finally melted away, as well, leaving no proof to newly arriving snows that Ashburn could be the land of the snow angels. When there were only patches of snow remaining, Floyd and Aly showed up on the porch railing early one morning. As Helena and Barbara were out the door, on their way to school, the two snowflakes flew up onto their noses with a hearty

JL CRAWFORD

"Good morning, girls!" "Well, hello," they both responded, thanking them for the wonderful time they had been enjoying over the past three weeks. "What are you doing here?" Helena asked them.

Floyd, who was looking a bit crustier than he usually did, told them that the warming weather was starting to take its toll, which was obvious for all of the snow that had already melted. Aly joined in, telling them that the remaining snowflakes could either, catch the next Mother Nature wind and go to another, colder land or, they could remain here and serve the greater purpose. Having discussed it amongst themselves, the remaining snowflakes had decided that they would like to stay in Ashburn and serve the greater purpose here. Barbara and Helena thanked them profusely for everything and wished them well however, the two snowflakes were not finished.

Riding along on the girls' noses as they made their way to school, Aly finally said, "We would like to serve the greater purpose not *just* in Ashburn, but in a very special place in Ashburn." "Yessiiirrreeee Bob," Floyd added, "That's what we want to do!" Helena and Barbara thought this was a wonderful idea and asked if they could help them locate a very special place. "Well," Aly answered, "We have already been thinking of a special place, but we don't know the exact location. Perhaps you could help us find it and we will have all of the remaining snowflakes meet you there tomorrow morning."

"Of course we can," Barbara shouted. "That's the best idea of all time. What's the name of this special place?" "Well," Floyd answered, "We don't reckon that it has a name 'xactly. It's more just like a place. One of them places where food grows." "Do you mean like a pasture or a field?" Barbara inquired? "No, not quite that big," Aly replied. "Do you mean like a garden?" Helena joined in. "Yepperr, that's it! That's what they call them places," Floyd answered. "But we want to serve the greater purpose in a very special garden," Aly said. "In fact, we want to serve the greater purpose in your grandma's garden, of course, if it's okay with her." "Oh, you two wonderful snowflakes," Helena said almost in tears. "If I wasn't afraid that you would melt right this second, I would give you both the biggest, best hugs of all time!" "Me, too," shouted Barbara, "I would give you the biggest and best hugs of all time, too!" Sure enough, the very next morning, all of the remaining snow in Ashburn came to rest in grandma's garden, serving the greater purpose for which it was created!

Before then, the children had enjoyed three wondrous weeks of sledding and Barbara had become the most-feared saucer-rider in all of Ashburn, boy or girl! She told Petey that, if they got enough snow to have the big race, she was going to enter in the saucer division, not the sled division. Cracking wise, Petey was quick to say, "You're just afraid I was going to beat you this year; you can't fool me!" Barbara had told him, "No, Petey, I just don't have room on the mantle for a saucer-race trophy . . . and another sled race trophy!" She zoomed by him in her saucer, laughing all the way down Wilkins Hill.

Helena and Johnny had gotten in a lot of sled practice as well, but never against each other, easily beating everyone against whom they raced. There was no doubt in anyone's mind that they would race for the championship once more. Noticing that Johnny was not nearly as boisterous and obnoxious as in years past, Helena remarked one day, "Johnny, aren't you anxious about the big race? You don't seem very excited about racing for the championship!" To her utter surprise, instead of bragging about how badly he was going to beat her in the race and take back the trophy, Johnny told her, "You know, Helena, I'm just looking forward to having a good time. If I win, I win, and if I don't, it will be just fine, because one of the two of us will win for sure, and I'm fine with that." Helena was so stunned, she couldn't even think of a reply and, when Johnny offered to carry her sled for her all the way home . . . well, let's just say that the future was looking brighter, snow or no snow!

Chapter 11

THOSE THREE WEEKS had flown by so fast for the children they didn't even realize that it was now Thanksgiving week already! They would only get two days off from school, plus the weekend, but there wasn't any snow left on the ground. In spite of that, every child in Ashburn was just grateful for the three wonderful weeks of snow they had just been enjoying. Unlike last year at this time, there were no sad, forlorn faces. In fact, all of the children and most of the adults were going on and on about how nice this snow had been. The comment heard by almost every grown up included, "Wasn't it wonderful how the snow was only in areas where children could play and not all over the steps and roads!" They remarked how no one they knew had slipped or fallen, nor had any wagons gotten stuck in drifts. It had been literally, the 'best snow' anyone could remember.

It seemed that everyone in Ashburn loved the snow again, at least this past snow. At Sunday service, even Reverend Hastings added a special sentiment to his sermon, asking the good Lord, "And Father, last but not least, please tell Mother Nature what a wonderful snow we just finished enjoying and, and, and if I may impose, Father, ask her to deliver all snows to Ashburn just like the last one. Well, maybe deeper of course, but have it fall the length and breadth of Wilkins Hill for the children, but not on any steps, or porches, or on the roads for the grown-ups!!!" Before lightning could possibly strike him down for asking the good Lord a favor in his sermon, he quickly signed the cross and called out "Amen, peace be with you, go in peace, brothers and sisters!"

To his complete surprise, he got a standing ovation from the entire congregation!

December arrived with plenty of cold arctic air, but no snow had fallen. The peaks of Daedalus and Colossus were covered, but not much more than usual, and snow had been seen in Ashburn, but only flurries. Once again, the children and the adults too, wondered whether they were going to get any more snow. While all of the families still had enough food to get through the winter, Mrs. Gunder having seen to that, they knew they had to get a good crop into the ground come spring, and as early as possible. The ground was quite moist right now for the recent snow having stayed around long enough and melted where it lay, but as the temperatures started to rise, it would quickly dry up, and well before a good spring crop could grow to its full promise. Grandpa kept telling everyone that winter had only just started, but even Buddy Cranford told him, "I know what you're saying Walter, but that's the same thing we thought last year, too!"

Helena had been giving the matter great thought. Like many children, she had seen flurries and had seen what looked like great snow storms flying very high overhead, but wondered why it had not fallen on Ashburn. "There just has to be a reason," she said one day as she and Barbara were coming back from playing with Samson and Duchess. Barbara asked, "Do you think the snow we have seen high overhead is looking down on our land in hopes of seeing snow angels, and because there are none to be seen, they are flying on to other lands?"

Helena was so startled by her younger sister's brilliant observation that she was almost speechless. Throwing her arms round her smart little sister, she said, "Oh Barbara, that's it, that must be it! Why have we not realized it before now? You are the smartest person in the whole family!" Giving it some very serious thought, the two girls were absolutely convinced that no snow would ever again land in Ashburn if newly arriving snow could not identify it as the land of the snow angels! Surely, they were both convinced that, if every new snow forever and ever would hear about the land of the snow angels, it would only want to land and serve the greater purpose there!

They rushed into the house screaming, "Grandma, grandpa, we know what's wrong! We know why there is no snow!" Helena added, "And the smartest little girl in the whole world figured it out! Barbara figured out why the snow is not falling on Ashburn. Oh, grandma, grandpa, we must do something about it!" "Whoa, slow down little angels," their grandparents said in unison. "Tell us what you figured out, Barbara," grandpa said. "Wait just a second, young lady," grandma offered, "Let's give both these smart girls a little hot chocolate to help warm them." "Oh, thank you, grandma," they both replied and plopped down into kitchen chairs. Once they had warmed themselves through and through, Helena said, "Go ahead, Barbara, it was your absolutely brilliant idea. You tell them."

Barbara proceeded to tell them how, when the last snowflakes were all set to leave Ashburn and go to another land to look for snow angels, they had seen the snow angels on Wilkins Hill and decided that was all the proof they needed to declare Ashburn the land of snow angels! Then, she reminded them that the snow of last season had also seen all of the snow angels, on Wilkins Hill, in their own yard, and in Mr. Cranford's pasture and, based on those observations had declared Ashburn to be the land of snow angels. "But," she concluded, "All of the snow that we have seen flying high overhead doesn't have any snow angels to see when they gaze down upon us, so they keep flying off to the east in search of the land they think is the real land of the snow angels." Crying now, she muttered, "Grandma, grandpa, how do we let them know that Ashburn is the real land of snow angels?"

Grandma and grandpa both had their arms wrapped round her, grandpa telling her, "Now, now, my precious little angel, we'll think of something." Grandma reminded her and Helena, "You girls seem to have forgotten that Christmas is just three days away. It's a great season for prayers and we must be certain that everyone in Ashburn is saying prayers for snow." Not even believing what she just said, she did a quick sign of the cross, folded her hands, bowed her head sharply, and said, "Dear Lord, please forgive my selfish thoughts. I just told my granddaughters to pray for snow in the season of your birth, completely forgetting to tell them to think of your Holy name. I ask your forgiveness, Father, and I promise to be more mindful, Amen." Looking at Helena and Barbara, she reminded them, "What I meant was to make sure that everyone in Ashburn, the four of us included, says prayers for snow *after* we pray to Jesus!" Looking over at grandpa, she quipped, "Walter, what are you doing way over there?" "Oh nothing mother. I just didn't want to be too close in case any lightning came through the window," and they all had a little chuckle. Well, maybe not grandma.

Grandpa was first to ask the girls, "Helena, Barbara, am I correct in thinking that neither one of you has asked your grandma or me for even the first Christmas gift? I'm not sure that Santa can fit all that you might ask for in his sleigh." Grandma joined in, "Father, I just figured they had gotten too old for Christmas or, had received so many gifts last year that they just didn't want anything this year." "Oh well, that's wonderful," grandpa replied. "Those precious little angels sure are thoughtful. I guess I'll go out to the workshop and find something to do since I don't have anything to make for anyone."

He started to get his coat and was half-way to the door when Barbara squealed, "Hey, wait a minute. I sent Santa a big list, bigger than last year, and I had a list for you, too, but it's not on my bed table anymore. I almost forgot all about it!" As grandpa and grandma tried to stifle their laughs, Helena put her arm around Barbara, gently reassuring her that grandma and grandpa wouldn't ever forget Christmas; especially for their two 'precious angels!' Realizing the joke that had been played on her, Barbara turned to look at her grandparents, her hands on her straight hips, her bottom lip sticking out as though she were about to cry, and said, "Fooled you! Ha, ha, ha! I fooled you!" Just as she started to stick her tongue out at them, grandpa rushed over to her and swooped her up in his arms. Laughing at her ten-year old silliness, he gave her the best hug of all time! They all sat down to a wonderful dinner and finished it off with another cup of hot chocolate!

Later, when the girls were in their room by themselves, Helena looked over at Barbara and said, "You know, just because you figured out why the snow is *not* falling on Ashburn, doesn't mean we have figured out a way to convince the snow *to* fall on Ashburn." "But Helena," Barbara responded, "What can we do? The snow is only going to fall where it sees snow angels on the ground and you and I both know that *we* are the real snow angels, remember?" "Well, I'm not so sure about that anymore, Barbara," Helena answered. "Yes, we made the snow angels in our yard and in Mr. Cranford's pasture, but the other kids must have made them on Wilkins Hill that first time. And we made them again in our yard this season, but who made all twenty-seven snow angels on Wilkins Hill this last snow? It wasn't you or I, and there wasn't even enough snow for sledding, so no kids would have gone there. Who do you suppose made those snow angels that Aly and Floyd found? Maybe there are real snow angels!"

"Wow, I never even thought about that! You're right. I wonder who did make all of those snow angels. Do you think grandma and grandpa are correct about real angels coming down from heaven, like mother and father, to give us a sign that they are looking over us?" Thinking about what Barbara had asked, Helena told her, "Well, there's absolutely no doubt that mother and father love us, and for sure, they are looking down upon us every day, but even if they did make those snow angels, or other angels visiting someone else made them, there isn't any more snow left for any visiting angels to make snow angels, for the new snow to see." Before they turned down the lamp, they agreed that they had to think like they had never thought before, agreeing that it was up to the real 'snow angels' to figure out an answer.

Christmas was only two days away and the girls had one last day of school before their holiday break. On the way to school they met up with some of their classmates, explaining to each one they encountered the problem they thought was the reason for no snow falling on Ashburn. Most of the kids thought that too many people still were not saying enough prayers. Kathy Clements assured them that even her father was praying for snow, which prompted Helena to ask, "Say, isn't Mrs. Gunder spending a lot of time with your dad?" Looking as though she wasn't supposed to say anything, she leaned in close and whispered to them, "I think my dad just might have the best Christmas present ever for Mrs. Gunder," which made all three girls scream and squeal so loudly, the two boys walking with them yelled, "Hey, cut that out," and ran off ahead of them. Kathy, Helena, and Barbara giggled the rest of the way to school, with Kathy reminding them just as they got there, "You mustn't say anything to anyone. Promise, you won't say anything," which Barbara and Helena did.

In school, Mrs. Gunder had the kids do only fun things. She gave them all a few assignments to do over Christmas break, but nothing that would require a lot of time, and nothing too unbearable. Acknowledging that there wasn't any snow at the time, but still hoping and hoping and praying that it would snow over their break, Mrs. Gunder decided to have all of the children make paper snowflakes and icicles. When they had made bunches and bunches of them, she said they could take them home and hang them up outside on their porches. "Just because there may not be any real snow right now, doesn't mean we can't pretend to have some snow," she reckoned.

Most of the boys thought this was a stupid, sissy thing to do, so Mrs. Gunder told them they didn't have to do it. However, when the very first boy laughed at the girls for having to make snowflakes and icicles, she told them all, "You're right, boys, that is a sissy game. Perhaps you will all enjoy making paper angels, instead!" They moaned and groaned for the rest of the day, while the girls just giggled and giggled. Near the end of the day though, Helena had the most remarkable thought. During lunch, she and Barbara had told Mrs. Gunder about their theory as to why snow was not falling on Ashburn, and to their delight, she absolutely, one hundred percent agreed with them. Of course, they didn't dare tell her who had actually made almost all of the snow angels.

Just before school was to let out, Helena asked if she could meet with Mrs. Gunder after school. Surprised that she would want to stay after on the day before Christmas Eve, she nonetheless agreed, for she knew Helena must have a very good reason. Shortly thereafter, the bell rang and the throng of kids poured out the door like water through a broken dam. The noise level was deafening, with every child wishing each other well, merry Christmas, see you next year, and everything else kids could think of to say. Helena told Barbara to come and listen to the idea she had developed as they were making snowflakes and icicles.

When Mrs. Gunder finished what she was doing, she sat at her desk and told the girls to pull over two chairs. "Now, what on earth could be so important to keep you two after school on the day before vacation?" she asked right off. Barbara had no idea what Helena was thinking, and that was clearly evident by the questioning look she gave Helena, like "Beats me!" Helena looked from Barbara to Mrs. Gunder and back again, before Barbara yelled, "Spill the beans, Helena! What is it?" Hesitating ever so slowly, Helena said, "I think I know how to get the snow to fall on Ashburn!"

Before Mrs. Gunder could utter the first sound, Barbara issued forth the loudest scream ever heard in the history of Ashburn, maybe even of all time. Jumping up from her chair, dancing round in circles, she screamed, "Oh, Helena, how can we get it to snow? What is your plan? What have you thought of? Can I help? Can I? Can I?" Mrs. Gunder had to actually place her hands on Barbara's shoulders to get her to stop jumping, finally directing her to her chair, saying, "Barbara, let's hear what your sister has to say, then we can all three jump for joy!" Settled finally, she stared at Helena with the amazed look of excitement that only a young child can produce; her mind conjuring up a million scenarios of her own that would certainly issue forth from her brilliant, older sister.

"Well," Helena started, "I was thinking about Barbara's theory that the snow wasn't falling on our land because the arriving snow had no snow angels on the ground to see from high above as they flew over." Looking directly at Mrs. Gunder now, she said, "So, when you told the boys that they had to make paper snow angels today, I thought, well, I thought that maybe we could make really big paper snow angels and place them on the ground at Wilkins Hill." Jumping up again from her chair, Barbara screamed, "Oh, Helena, you are the smartest person in the whole world, maybe even smarter than Mrs . . . . I mean than Mr. Clements! Oh, you are the best! It's a great plan and it will definitely work. I just know it will!" "Barbara!" she heard Mrs. Gunder shout. "Please come back over here and sit down and let's think this through."

When Barbara had once again settled down, as much as any ten-year old can, Mrs. Gunder suggested they plan a strategy and consider every possibility. After talking it through a bit, the biggest problem they could think of was how to make paper snow angels large enough so that the arriving snow would see it from high up in the sky. When Barbara suggested that they make them bright, instead of big, like bright orange, or red, or yellow, Helena asked her, "When have you ever seen an orange, or red, or yellow angel? I think we have to make them white," to which they all agreed. When Mrs. Gunder asked, "How do we know what size to even make them," Barbara absent-mindedly plopped right down onto the floor, spread her arms and legs, flailed them in and out ten times, and said, "This is the exact size that we made them when we . . ." Just as she caught herself saying what she and Helena had decided they couldn't tell anyone—ever, Mrs. Gunder said to them both, "Why don't we have a seat in our chairs and have a little talk, before we go any further. Shall we, girls?"

Over the next twenty minutes, Helena and Barbara told Mrs. Gunder the entire story, from the first time Helena spoke to the snow, how the snow helped them each win their big sled race, grandpa's first time speaking with the snow, about Aly and Floyd, to grandma being covered in snow like a snowman, and the snow agreeing that Ashburn was indeed, the land of the snow angels and covering Wilkins Hill for three weeks when there wasn't another snowflake in all of Ashburn. Mrs. Gunder thought about trying to write it all down, saying how it would make the most wonderful book, but could hardly find herself believing all she was hearing. Yet, at the same time, she couldn't dispute a single thing the girls told her, and when they suggested she confirm it with grandma and grandpa, she was convinced. They were still left with formulating a plan, but Mrs. Gunder was convinced that, if they could come up with a sound idea to somehow fool the snow into falling on Ashburn, it might just do the trick!

It was getting late and Mrs. Gunder told the children they needed to be on their way before it got dark and their grandparents became worried. She promised to give the matter serious thought that night and would even ask Harold, I mean, "Mr. Clements," she said, "For his valued opinion." Barbara and Helena looked at each other and giggled, knowingly, and Helena clasped her hand tightly onto Barbara's mouth for fear she would let one more cat out of the bag!

On the way home, they talked about the paper snow angels, but Barbara said, "What if it rains and they get all mooky and yucky? The snow won't think those are snow angels." "Yeah, you're so totally right, Barbara," Helena told her. "We can't even make snow angels out of large pieces of paper because of that. What can we possibly make them out of that will really fool the snow into thinking they are real snow angels?"

Somewhat despondent for lack of an answer, Barbara told Helena, "I think we should ask grandma and grandpa for their help." "Yeah," Helena agreed, "I just wish we knew how those twenty-seven snow angels got onto Wilkins Hill the last time."

As they crossed the Cranford's farm on their way home, Helena noticed the clothes hanging on the clothes line. Heavy coats that were wet from the snow hung like boat anchors, pulling the line almost to the ground. Shirts, and dresses and pants, and Barbara noticed, "Men's long underwear!" flapped lightly in the breeze. "Hey," she shouted, "What if we laid out long underwear like that on Wilkins Hill! Do you think the snow would think they were angels?" Helena stopped and thought for a minute, then said, "Well, I guess it's possible, but they would be awfully skinny angels, and we would have to make something for the shape of the heads. And, where would we get a bunch of long underwear from? I think we better give it some more thought, but it was a good idea, Barbara!" "Well," Barbara answered, "Just like Mrs. Gunder says, it's better than using your noggin for a hat rack!" They laughed at that and other girl things as they came towards the back porch at their house.

Just as they were about to step up onto the porch, Helena froze dead in her tracks, put one hand to her mouth, looked right at Barbara, and whispered, "Oh my gosh, Barbara, I've got it! I know what we can use to make snow angels with!" Filled with anticipation, Barbara grabbed Helena's arm and squealed, "What? What can we use? Tell me, tell me Helena!" Turning towards the side yard, where grandma's laundry was also hanging on the line and blowing madly in the breeze, she pointed so Barbara could see the many sheets and blankets, telling her, "Look, Barbara, those would be perfect! We could cut them into perfect snow angel shapes, some small, some medium, and some big, and put them all over Ashburn. That way, wherever the snow might fly over our land the snowflakes will be certain to see them and land here! Oh, Barbara, I just know it will work!"

JL CRAWFORD

Barbara was jumping up and down in total excitement, hugging her smart older sister until they were both jumping for joy! "But, Helena, where will we get all of the sheets and blankets from? Surely, grandma will not let us cut up all of her sheets and blankets!" That sound reasoning from her smart little sister brought them both back down to earth, just as they heard a voice from the back door, "Girls, what on earth has you jumping up and down, and why are you so late getting home? Your grandpa and I were worried sick!"

Coming up the steps and giving grandma a little hug, Barbara offered, "Oh, grandma, we stayed after school to talk with Mrs. Gunder about how we can bring snow to Ashburn. Helena has the best idea of all time and Mrs. Gunder agrees. She's even going to talk to Harold about it . . . oops, I mean, Mr. Clements, you know, Kathy's dad. Let Helena tell you and grandpa all about it because we need your help." "All in good time, young ladies," grandma replied, "But first, you two go up and get cleaned up for dinner and we'll talk about it with grandpa. Lord only knows where that man is now, or what he's up to."

Grandpa came in shortly thereafter, just as the girls were coming down for dinner, and they heard her ask him, "Walter, why are you covered in wood shavings? What are you doing out in that barn?" He stepped out onto the back porch and, with the door still open, told her, "Oh, nothing, mother. I'm just working on a little project. My, oh my, what have you cooked for dinner, my love? It sure smells wonderful in here!" Barbara and Helena always giggled when he called grandma, "my love!" For the rest of the evening, as they usually did, they would address each other as "my love," giggling all the while until grandma would tell them, "Okay, that's about enough of that!"

Plopping into her chair, Barbara said, "Hurry grandpa, you have to sit down so Helena can tell everyone about her fabulous idea to bring snow to Ashburn! Oh, sorry grandma, after we say the blessing, then Helena can tell us all about it," as grandma smiled approvingly. When everyone's plate was loaded up with food, Helena told her grandparents about her idea to bring snow. She told them how Barbara had accidentally blabbed about who really had made the snow angels, only to see Barbara looking at her in total disbelief. Barbara had her hand on her mouth, which was wide open and showing all of her mashed potatoes, but couldn't begin to say a word.

Just as Helena started to say "What, Barbara, you know you blabbed it," grandpa asked her, "What's this about you two girls making all of those snow angels?" "That seems to be a very good question your grandfather has asked, Helena. I presume you have a very good answer?" Realizing that she had just blabbed the same thing to her grandparents that Barbara had done to Mrs. Gunder, Helena suddenly fell silent. She looked up at everyone, only to see all of them staring at her, waiting for an answer, but she could only manage a weak, "Gee, I don't think I feel very well. Maybe I should go up to bed." Waiting for approval, the dining room as quiet as night, she heard grandma answer, "Yes, I suppose so, Helena. I'll have father send for Doc Smithers and have him take a look. You'll probably miss Christmas Eve dinner tomorrow, and maybe even Christmas, but you can go upstairs if you wish."

Feeling as small as an ant, she pushed her chair away and started to walk away when she turned to look at them, tears having filled her eyes and, about to let loose a torrent of tears, wailed, "Oh, grandma, grandpa, we didn't mean to tell a fib. We didn't want to tell anyone for fear that the snow would find out and wouldn't believe that Ashburn is the land of the snow angels. We never did anything on purpose. We didn't even think we were doing anything at all, just playing in the snow and it was so much fun, and then, all the kids were doing it at Wilkins Hill."

She went on and on about the first time the snow told them they had seen angel impressions and were convinced angels had come down from heaven and made their mark in the snow. They thought it best to just let the snow think that, especially after the elder snowflake had proclaimed

JL CRAWFORD

Ashburn to be the land of the snow angels. When they found out that their grandparents and Mr. Cranford believed the shapes to be made by angels from heaven, and possibly in the spirit of the girls' parents, she said, "Oh, grandma, grandma, we just couldn't tell you differently and possibly break your hearts." "But wait, Helena," Barbara interrupted. "It just might be true because you and I did not make the snow angels that the last snow saw on Wilkins Hill! There wasn't even enough snow for sledding or saucers or snowball fights on Wilkins Hill, or anything, but somehow, twenty-seven snow angels, bigger than Helena or I, showed up on Wilkins Hill and the snow came back and showed us. We haven't figured that out yet, but maybe there *are* angels visiting Ashburn as well. Do you think it could be true, grandma?"

Grandma started to open her mouth, but grandpa jumped ahead of her. Motioning for Helena to come sit on his lap and for Barbara to sit with grandma, grandpa told them, "Girls, it's clear that you didn't intend to do anything wrong or to tell any fibs, but it's not always right to let people think things when you know the truth to be otherwise. Now, I'll be the first to say that, thinking some impressions in the snow could be angels from heaven might not fly with everyone, but it also made me feel pretty good. Your grandma and I liked thinking that your mother and father were up above, watching down on their two precious angels. In fact, I've often wondered if they tell the real angels up above that they're looking at real angels down on earth, and what the angels think!"

"I guess it probably was a pretty good idea to let the snowflakes think what they wanted to about the shapes they saw and, from what Aly told us, they seemed to form that impression all on their own. Let me ask you though, you haven't actually told anyone that angels have visited Ashburn and made those impressions, have you?" In unison, the girls blurted out, "Oh, no, grandpa. We haven't told anyone about the snow angels . . . well, except now for you and Mrs. Gunder. That would be lying and you have taught us to never, ever lie." Setting her down on her feet, but not before he got a big hug and gave her a kiss on her cheek, grandpa said, "That's the answer we were hoping for, sweet girls. Now, we better sit back down and finish our supper and talk about this big plan of yours!"

Having agreed at least that letting the snowflakes think the impressions in the snow were snow angels leaving their mark for all snow to know that Ashburn was the land of snow angels, the idea of possibly doing something that would further that belief wasn't a bad thing in any way. So, when Helena told them about using sheets and blankets, cut up in the shape of angels and laying them down on the ground throughout Ashburn, grandpa and grandma thought it was absolutely brilliant! Grandma was concerned about how they would get enough sheets or blankets to use though, for she did not have nearly enough. After some more thought, they all agreed that using just sheets was probably the better idea, because they didn't have but one, single white blanket, and they were in complete agreement that all of the angel shapes had to be white!

Grandma was doing dishes, grandpa had gone back out to the barn, and Barbara and Helena were busy drawing angel shapes on paper. Helena had brought in one sheet from outside and had laid it on the floor in the living room. She told Barbara to lie down and make the shape of an angel. Before she made any marks on the sheet though, she asked grandma for permission, and then proceeded to trace Barbara's angel shape, first with pencil, then more boldly with charcoal from the fireplace.

Grandpa walked through the door, saying, "Well, look who just came into the yard when I was coming out of the barn. Look everyone, it's Mrs. Gunder and Mr. Clements!" Drying her hands on a dishtowel and tossing aside her apron, grandma welcomed them in, asking, "Harold, Lorraine, what brings you over here at this hour? Please come in. I have a fresh pot of coffee on the stove and there's plenty of apple pie leftover from dinner." Mrs. Gunder was beside herself, telling grandma, "Oh, Helen, thank you, but we've already eaten and we just had to come over and tell you what we're thinking about Helena's idea! She did tell you, didn't she?" "Oh, yes, she spilled the beans alright," grandpa informed them, "And we've been giving it some good thought as well." Between them, they chatted about the idea of using bed sheets, with Mrs. Gunder saying, "That's exactly what Harold suggested!" Barbara added, "That was Helena's idea too, and we think it's just the best idea ever!" Grandma nodded her head at what Barbara was saying, but interjected, "There just seems to be one big problem, however. Where do we get enough bed sheets to make as many angel shapes as we might like?"

Mrs. Gunder jumped to her feet excitedly, exclaiming, "That's no problem at all, at least not anymore! Thanks to the extraordinary generosity of this wonderful man, we'll have more than enough bed sheets to make a hundred angel shapes!" Barbara and Helena were jumping up and down, screaming, laughing, giggling, and carrying on so much, the grown-ups could only look and stare . . . and laugh with them! Grandpa looked over at Harold and asked, "Harold, do you have a storeroom full of bed sheets that nobody knew anything about?" "No, of course not, Walter, but what I do have is enough community-profits money left over strictly for community support, to buy ten bolts of material from Jim Godsey! We'll use that to make as many angel shapes as we can." Mrs Gunder added, "And we think the best idea is to put as many up and down Wilkins Hill as we can, with others placed at both ends of town, some more in your yard and Buddy Cranford's pasture; maybe even a few on the slopes of Daedalus and Colossus!" "Well," grandma concluded, "Some people around here sure have been using their noggins for more than just a hat rack!" Hearing that, Barbara just looked at Helena and they both burst out laughing. Grandpa looked over at Mr. Clements and said, "How about some of that apple pie and coffee that Helena mentioned?" and they made their way to the kitchen. Out of earshot of grandma, grandpa told Harold, "I might even have something to spice up the coffee!"

Even though it was Christmas Eve, Jim Godsey was more than happy to open up and sell Harold the bolts of material. They had arranged it the night before and Harold was at the store at 7:00am. Mrs. Gunder had told him that there was a lot of work to be done. Over coffee and apple pie the night before, they had hammered out the final plan. Okay, there was a lot of ice cream, too, which seemed to keep the girls interested in what was going on. It was decided that everyone would meet at the church, where there were a lot of big tables to work on. Barbara, Helena, and Kathy were in charge of drawing the angel shapes. They took turns lying down on the spread-out fabric, one another drawing the outline of each girl. They were three different sizes so it was just perfect. When Helena asked grandma if she wanted an angel shape in her size, she just made a loud, "Hmmpff," and went about what she was doing.

Grandma and Mrs. Gunder were cutting out all the shapes, because they knew how to use scissors better than anyone else. Grandpa and Mr. Clements were stacking the angel shapes between flat pieces of wood so they wouldn't get all wrinkled or, as grandpa said, "We don't want all the angels' toes to curl up!" It was a serious team effort and by the time grandma asked, "Who wants a triple-decker peanut butter and jelly sandwich, boiled eggs, pickles, and a slice of key lime pie?" the whole job was done!

The entire team was sworn to secrecy, just to be sure that no word leaked out and any arriving snow didn't get wind of the fact that there might not really be any snow angels. The rest of the plan was to be carried out after dark, and that's where grandpa, Mr. Clements and Reverend Hastings came in. It was their job to put out all the snow angels after dark and they had to secure them into the ground so the wind didn't blow them away. Grandpa had brought along all the stakes he could find and he even cut some more that afternoon. The sky was as grey as it had been in months and the temperature was well below freezing. In years past, this was the perfect weather recipe for snow! Everyone knew that this plan was going to be the greatest success of all time!

Grandpa's wagon was filled with angel shapes, as was Mr. Clements, and both were covered with tarps so no one would see what was underneath. Before everyone left to head home, it was Christmas Eve, after all, Reverend Hastings gathered everyone in a big circle. Holding hands, he led them in the Lord's Prayer and then asked Jesus to answer the one prayer that everyone in Ashburn was going to ask tonight, saying, "Father, we need you this night like never before. Please answer our prayers this night as you so often do. Allow good enough weather for Santa to make his rounds, and be sure to tell Mother Nature that this land loves snow more than any other. Amen." After hugs all around and wishes for a merry Christmas Eve to everyone, they headed home; all just a bit closer for having shared in another community effort.

As soon as it was dark, grandpa headed over to Wilkins Hill. Mr. Clements lived on the other side of town, so he and Reverend Hastings placed angel shapes in various yards and fields, on hillsides and in pastures; making certain the snow would see the shapes, but not any curious children who might pick up the material wondering why it was there. Grandpa placed thirty-one angel shapes up and down Wilkins Hill, four on each side of the creek, which was still frozen, six in Mr. Cranford's pasture, and five throughout the yard and farm. When he was placing them in Mr. Cranford's yard, Buddy had come outside to let Samson and Duchess run around and do their business. They must have smelled grandpa because they came running over to him, jumping up and down, barking and barking. Grandpa was trying to shush them so Buddy wouldn't come over and see what he was doing, but it wasn't until they had given his face a complete licking that they ran back to their own house. Walking back to his house, Mr. Cranford was looking towards the pasture the whole time, trying to figure out what those two silly pooches had been doing.

Chapter 12

IT WAS QUITE late when grandpa walked back in the house and he quickly plopped down into his big, soft chair. He was cold and tired and grandma had a steaming cup of hot chocolate for him, some more apple pie, and the biggest scoop of ice cream of all time, or so the girls thought. Knowing what the girls were waiting up for, grandma suggested they forego opening presents tonight because grandpa was so tired. "Awwww, grandma, do we have to?" they both moaned. "Do we have to what," grandpa inquired, not certain of what was going on. Grandma told him that she thought it best for everyone to get a good night's sleep after all of the hard work they had put in, and they would open presents in the morning, before going to church, but before she could get another word in, grandpa boldly said, "We have traditions in this house, mother, and by golly, we're going to stick with them. Let's open up a couple of presents, shall we?" Grandma just looked at him and gave him her best smile, for she knew he could never disappoint his two precious, little angels.

As the girls were going through the pile of presents, grandpa said, "Actually, Barbara and Helena, I would like very much for you to open a present that I suggest." "That's a wonderful idea, grandpa," the girls replied together, "Which one? Which one?" Grandpa pointed out two identical packages that were leaning up against the wall, just to the side of the tree. They were only wrapped in paper and the top and bottom had a bit of string keeping the paper from coming loose. Grandma looked quizzically at grandpa, not having the first clue as to what they could be.

From the shapes of them, the girls were absolutely certain that grandpa had either made them new wooden crosses to hang over their beds or, they were some new, useful project that he was always making for them.

Each girl squeezed, rubbed, turned it over and over, checked the weight of it, and Barbara even knocked it against her head, trying desperately to figure out what it was before the other. Helena said, "I'm certain it is a new cross for over my bed, but it's a bit too big." Barbara, holding it in both hands with the long end pointing to the ground, was walking around in a circle saying, "I know, it's one of those things they use to find water in the ground!" Grandma chuckled at that and told them, "Your grandpa is certainly a 'divine' man, but I don't think he knows the first thing about making a divining rod! If you can't guess, go ahead and un-wrap them. I want to see, too!"

The girls tore into the paper, each ripping through it successfully at the same time. Somewhat bewildered, they looked at grandma and grandpa and said, "Thank you, grandpa." Helena said, "I was right, it is a new cross for above my bed, and it is a very nice one, grandpa." Barbara added, "It is so smooth and it feels as though it has some engraving on the other side. What did you make grandpa?" Grandpa sat in his chair, a little bit too smug for grandma, and said, "Well, why don't you silly girls turn them over and see." Barbara quickly looked at Helena and said, "We do it on the count of three, okay?" Locking fingers as they do when they make solemn pacts, they each said, "Deal!"

Grandpa said, "Mother, why don't you do the honors and count to three?" "Oh, Walter," she replied. "Always the showman! Okay girls, one, two, and . . . THREE!" The girls turned the crosses over, their eyes busy reading what words had been engraved on the crosses, their mouths wide open, slowly deciphering grandpa's work. Helena was the first to shout, "Oh, grandpa, it is a cross! No, I mean it isn't a cross, but yes, it is a cross, I mean, I mean . . ." Barbara had just figured it out as well and when Helena couldn't spit the words out, she yelled, "It's a garden cross,

Helena; they're garden crosses. Grandpa made them for our dear, special friends. Oh, grandpa, they will remember us forever and ever!" The girls were hugging and kissing grandpa while grandma was sitting as though in a cloud.

Getting their attention, grandpa pointed toward grandma and suggested maybe they should show them to her. They raced over to grandma and jumped in her lap, thrusting the garden crosses in her face. "Garden crosses," they explained. Finally, when Helena allowed grandma to hold it and look at it more closely, she saw just what the girls were trying to make her understand. "Mine says Floyd's Garden," yelled Barbara as she handed it to grandma. "And mine says Aly's Garden," Helena added. "We're going to put them in opposite ends of your garden, grandma, where Floyd and Aly spent their last days. They told us they wanted to serve the greater purpose in a special garden." "Yeah," Barbara echoed, "They got the last of the snow and came to your garden, grandma. They said they wanted it to be the best garden ever . . . and it will be, I just know it will be!"

Grandma removed the cloth-square she had from her pocket and dabbed her eyes. As she held Barbara close, Helena went over and sat with grandpa. They spent some time talking about the snowflakes and how they had impacted their lives, fondly recalling Floyd and his funny, crusty old voice, and how Aly, through her strong leadership, for such a tiny little snowflake, commanded such a presence with the billions and billions of other snowflakes. They recalled being covered in snow during the furious little snow cyclones that the snow could produce, almost instantaneously, it seemed. Before anyone knew how long they had been reminiscing, Helena and Barbara had both fallen asleep in the laps of their grandparents, clutching their garden crosses as though they were crosses of Jesus Himself, cast in gold. Grandma and grandpa carried the girls to bed, certain that their dreams would be only the dreams that all princesses should have—the sweetest of dreams.

Grandpa went back downstairs to turn down the oil lamps and check the doors. He stepped out onto the back porch and felt a light, cold mist falling on his face. He looked toward the heavens, asking no one in particular, "Why aren't you coming down as snowflakes? Surely it is cold enough. Are you going to answer the prayers of all those who wish for snow?" Then, as though somewhat frustrated, he concluded, "If for no one else, could you please answer the prayers of two, precious angels?" He went outside to his workshop, moved away the many boards that were hiding the different presents that were supposed to be from Santa, along with the gifts that he and grandma had made or purchased for the girls. It took three trips back and forth before he had brought everything inside and placed them around the tree.

Grandma and grandpa had decided from the very first Christmas when Helena and Barbara came to live with them that, every Christmas, from the first one on would be, as the girls were so fond of saying, "the best ever!" This one, grandpa was certain, would be the very best of all! Before he turned down the lamp in their bedroom, he kissed grandma, as he did every morning and night, and told her about the misting rain. She gently touched his shoulder and then, grasping both his hands in hers told him, "Walter Broadhurst, you're a wonderful man and an even more wonderful grandpa. Those garden crosses that you made for the girls were a very special, warm, and caring idea; gifts that will last forever. How you manage to come up with the sweetest thoughts and ideas will always be a source of wonderment for me, and great pride, I might add!" Pulling her closely too him and hugging her tightly, he looked into the most beautiful brown eyes he had ever seen, telling her, "My dear lady, it's helps to have the constant devotion, love, and inspiration of the most wonderful woman in the world!" As he started to turn down the lamp, he looked one last time toward the window and, turning back to grandma exclaimed, "Look, my dear, the rain has turned to snow. Maybe this will be the "best Christmas ever!"

Christmas morning greeted the family with a snowy white landscape blanketing almost everything, though very light. Happy nonetheless that snow had finally fallen on Ashburn the girls were as giddy with excitement about the snow as they were about the prospect of opening presents. Barbara was the first to remember, of course, that they had only opened one present on Christmas Eve, quickly reminding everyone, "Hey! We only got to open one present last night and the family tradition calls for opening two! Can we open another present before church? Can we? Please, oh please?" Grandma and grandpa looked at each other knowingly and, in unison, said "Traditions are traditions. Of course we can open another present!" Still in their night clothes, each sipping a steaming cup of hot chocolate that grandma had made them, they searched the mountain of presents spread out around the tree. Helena remarked that Santa must have been very busy last night and Barbara, giggling, said, "Yes, he must have been. I wonder what time he went to bed!" They looked at each other, then back and forth to grandma and grandpa, and they all laughed!

The first loud, shrill scream came from Barbara, as she opened what she thought for certain was a baby rag doll to go along with the two she had, only to discover that grandma had made her a new fancy dress, very much like the one she had made for Helena last year but, as she disclosed to all, "even prettier than Helena's!" She had no sooner given grandma a hug and kiss than she ran upstairs telling them she was going to get dressed for church. At the top of the steps she turned to face them and, holding the dress up for all to see said, "And I will be wearing the prettiest dress of all time!" Helena, grandma, and grandpa all laughed at how everything, no matter what it was, could possibly be the "best of all time!"

Helena had picked out a present that was about ten inches long, three inches wide, but flat as a pancake. She kept squeezing it between her fingers, trying desperately to guess what it could be; feeling movement inside the wrapping as she kneaded the package gently between her fingers. It felt as though there were tiny pebbles and wire throughout. Looking at the wrapping once again, she saw that it said "To Helena, from grandma and gramps, and . . ." Looking inquisitively at grandpa, like he might offer some sort of hint, he just shrugged his shoulders and said, "Don't ask me!"

Her curiosity having reached its peak, she tore through the wrapping, the same soft, doe-like, brown eyes that were a match to her grandma's filled with excited expectation. It was only when the precious gems and gold necklace slipped from the package into her open hand that Helena's mouth fell open. Clutching the beautiful necklace in one hand, the most exquisite thing she had ever seen, let alone held, she thrust her other hand to her mouth. Gasping for air, she looked for the wrapping paper and, holding it in her hand so she could read whom it was from, she asked, "It says it is from grandma, gramps, and . . . is it from whom I think it is?"

Grandma reached for the necklace and, opening the clasp, placed it round Helena's neck and fastened it securely. Turning her so she could show it to grandpa as well, grandma said, "Yes, Helena. This is from your mother. It was given to her by your father on their first Christmas after they were married." Helena raced over to the mirror in the entryway, admiring the absolute, most wonderful gift she could possibly imagine. Turning to them, fingering the necklace in both hands, she told them, "I thought I recognized it as soon as I un-wrapped it, but never in my wildest dreams did I think it could be mother's necklace."

Beckoning her forth, grandma told her when Helena's mother had first un-wrapped the necklace many Christmases before, she told your father, grandpa, and me that, "One day, when we have a little girl and she is old enough to wear and appreciate this, I will give it to her." "Well, Helena," grandma said, "Your grandpa and I feel that you are old enough to appreciate this special remembrance of your mother, and we are certain that you will wear it with great pride and take good care of it." Hugging them together, her arms round both, she was completely in tears as she tried to thank them each, but all she could manage to utter were whimpers and sniffles. She turned and ran up the stairs, calling out to Barbara to come see the special gift she had gotten, saying, "Oh, Barbara, this has got to be the best of all time!" Holding grandma's hand, grandpa looked at her and said, "Helen Broadhurst, it seems as though I don't have the market cornered when it comes to wonderful ideas," and gave her a warm hug.

Dressed and ready for church, grandma asked grandpa to sweep the steps before they went out just to be certain no one slipped on the way out. Barbara had on her new dress and was dancing and twirling until she was dizzy, the bottom of her dress fanning out in a huge circle. She was in her own little world and grandma could hear her saying to no one at all, "Yes, Romeo, this is my new dress for the ball. Oh, why yes, Romeo, I would be happy to go to the ball with you!" Helena had her necklace round her neck and couldn't stay away from the hall mirror, so enamored of its beauty was she. Grandpa stepped back inside and told grandma, "That's odd, there isn't the first bit of snow on the steps or the porch, and there is none on the drive; only on the grass." Grandma agreed it was odd, but glad for it, resolved that the steps and drive must not be as cold as they thought they were.

As they drove to church in the wagon they remarked how there was no snow anywhere, except for on the grass and in the fields; not even on rooftops. They could see the high peaks of Daedalus and Colossus in the distance and they were covered in snow; a great swirling of snow almost completely obscuring the very tops of each. "Looks like we could get some more snow pretty soon," grandpa remarked. Helena and Barbara said, almost simultaneously, "Grandma, grandpa, it appears that our snow angels worked. We must be certain to talk to the snow and ask them why they came to Ashburn."

It was only just then that the four of them realized they had not spoken to the snow at all! "What a blundering idiot I have been," Helena blurted out. "Oh, grandpa, please stop for a moment and let us see what the snow has to say." Grandma said they needed to be on their way or they would be late for service, and could talk to the snow after church. As they drove on, Barbara and Helena were filled with talk about the snow and their success with the snow angels, until Barbara offered out, "But why did so little snow fall, Helena? Do you think the rest of the snow went to another land? And what will happen when the next snow comes and they cannot see the snow angels that are now covered?" A pensive silence accompanied the family as they made their way on toward town.

Arriving at church, Barbara and Helena were not at all surprised to see Johnny and Petey hiding stealthily behind trees, having seen them run for cover as they drove up to the church. As grandpa tethered their horse to the post, the girls jumped from the back of the wagon, each of them getting ready to make a couple of snowballs while behind the cover of the wagon. They were prepared to burst forth with snowballs at the ready. Formulating their plan of attack from behind the wagon, they heard loud, excited voices coming from the trees that sounded just like Johnny and Petey's. "Hey, that's not fair," the girls heard Johnny yell, followed by Petey yelling, "Yeah, you throw too hard, no fair!" Poking their heads around each side of the wagon, they saw grandma with snowballs in each hand. Looking at where Johnny and Petey were standing behind trees, they could see where grandma had fired off a few snowballs at each tree, splattering the boys' faces with snow. Armed and ready for more action, grandma called out to them, "What did I tell you about throwing snowballs at girls! If you want some more of my furious fastball, just keep it up!"

A roaring laugh was then heard from the direction of the church that caught everyone's attention. Turning to see the source, they all saw Reverend Hastings bent over to his knees, laughing so hard his face was red, slapping his knee with his hand. He called out to them, "Helen Broadhurst, I still want you to pitch on the church ball team this year!"

Everyone dropped their remaining supply of ammunition and headed into the church. Frustrated once more, Johnny and Petey looked across the lawn at each other. Realizing there was nothing they could do about it, they each spread their arms and legs, fell backwards into the snow, and flapped their arms and legs, laughing it up all the while!

Harold Clements, his daughter, Kathy, and Lorraine Gunder all arrived in Mr. Clements' wagon, just as Helena and her family were walking in. At the top of the steps, Reverend Hastings was greeting everyone as was his custom, thanking them for coming and wishing all a very merry Christmas. When no one else was in earshot, he looked at all of the "special Ashburn eight," as he had nicknamed them and winked, saying softly, "Looks like our plan may have worked! Great work, everyone!" Inside, the congregation was all abuzz, neighbors greeting each other, merry Christmas wishes heard throughout, children trying to out-do one another with the best gift they had received. The smaller children were telling each other what Santa had brought them and everyone was thankful that some snow had fallen, while wishing that more had fallen. Buddy Cranford had found grandpa and was telling him how no snow had fallen on his steps, his porch, the roof of his house or the barn. He had left two horses out in the pasture overnight, with blankets, of course, but there wasn't even the first flake of snow on them either. All in all though, it was a very festive crowd that greeted Reverend Hastings as he made his way to the pulpit.

The church had been prepared in all of its seasonal finery. A large Christmas wreath adorned the front door as all had come in, with a large red ribbon, pine boughs all around, and small pine cones decorating it further. Inside, all the pews had pine boughs draped down their entry; the fresh pine smell filling the church. Decorations of every sort were strung throughout and the sun's rays made the stained glass windows more beautiful than kaleidoscopes. All of the girls and women wore what appeared to be new Christmas dresses and many women obviously had brand new bonnets. Reds and greens, silver and gold, all of the colors of the season filled the church. All of the men, including the boys, had their Sunday-best suits on, the younger boys twisting and squirming all the while, anxiously pulling at the knots of their ties, certain they were going to strangle before Reverend Hastings finished his sermon. Half-way through the service, grandpa notice a dimming of the brightness through the stained glass windows. Unable to see out of them of course, he turned to see Buddy Cranford craning his neck around as well, no doubt wondering if some rain clouds weren't headed their way.

Reverend Hastings had greeted the citizens of Ashburn with a hearty and heartfelt merry Christmas. As was his custom on Christmas Day, he spoke of Christ's birth and the majority of his sermon was devoted to the story of Jesus. He led his parishioners in many prayers, read from many appropriate verses, and to everyone's delight, made sure they sung at least ten different songs, both hymns and Christmas songs—including Jingle Bells! Of course, "Silent Night" was still everyone's favorite, followed by "Oh Come All Ye Faithful," for which, no one needed their music books. Many parishioners were very good singers and while they had never formed an official choir, Reverend Hastings was convinced beyond belief that the people of Ashburn could out-sing any other congregation in the land.

On this Christmas Day though, a new and very bold voice came forth, one that no one could remember hearing previously. By the third song, everyone in the church had stopped wondering where this magical voice was coming from having turned to witness Harold Clements produce vocals that all thought could have only been heaven-sent. Mrs. Gunder looked on in admiration, her arm discreetly intertwined in his. By everyone's account, this just might have been the 'best Christmas sermon of all time!'

Every Sunday, before he wished everyone, "Go in peace," Reverend Hastings asked the congregation if anyone needed anything, if anyone needed any help, if anything was needed in any way, reminding all that Ashburn was a community; a community where everyone looked after everyone else. More often than not, someone needed something and without fail, there was always a solution offered by one, or by many people, such was the warm, loving community that Ashburn was known to be.

Surprisingly, not the first person raised their hand, but just as Reverend Hastings was about to wish everyone well, Harold Clements raised his hand. Recognizing him, Reverend Hastings asked him to come forward. Grasping Mrs. Gunder's hand and whispering to her, the two of them made their way to the front of the church. Still holding her hand in his, Harold looked to Reverend Hastings, then to the congregation and said, "Well, we really don't need anything, but we just wanted everyone to know that I have asked Lorraine Gunder to marry me, and last evening she said, yes!"

The church erupted into an uproar, people spilling out into the aisles to come forward and offer their congratulations. Hugs and handshakes were given to both, by everyone; well-wishes offered a thousand times! Finally getting some order restored, Reverend Hastings asked Harold and Lorraine, "So, when is the big day? Have you set a date?" Looking at each other, then at the congregation, and finally back to Reverend Hastings, they replied, in unison, "Well, Reverend, since all of our family and friends are gathered here today, we would like to get married today! We would like to get married right now!" The entire church went berserk with glee and excitement! The noise level was so great that the organ player's music was completely drowned out.

The women were fussing over Lorraine, offering to help with this and that while the men were talking about going outside for a cigar. Harold and Lorraine finally put a stop to all of the activity and fuss, telling everyone that all they wanted was a simple service in front of all of their friends, the people they loved the most. When everyone had taken their seats again, and as tradition held, Lorraine walked down the aisle, accompanied by Kathy Clements. The organ player piped out the Wedding March, as she met Harold at the altar. Jim Godsey filled in as Harold's impromptu best-man and Lorraine asked Helena and Barbara to join Kathy as part of her entourage. Grandpa looked at grandma with a worried look, telling her, "I sure hope they don't get any ideas!" When Reverend Hastings introduced the happy couple as "husband and wife," there was one, final uproar, and even more congratulations were offered all around. Hugs, kisses, and handshakes were in great abundance. If anyone doubted now, that this wasn't the 'best Christmas service of all time," let them forever hold their peace!

Buddy Cranford told Harold it was high time he had a congratulatory cigar, and made his way to the door to retrieve them from his wagon where, he told Harold very quietly, "I keep a stash of them under the wagon seat!" Opening the door of the church, Buddy was met with a blast of cold air and a torrent of snow! While the citizens of Ashburn had been celebrating the wedding of Harold and Lorraine, a blizzard had descended on Ashburn! Snow blew furiously into the church and by the time Buddy had pushed the door shut, he was covered in snow from head to toe. When he turned toward where everyone was watching, he was met with gaffs and guffaws from all, for he was barely discernible from a snowman!

Overcoming his surprise, he sputtered out, "Wow, everyone, it's really snowing out there!" All of the children burst into an uproar of cheers and screams, as did many grown-ups. Wiping the fog away from the glass in the front doors, Buddy looked out to see just how bad, or good, it really was. When he turned back to face everyone, his face was as white as the snow itself. Waving Walter to come forward, he was almost frantic. When Walter got to the door, Buddy told him, "Walter, see for yourself. It's just like this morning. The snow is only falling on the grass, yet it's a blizzard out there! There is no snow on the steps, nor is there any on the drive. Not the first horse or wagon has any snow on it. Look! See for yourself!" Looking out through the glass, Walter couldn't believe his eyes. Everything Buddy was telling him was true. Putting his hand on Buddy's shoulder and leaning in closely, grandpa told Buddy, "We need to find Reverend Hastings and talk to him about this. It's some kind of miracle, or something!"

Chapter 13

HELENA AND BARBARA and many other children had gone outside to witness the blizzard first-hand, exuberant that this snow would be maybe, the best of all time! Johnny yelled up from the front lawn, "Wow, there must be two feet already, and it's still coming down!" Petey called over to him, "The big race is going to be on for sure. Christmas break is going to be great!" That brought cheers from all of the kids and the snowballs began flying, except for Johnny and Petey who were certain that grandma and her furious fastball were lurking close by! "Hey," Johnny suddenly called out, "Why isn't there any snow on the steps, or on the roof, or on the horses, or the wagons, or on the road?" Whatever any child was doing, they stopped to consider what Johnny had revealed, yet no one could offer a single explanation. Helena looked at Barbara, and so no one could hear her said, "Like I said on the way to church, we need to talk to the snow and find out what's going on. Come on, Barbara, let's go somewhere where no one will see or hear us," and around to the back of the church they went.

When they were certain that no one else was around, the girls each picked up a handful of snow and tossed it high in the air, exclaiming, "We love the snow! Barbara and Helena love the snow! We want to talk to you, snowflakes . . . about snow angels!" The blizzard around them was already furious, but it seemed to move away from the girls, as though it was snowing everywhere, except for where they were standing. "This is so incredible," Barbara remarked, and no sooner had she said that then a small swirl of snow started round their feet and rose into the air, ultimately encapsulating them. Helena was the first to say something, not sure if this snow would be the same as the others. "Hello, snow," she said. "Is there anyone here who would like to speak with us? We live in the land of the snow angels, the land where snow is loved and wanted more than any other land!"

They waited and waited, but heard nothing. A moment later, Barbara said, "It is true, snowflakes. We are the land closest to the highest mountain peaks, where the snows of last season and two seasons past proclaimed our land, Ashburn, to be the land of the snow angels. I am Barbara and this is my sister, Helena. Will you speak with us?" The swirl around them stirred even more and the girls weren't sure whether they had angered it or if it was just not certain about them. Helena finally said, "We are telling the truth, snowflakes. We truly love the snow and want it to come here, where children can play and where the snow can serve the greater purpose for which you were created."

A furious swirl of snow soon had them covered and Barbara told Helena that she was getting scared. Helena reminded her that it was important to trust the snow for, as they had learned from snows past, the snow was their friend. Barely able to see past the end of her nose, Helena caught the shiny sparkle of a large snowflake just at the tip of her nose, asking it, "Snowflake, do you wish to speak with us? We are your friends." With that, a strong man's voice came forth, saying, "Well, hello. You have made mention of the greater purpose and the need to trust the snow. What do you know of these things?"

Convinced that they had gotten their attention, Helena and Barbara spent the next few minutes telling the snowflake, whose name they learned was Carl, all about having spoken with the snow for two seasons, about snow angels appearing, about the first elder snowflake who had traveled back to the land where snow was created and proclaimed Ashburn to be the land of snow angels, and everything else. They told them of their knowledge about Mother Nature and why she created snow

JL CRAWFORD

in the first place, of the terrible time they had last year because no snow had fallen—the first time ever. And, to be truthful, they told them about people in Ashburn who had said prayers against snow, but assured them that now, almost everybody was praying for snow and really wanted the snow to come back and stay forever and ever.

Another snowflake, named Julia, had joined the conversation, resting on Barbara's head until she had shaken her down onto her nose, telling her, "I can't see you way up there on my head!" They became friends almost immediately. Julia asked the girls to tell them about the snow angels. She had arrived last night, telling them that as they were flying overhead they saw what appeared to be snow angels on the ground, even though there was no other snow anywhere around. Barbara and Helena looked at each other, certain that their attempt to get the snow to believe the sheets were real snow angels, had been found out. They wondered whether the snow would just fly away right now, but they just didn't know how to explain themselves.

Without really thinking, Barbara blurted out, "What snow angels? When we went to bed there was no snow on the ground at all, and there was barely any when we woke up this morning!" "Yeah," chimed in Helena, "Are they still here? Where are the snow angels you speak of?" Julia looked at them each very slowly, finally saying, "Well, I'm not sure now because too much snow has fallen to see them, but there is a very big hill not far from here, and there were many, many snow angels on that hill." The girls knew that grandpa had placed a whole bunch of make-believe snow angels on Wilkins Hill and were glad that so much snow had fallen that they might not be able to see them, until Julia said to Carl, "Maybe we should go to that hill and have all of the snow fly away and we will see if there are any real snow angels there."

Barbara was shaking almost uncontrollably by this time, certain that their plan had been foiled and that the snow would leave Ashburn for all time. With tears streaming down her face, she told Julia and Carl all about their plan to make sure the arriving snow knew Ashburn was where the snow was supposed to land. She explained how Helena had come up with the idea, not to fool or trick the snow, but just to send the new snow a sign that this was the land where they should serve the greater purpose. She asked them both, "How else would the snow know where to land? Many snows have flown by already this season and we were afraid that no snow would land here at all, just like last season," tears flowing forth as though from a spigot. "Really, you must believe us. We have learned to trust the snow like never before and we would never do anything to deceive it." Helena quickly joined in, apologizing for coming up with such a half-baked idea, but assuring them, as Barbara had, it wasn't an attempt to trick the snow as much as it was to help them recognize the land of the snow angels.

Before they had a chance to say anymore, Carl and Julia flew away, with great swirls of snow following them, leaving Barbara and Helena in total shock, convinced it would never return again. Helena suggested they go inside and tell grandma and grandpa, Mr. and Mrs. Clements—it sure sounded funny calling them that, and Reverend Hastings. The grown-ups would probably come up with a new plan, but after all, as she pointed out to Barbara, the snow was stilling falling in a blizzard. Why hadn't all of this snow followed Carl and Julia?

Inside, they found grandpa and Mr. Cranford huddled together with Reverend Hastings. Grandma was still fussing over Mrs. Clements, but this was just too important to wait. Asking if they could interrupt to speak with them about something very important, grandma told her that this was a very special day for Mrs. Clements, telling them that they could probably wait until later. Leaning in so only grandma and Mrs. Clements could hear them, Helena said, "But, grandma, this is about the snow and the snow angels, and it is very important." Better understanding the possible gravity of the matter, grandma and Mrs. Clements excused themselves from the group, promising to only be a matter of minutes.

JL CRAWFORD

When grandma asked if gramps knew about this, Helena told her that he was speaking with Reverend Hastings and Mr. Cranford, reminding her that Mr. Cranford didn't know anything about it. "Well," she said, "It may be time to let one more believer into our little plan."

Sensing something was afoot, Harold came over to join them. Kathy was outside with the other kids and they decided it was probably best to have her keep them occupied. Helena and Barbara told them about the conversation they had just had with Carl and Julia, and for Mr. Cranford's benefit they had to go over the whole story, from start to finish. When he had digested everything they had to tell, he was so stunned that he had to get a glass of punch before he could go any further. Reverend Hastings told him, "Buddy, I know how incredible this is to believe, but the good Lord and Mother Nature are two very powerful forces. I can't say as I would blame you if you wanted something to drink a bit stronger than that punch. If I had something here I might even join you." Grandma quickly cut off any further talk of that with a loud and firm, "Hmmpff!"

After some serious thought, it was agreed that the truth was the best way to proceed. Helena and Barbara had told Carl and Julia what the group had done, and when it was all said and done, it was as much a means of giving the arriving snow a way to identify Ashburn as the land of the snow angels as in trying to trick the snow. After all, the elder snowflake and the snow of last season had proclaimed Ashburn to be the land of the snow angels, even if they didn't know that the two real snow angels were Helena and Barbara! It was a unanimous decision, that was their story and they were sticking to it. Helena and Barbara even made everyone lock fingers and say, "Deal!" However, they didn't know how they were going to proceed any further, so it was decided that everyone should just go home because, it was after all, still Christmas Day!

The blizzard-like conditions continued the entire trip home, yet no snow stuck to the road, on the horse, nor on the wagon. It was, everyone agreed, the most unbelievable thing they had ever witnessed. In snows past, these conditions would have had everyone inside, safe and sound. As they neared Wilkins Hill, the snow was even more intense than it had been the entire way. The snow wasn't just falling, it was rising and falling, blowing sideways, and every which way, as though in a mad frenzy. Grandpa suggested they take a wide path around Wilkins Hill, lest they get caught in a blizzard so bad they not might make it home, and everyone agreed.

With only a half-mile left until they arrived home, just coming up on Mr. Cranford's farm, Helena and Barbara turned to glance back in the direction of Wilkins Hill. What they saw so scared them, they could only poke grandpa in the back and point when he asked them what they wanted. He and grandma turned to see what appeared to be a full-blown nor'easter headed their way. Normally, the snow moved from their farm eastward, across Mr. Cranford's farm, toward Wilkins Hill, but this storm was headed toward them, from Wilkins Hill.

Grandpa put the whip a little more firmly to Bernie, their trusted horse and, apologizing at the same time to him, said, "There's an extra apple in it for you Bernie, it you can get us home pronto!" Grandma leaned forward to Bernie's ear and told him, "I'll double that offer, Bernie. Let's get a move on!" Turning to the girls, grandma told them, "Hold on to your hats, girls, we're about to skee-daddle," and Bernie had them home in record time! Bernie skidded to a halt right in front of the back porch. With the steps clear of any snow at all, grandpa told the girls and grandma to get inside, saying he would be in shortly, needing to put Bernie in safely. Grandma reminded him to be sure Bernie got two apples, and added, "And an extra half-serving of grain, too!" Bernie pawed the ground twice in approval and let out a loud whinny!

Safely inside the house, the girls and grandma looked out the window, wanting to be sure that grandpa made it back inside. The snow was so heavy and blowing so wildly, they could not even see the barn. Grandpa had put Bernie inside his stall, covered him with two blankets, gave him

JL Crawford

three apples and an extra half-serving of grain as grandma had suggested. Patting him on the rump he told him, "Better have an extra apple old buddy, just in case it snows so hard I can't get the door open in the morning." He forked in another load of straw as well and leaving, told Bernie, "You stay nice and warm." He smiled as he saw Bernie turn his head toward him and swished his tail a couple of times.

Grandpa had to use all of this strength to push open the barn door, so strong were the wind and the snow's fury. He wasn't sure he could find his way to the back porch, even though it was only about fifty yards and he had made the trip thousands of times over the years. The heavy snow had visibility down to only arms length and grandpa had to lower his head and hold onto his hat. He grabbed the fence rails that bordered the corral, knowing that they would get him more than half-way to the house. From there, he would just have to aim himself in the right direction and hunker down until he saw the porch.

As he reached the last fence post, the snow lightened dramatically, almost coming to a stop, just as he started in the direction of the house. Thinking for a minute, not wanting to start toward the house and suddenly get caught in another furious storm, he held onto the last post. Looking skyward, grandpa said, "Snowflakes are you helping me? Is that why the storm has lightened up, so I may make my way to the house?" He noticed the small swirl round his boots and watched as it slowly rose toward his head and his hat which, he discovered, didn't have any snow on them at all. In fact, there was no snow on him anywhere, neither his boots nor his coat! Completely beside himself, he asked one more thing, "Is this all a dream, snowflakes?"

No sooner had he asked the question than Carl and Julia settled onto his nose, sparkling and shining and glittering away. Carl was first to answer, "Why no, sir. We don't think you are dreaming. Are you not awake?" "Well, I think I am. At least I was awake at church and most of the way home, but I can't explain why I have no snow on me. Why wasn't my horse covered with snow, and why aren't the roads and rooftops completely covered? Why is there no snow on the porch steps that requires sweeping? It's as though we are all dreaming!" Julia didn't answer him at first, but asked him instead, "Why were you running away from us at the big hill? Why did you make the wagon go faster when we were trying to catch up with you?"

"What," grandpa asked incredulously. "We were trying to get home before the blizzard caught up with us. We didn't understand why the snow was moving from east to west instead of from west to east as it always does. I needed to get the girls and mother back home safely, and to get my horse in from the snow and cold." Julia looked at Carl and they both started laughing. Grandpa was about to ask what was so funny when Julia motioned for Carl to stop and told grandpa, "Sir, I'm sorry; we're all sorry. We were waiting for you at the big hill to tell you the good news. When we saw you turn and go around that special place, we were just following you. We wanted to tell you what we had learned."

"So, it wasn't a ferocious blizzard that we thought was moving in our direction?" grandpa wanted to know. Carl then piped in, telling grandpa, "Oh no, sir. Not a ferocious blizzard in any way. If you want to see a ferocious blizzard, you should see us high on top of those big peaks that surround this land!" Feeling calmer than he had just a few minutes earlier, grandpa told them, "Well, it sure looked like a blizzard to us, and when I tried to make my way from the barn to the house, I was afraid I might not make it the rest of the way!" Just then, grandma's voice was heard from the porch, but she was just barely visible for the snow that was still swirling. "Walter," she called out. "Are you okay? Can you find your way? Do you need help?" And the snow came to a complete stop between the house and where grandpa was standing! Her hands on her hips and her mouth dropping open, grandma said in utter surprise, "Will miracles never cease!"

Walking toward the house, grandpa told her, "Yes, mother, I'm just fine. The snow was telling me all about . . . well, wait a minute. Why don't we let the snow tell us the good news that Julia and Carl say they have for us. Tell Barbara and Helena to come outside." Moments later, each of them holding steaming cups of hot chocolate, the girls came onto the porch. Barbara asked, "What is it grandpa? Hey, when did it stop snowing?" Helena added, "Grandma said you told her the snow had some good news to tell us. What is it, grandpa?" "Well," he said, slowing them each down a bit. "I don't know. Let's let Julia and Carl tell us, shall we?" The look of anticipation of their faces was without equal.

At that moment, the snow started a small swirl once again, finally settling onto the porch railing, where Julia and Carl stood next to each other in all their sparkling glory. Carl told them about waiting for them at Wilkins Hill and then following them home when they had gone a different way, having to fly so furiously because their wagon was going so fast. Barbara and Helena kept trying to ask questions, but grandpa motioned them to just wait until the snow had finished telling them all they had to say. Julia told them about arriving the night before and seeing the angel shapes on the ground all over the land between the two big mountains, and particularly the great many on the big hill. From high above, the snow was certain that this was the land they had heard about, but flying lower, they wondered why there was no other snow on the ground.

They had finally decided that, after such an already long journey, and having just cleared the two high and treacherous mountains, much of the snow didn't want to go any further. The snow that wished to stay fell on Ashburn, but so much more flew on to find another land where it might be wanted and loved. Julia and Carl had decided to stay in this land, but were very skeptical about the angel shapes, as was all of the snow that flew on elsewhere. During the night, they had flown all around the mysterious shapes on the ground, over and under them, around the edges, trying to get the snow to rise up and fly with them. Carl said that he and Julia were convinced that these were not real snow angels, but many other snowflakes had asked them, "What is a real snow angel? What are we actually looking for?" Not being able to give them an exact answer, it was decided by all that they would stay until the next day.

When Barbara and Helena had told them this morning the whole story about the snow angels, the snows of seasons past, how the snow elder had declared this the land of the snow angels, and their attempt to give the arriving snow a sign that this was the land where all snow was loved and wanted, Carl and Julia had told all the other snowflakes. Since no snowflake knew exactly what they were supposed to be looking for, they had all agreed that this was at very least, a land where snow was very much wanted and loved.

"So," Julia concluded, "All of the snowflakes decided this was the land where we would serve the greater purpose. When Carl and I flew away from you this morning, it was to tell the other snowflakes what you told us, which we believed to be the truth. At first, we thought the people of this land might be trying to trick the snow into coming here and might not really love or want the snow. And, there were quite a few snowflakes who thought that big hill was the center point of the land of the snow angels. We gathered there to talk this morning while you went into that building. As we were discussing the matter, more and more snow was blowing in from where we had come last night. Seeing all of the snow here, the snowflakes started falling furiously."

"We tried telling them what we were discussing, but they wouldn't believe anything except this was the land of snow angels that they had heard about. The new snow told us there were snow angels outside of that building you had gone into, so we flew over there ourselves to see what they had seen." "And sure enough," Carl jumped in. "On either side of two of those wagon-things, were angel shapes; and the ground had already been covered up by then. We figured that angels had come down

JL Crawford

to visit while we were over at the big hill." Barbara and Helena looked at each other befuddled, as did grandma and grandpa; the four of them wondering who, or what had created the snow angels while everyone was in church. Grandma tried to put an end to it, offering, "The good Lord and Mother Nature both, work in mysterious ways!" "Well," Julia added. "That's pretty much what we decided too, and if all of the new snow decided on their own that, this was the land where they wished to serve the greater purpose, who were we to argue. So, here we are!"

Helena and Barbara placed their empty cups on the railing and ran down the bare steps. Grabbing handfuls of snow they each threw the snow high into the air, watching it fall slowly back down. As it did, they each cried out, "We love you snow! Helena and Barbara love the snow!" They were quickly followed by grandma and grandpa doing the very same thing, yelling, "Helen Broadhurst loves the snow, too" and "So does Walter Broadhurst," followed by a chorus of all of them proclaiming, "We ALL love the snow!" Julia and Carl looked at each other, then to Helena, Barbara, grandma, and grandpa shining and sparkling like never before. Turning to face all of the snow, they shouted, "We don't need any more convincing than that! This must be the land of the snow angels!"

The largest swirl of snow ever before seen in the land rose up and encircled all of them. It flew all around the Broadhurst farm, the Cranford's farm and as far as the eye could see, dancing and twirling, shining and sparkling. Her face smiling like she never thought possible again, especially when it came to snow, grandma suddenly realized they were all outside without coats, except for grandpa. "Come along inside, girls. You'll catch your death without coats and mittens and hats," and they all started up the steps.

At the top step, grandpa stopped and turned toward the snow, calling for Carl or Julia. They landed next to each other on the porch railing, asking, "Yes, sir. What can we do for you?" His hand rubbing his whiskers like he was pondering the greatest problem of all time, grandpa asked them seriously, "Snowflakes, can you tell me why there is no snow on the porch? Why there is no snow on the steps? Why there is no snow on the roof of my house or the barn? Why is there no snow on the drive or the roads? Why was there no snow on Bernie, my horse, when we came home?"

"Well, of course we can," Julia answered. "Oh, you bet, that's an easy one," Carl added. "You see, we only land where we are wanted and loved. That is what Mother Nature tells all new snowflakes each year." "But," grandpa interrupted. "You know this is a land where snow is loved and wanted. Why is the snow not falling everywhere in our land?" Thinking he had explained himself clearly, Carl was miffed by grandpa's question. Standing at the doorway and overhearing the conversation, Helena and Barbara each chimed in, "Yeah," snowflakes, why is the snow only on the ground?" Julia flew up high into the air and settled on grandpa's nose.

"Let me explain it a bit more clearly and in greater detail. First, you must remember that we only go where we are loved and wanted. We have no doubt that the snow is 'loved' in this land of yours, but there are places where we are not 'wanted,' a fact we know for certain." "I can't believe that," Helena remarked. "We love you and want you everywhere. What could possibly make you think you are not wanted in places?" "It is what we hear from the higher power, Mother Nature's creator, who we must obey just as she must. Mother Nature is the creator of all snow, just as with rain, wind, and storms of every kind. We follow her direction, but she answers to a power even greater and more forceful than she. We must do what she tells us, but we must also do what the higher power tells us, even if it differs from what she tells us to do."

Grandma was spellbound by the conversation and asked, "Snowflake, do you mean to say that you speak to the Lord Himself." "Not exactly," she answered. "We don't actually speak to Him as much as He speaks to us, telling us what to do and we must absolutely obey Him or Mother Nature would . . . well, you know what they say about it not being nice to fool with Mother Nature!" "Then how does He speak to you, snowflake? Please, I am curious to know," grandma implored her. Looking to Carl for help, Julia said, "I think your word for how the higher power speaks to us is called 'prayer;' is that right, Carl?" "Yes, I believe that is the correct word and the higher power has many names as well. Good lady, you used the word, Lord, which is one name we know of, along with Jesus, Father, and Almighty. Do you not know that we hear the prayers of people of the lands where we fly over?"

"That's right, grandma," Barbara told her. "Don't you remember the snow of last season told us that, and the reason that snow did not fall on Ashburn was so many people were saying prayers for no snow." "Ah, that would explain it then," Carl said. "If too many people did not want the snow and the snow heard it in their prayers, the snow would fly on to other lands." "That's exactly what it did last year," grandpa told Carl. Trying to make sense of everything, Helena asked, "So, when we go to bed each night and tell Jesus our prayers, you can actually hear them?" "Yes, sweet girl," Julia answered. "Mother Nature has taught us that prayers are the words of the higher power and we should listen to and obey them just as she or the higher power was speaking to us directly."

Grandma suddenly put her hand to her mouth and gasped, "Oh my goodness! I have been praying each night for snow and at the same time, I have been praying that it would not fall on the steps, or on the porch, or on the roof! Do you think that is why the snow is not falling there?" Carl laughed loudly, stopping to say, "Good lady, you are not the only one saying prayers for that. We have heard that in many, many prayers all across this land, and we are obliged to listen and obey. So, yes, if the majority of prayers wish for something, we answer prayers as the higher power directs us to do." Fanning herself as though she was about to faint, grandma looked at Helena and Barbara and grandpa, saying to them, "Father, girls, how many times has Reverend Hastings told us about the power of prayer!" As they all absorbed what grandma was saying, convinced she was one hundred percent correct, grandpa asked Carl and Julia, "Do you think my horse, Bernie, could have been praying for no snow to land on him?" Laughing at the thought, Julia and Carl said, "The higher power answers all prayers. It's not for us to ask from whom or what."

The snow continued falling on Ashburn throughout the Christmas break. The children went sledding, ice skated, made snowmen, had snowball battles, and raced saucers every day. Whatever snow fell on Ashburn fell only on the grass, in pastures and fields, and on the rivers, streams, and creeks, all of which were still frozen. The roads remained clear all winter, as did everyone's porches, steps, and roofs. Convinced that the power of prayer was the answer, each Sunday, Reverend Hastings implored the congregation to keep praying for snow, telling them also, it was actually okay to pray for snow to 'not' fall in certain places. Helena and Barbara played with Samson and Duchess every day, but were sure to get in plenty of practice on their sled and saucer. Mr. and Mrs. Clements went to some place warm and sunny for a whole week, and Kathy stayed with Helena and Barbara while they were gone. They had the best time ever! Not a day went by that the girls didn't speak with the snow, reminding them each and every day how much they loved the snow and wanted it to stay as long as possible. Carl and Julia were convinced they had made the right decision—Ashburn was the land of the snow angels; the land where snow was loved and wanted by all!

Chapter 14

SOONER THAN ANYONE could want, Christmas break was over and it was time to go back to school. Mrs. Clements was her same old self, just happier, or so it seemed. Before long, most of the boys were talking about the big race, which was still three weeks away! Brother, it's all they seemed to talk about, even though there were more girls as reigning champs than boys. Johnny Cranford was much more subdued this year than in years past, but Petey Braun was as big a blabbermouth as he had ever been. "What do you expect from an immature ten-year old," Barbara would say every time he mouthed off, and all of the girls would laugh and poke fun at him. Everyone in Ashburn it seemed, was as happy as they had ever been; even many of the grown-ups whom the children used to call 'old fogeys,' when they were out of earshot!

The snow on Wilkins Hill had been trampled down hard and deep, and the courses for the sleds and saucers were in the best shape ever. In some areas, the snow drifted to eight feet, yet the roads and areas where people prayed snow wouldn't land, remained clear as could be. Visitors to Ashburn from other lands where there was a lot of snow, had asked over and over, "Say, who clears all the snow for you folks? They sure do a good job! We sure wish it could be like that where we live!" Every time Reverend Hastings heard someone say that he would reply, "Maybe you should stop 'wishing' and do a little more praying!"

Julia and Carl seemed to like staying around the Broadhurst farm, always looking forward to the time when Helena and Barbara would come outdoors to play. They got the biggest chuckle when the girls would launch themselves from the top step of the porch and land deeply into a big drift of snow, always coming up laughing, covered from head to toe. When the girls would go and play with Samson and Duchess, which was every single day, the snowflakes would follow them, sometimes landing on the pooches' noses. Dancing on their noses would tickle Samson and Duchess and they would try and catch the snowflakes with their long tongues, but Carl and Julia would always fly away, just out of reach!

When Bernie would be brought outside from the barn, Carl and Julia would tickle his nose, too, which would inevitably provoke a loud sneeze, blowing the two snowflakes skyward. Barbara told them one day how much it reminded her of their snowflake friend, Floyd, and how he loved to be blown sky-high, laughing and screaming all the way down. Julia told her she was pretty certain that she and Carl would have been great friends with Floyd and Aly. When Helena told them about Aly and Floyd serving the greater purpose in their grandma's garden, the two snowflakes thought that was the most special thing they had ever heard.

Just a few days before the big race, Petey Braun told Barbara in school one day, that he was going to enter the saucer race and the sled race. He had been practicing on his saucer, Barbara had noticed, but was always falling off whenever he went over a snow mound, which got laughs from all of the kids within sight of him. Nonetheless, he was convinced that he was as good as anyone on the saucer and would come home with two trophies! "Oh brother," Barbara had told him when he revealed his plan to her, telling him that he had better spend as much time practicing on his sled as he was on the saucer. She reminded him that he wasn't even the reigning sled champ, but he remained convinced of his "male superiority," as he kept referring to his sledding and saucer skills. Whenever he used that term the girls would put their hands on their hips and, mocking him, would say, "Oh yeah? Girls rule and boys drool!" Petey Braun never got a bit of respect from anyone!

JL CRAWFORD

The day of the big race was sunny, cold and crisp. Not a single cloud graced the sky, only brilliant sunshine. A light breeze had snowflakes swirling round and round. So bright was the sun that the billions of flying snowflakes gave the air the appearance of crystal fragments. The sun was just strong enough to lightly melt the long, glistening, sword-like icicles that hung from every porch, tree branch, and barn eave. All it took was a single icy drop down the neck or worse, all the way down one's back from a melting icicle to produce loud yelps from those who lingered too long in the wrong place. Nothing though, would keep any citizen of Ashburn away from town and the scene of the big race.

The streets and shops were so full early in the morning it prompted grandma to tell grandpa, "Walter, I think the whole town must be outside this morning. I've never seen it so busy!" Surveying the crowd, grandpa concurred, telling her, "My love, I think the whole town has finally come to grips with the importance of snow and this is one fine way of showing Mother Nature that she is appreciated." Looking into his eyes, one arm round his waist, she told him, "Don't forget the good Lord, Walter. I think he had a lot to do with this, too!"

They continued along the main street of town, making their way toward Wilkins Hill, getting a close look at all of the wonderful treats that people had made this year. When they reached the tables where warm dishes were being displayed, grandma spied Mrs. Kendall, who was once again in charge of all of the food items, from pastries, pies, brownies, and cookies to meats, vegetables, casseroles, and more. Mrs. Kendall, the proprietor of the boarding house and the only restaurant in Ashburn, was well-regarded as the best cook in town. Between herself and her three assistants, it was pretty well acknowledged that any dish that anyone could ever want could be made by one of them. Seeing grandpa and grandma with their arms full of food, Mrs. Kendall quickly corralled two assistants to lend them some help and asked grandma, "Helen, what have you made this year? Is it warm or room temperature?"

Looking a bit befuddled, grandma told her, "Why, Elizabeth, we don't have a name for this dish. It's just something I've been making for years and years at our house, but it is best served warm, if not even piping hot!" Directing them to the table under which one of the men had rigged a controlled fire, she had them place the metal trays on top. Still curious what grandma had made, Mrs. Kendall asked, "May I try one?" "By all means, Elizabeth," grandma told her, "Please, try one. I would like to have your 'professional' opinion." Grandpa reached under the cover to get one himself, but received a quick slap on the back of his hand, along with the admonishment from grandma, reminding him, "You've had enough already, Mr. Broadhurst!"

Mrs. Kendall took a small bite and allowed herself to slowly taste the many flavors in the dish that grandma had made, but said nothing. Then, she took a large bite and grandma watched as she gently chewed, her eyes closed, savoring every taste and texture as though she was judging an exotic cooking competition. Finishing, she opened her eyes, wiped her mouth delicately with a napkin, and even licked her lips, which drew a look of amazement from grandma and grandpa. Looking right at grandma, Mrs. Kendall said for all around to hear, "Helen Broadhurst that is the most delicious treat I have ever tasted! You must tell me the recipe and you must allow me to put it on my restaurant menu!"

Astonished at her reaction to what she had always considered to be just a snack she made for Walter and the girls, grandma told Mrs. Kendall the recipe. She said she started with an open-faced muffin, layered it thickly with a rich tomato sauce, topped that with a grated cheese, and cooked it for a few minutes in the big brick oven. Over the years, she told Mrs. Kendall, they had added items as toppings, including ham, sausage, vegetables, mushrooms, and occasional imported meats that she found in the mercantile, like pepperoni and kielbasa, and others, many of which she had included in the variety she brought along today.

Still fawning over the wonderful creation, Mrs. Kendall asked, "And you don't have a name for it? We must be able to tell everyone what it is they're eating and enjoying," to which grandma replied, "Well, we have just always called them 'muffin-melts,' and depending upon what topping one wants, you just ask for a ham muffin-melt, or mushroom muffin-melt or, as Walter likes, a muffin-melt with everything!" Everyone close by who was hearing the conversation immediately asked to try one and the response was overwhelmingly for approval.

After telling grandma that she had created, without any doubt whatsoever, the 'best new creation' of this year's event, she instructed two of her assistants to go back to the restaurant and make as many muffin-melts as they could. Grandma asked if she could go along and help with the cooking, which absolutely thrilled Mrs. Kendall, telling her, "Round up some young boys on the way and have them bring them over here as soon as they're out of the oven. Pay them in muffin-melts if you must!" Looking at her remaining assistant, Mrs. Kendall said, "I wish we hadn't made so many triple-decker peanut butter and jelly sandwiches this year. Muffin-melts just might put them out of business," which got a loud laugh from many people.

At Wilkins Hill, the younger-aged children had already finished racing and as always, every participant received a trophy and a coupon for a free item of food. Kids were streaming onto the main street, yelling and screaming about their victories, holding their trophies high for all to see. Proud parents, siblings, and grandparents were congratulating them, with plenty of hugs and kisses to go around. A few of the younger kids were crying, either from not having won their race or, from having been fished out of the trees and bushes where they had flown off of sleds or saucers. No one ever sustained any serious damage or injury on the day of the big race, and certainly nothing that some special treats or hot chocolate wouldn't take care of! Isn't it amazing how a torrent of tears can be dried up with a single double-fudge, walnut brownie, or a triple-decker peanut butter and jelly sandwich, a slice of key lime pie, or a cupcake loaded with icing! Wait until the children tried this year's best new creation—the muffin-melt!

In the ten-year old age bracket, Petey Braun proved to be worth his mettle, winning the event by a large margin in all three heats and the final race. Proudly presenting Barbara with his trophy, he was quick to say, "See, I told you who the real sled-champ is!" Rolling her eyes at him, Barbara reminded him that he still had not beaten the reigning champ, saying, "So, it's not really official!" Petey told her to watch herself in the upcoming saucer race, because, "I'm taking home two trophies today, missy!" As it turned out, it was a good thing Petey won the sled race, because he lost the very first heat in the saucer race, to a nine-year old girl, and it wasn't even close. On the very first snow mound, Petey had gone air-bound, landing in a six-foot snow drift while his saucer sailed all the way to the bottom of Wilkins Hill. By the time some older kids had pulled him out of the drift, he looked liked the Abominable snowman!

Barbara, meanwhile, had sailed through all three heats, winning each of them by such a wide margin that, when the final race was about to begin, her opponent withdrew, saying she didn't want to be embarrassed like all the other racers! Barbara became the very first person in all of Ashburn, girl or boy, to ever win a saucer and sled championship! Still brushing snow from his coat and cap when he found Barbara sitting in a chair eating a muffin-melt, her trophy on the table in front of her, Petey stuck out his hand and congratulated the champ. Stuffing a pepperoni muffin-melt in his mouth that Barbara had given him, he mumbled something that no one could understand. Knowing what he was boasting about, Barbara answered him, "Yeah, yeah, Petey. I know you're the sled champ this year, but we will race against each other after the big race is over and we'll see who is best between you and me." Wiping tomato sauce on his sleeve, Petey looked at her and said, "That's not what I was trying to say, Barbara. I just wanted to know who made these muffin-melts!"

JL CRAWFORD

While the next races were going on, Barbara and Petey sat next to each other, showing their trophies to all who came by, stuffing themselves with muffin-melts, brownies, and cookies.

In the big event of the day, the race between twelve and thirteen-year olds, there were no surprises. Johnny Cranford beat three boys by more than thirty-seconds each. The fifteen-year old who had entered before as a twelve-year old, whom Johnny had beaten very badly, convinced the race committee to let him race against Johnny this year, just so there would be some solid competition, promising not to claim a trophy if he won. Well, Johnny beat him by a greater margin than the two other boys. Throwing his sled into the woods when he finally got to the finish line, acknowledging that Johnny was the far-better sled-racer, the teen was heard to say, "That's it, my racing days are over!"

Helena had beaten two boys and one girl in her three heats and, like Johnny, was so far ahead in all three races, most people had lost interest before the racers were half-way down the hill. In her second race, against a thirteen-year old boy, the boy had quit two-thirds the way down Wilkins Hill, walking off into the woods rather than having to admit he had been whipped by a girl! Someone said he lived over in the direction of where he was walking and probably didn't want to experience the goading he was sure to get from the other boys.

The final race was all set to start. Every child that had been stuffing their face in town was now at the finish line or lining the course. The younger racers aspired to one day be the sled champ of Ashburn and no one was about to miss this repeat championship of two years before. As Helena and Johnny were about to start, just waiting for the whistle, sleds grasped firmly in their arms, Johnny looked over to Helena and winked, telling her, "Good luck, Helena, I really mean it!" Thinking momentarily that it might have just been a trick, Helena had a look of skepticism on her face, but when Johnny followed it with a nice, well-intending smile, she knew he had been serious. Realizing this, she gave him her best smile, saying, "Thanks, you too, Johnny. Good luck!" And the whistle sounded. They both ran as fast as they could on the hard-packed snow, Helena a lot faster this year than before, but still not as fast as the one-year older Johnny. As they reached the precipice of Wilkins Hill, Johnny only had a lead of about five feet, far less than the race two years ago.

At the edge of the hill they both launched themselves straight out. People lining the coursed "Oohed" and "Ahhed," wondering how far they would fly through the air before landing hard on the snow-packed earth. When they each landed, Johnny was in the lead by about half a sled length, but both of them were flying. Separated side to side by only two feet, Helena looked over at Johnny and saw a swirling of snow start to rise around the front of his sled. Remembering how the snow had helped her and Barbara win the last time, she thought this was happening again. Along the course, grandma and grandpa saw the snow swirling as well, pointing in Johnny's direction, remembering what Helena had told them about the last race.

Barbara looked to Petey and said inadvertently, "Look, the snow is going to help Helena again." Baffled at what she was telling him, he looked at her and said, "What are you talking about? The snow is going to help both of them." Realizing her unintended gaff, Barbara collected herself and, admonishing herself for her lapse in judgment said, "Oh, I don't know what I'm saying. It's just me, silly Barbara," and they watched on in silence and in awe of the two best racers in Ashburn.

Around and through the first turn, Johnny had the inside track so he gained about ten yards on Helena. The course was as fast as it had ever been and each of them was holding on tight into and through the turns. Grandpa had waxed Helena's sled like never before, promising to put it in the best condition ever! Johnny's dad had done the same to his sled, including putting streamers in the handle grips. As Johnny flew down the hill, the streamers made it appear as though he was going even faster. Into the second turn, Helena was on the inside and gained the distance

JL CRAWFORD

she had lost on the first turn. They were virtually even with half the race left. Once again, Helena saw snow swirling around the front of Johnny's sled, but she wanted to win this race without any help. Looking straight ahead, she glimpsed Julia and Carl on each mitten and Carl was telling her, "Don't worry, Helena, we're going to help you win this race," and they flew over to Johnny's sled, along with a billion other snowflakes!

Looking at the rapidly growing swirl of snow around him, Helena yelled over, "No, snowflakes, I don't want your help this time!" Not looking over toward her, but hearing her voice, Johnny called out, "What did you say? What about the snow? Did you say you need help?" They were just entering the third turn, one that would give Johnny another lead because he was on the inside again. With Johnny on her right and turning to the right, Helena could see him without having to turn her head. Realizing that she had almost spilled the beans, she yelled after him, "Oh, nothing. I was just saying how the snow this year is a big help." "Yeah, you're right," Johnny called out to her. "It's going to help me win," and he sped through the turn, gaining more than thirty feet in distance between them.

Helena saw Julia and Carl land on her nose, Julia asking her, "Did you say you don't want us to help you win? We can, you know. We'll create a big snow swirl in front of him and he won't be able to see!" "Yeah," Carl added. "He'll fly right into a big drift and be lost until spring!" Helena looked directly at her two friends and told them, "No, snowflakes. Thank you very much for offering, but this year I want to see if I can win the race all by myself. Please make sure that no snowflakes interfere with Johnny or help me in any way." "Okay," they both replied, adding, "Good luck! We'll see you at the bottom."

They were coming into the final turn, a left turn that would give Helena some advantage, but would it be enough to help make up and overcome the lead that Johnny had built. The noise along the hill was deafening as everyone was yelling and screaming at the top of their lungs.

This was the closest race anyone could remember seeing, by the two best racers in all of Ashburn. The excitement was so great that grandma was clenching her hands as tight as she could. Not realizing that he had even done it, Petey had slipped his arm around Barbara's shoulder, his mouth wide open as he watched the race unfold. It wasn't until Barbara turned and gave him a "What's going on?" stare that he realized what she meant and quickly dropped his arm to his side, but she did wear a small smile that she wouldn't dare let him see!

Through the turn, Johnny had veered a bit too wide and Helena had taken advantage of the error to make up the distance between them. With only seventy yards of straight-away ahead of them, they were neck and neck. Separated by only two feet or less, they were flying downhill faster than either of them remembered ever doing. They were both thinking that if they hit even the smallest bump or mound, they would be launched into the air like a bird! At the bottom of the hill, the race judges were lined up right on the finish line, so certain were they that this race might be the closest race in the history of Ashburn racing! Daring not glance over at the other for more than just a split second, lest they take their eyes off the course too long and end up in a drift, or the woods, their eyes met the other's, each of them realizing just how close this race was going to be.

Helena suddenly remembered what Johnny had said weeks before about, how winning wasn't the most important thing. He had told her that having fun was more important and as long as either one of them won, that was okay with him. She wondered whether he remembered saying that and whether he really meant it. Was it just a trick to distract her during the race? With just fifteen yards to the finish line, they were still dead-even. Reverend Hastings patted grandpa on the back and told him, "If I were a betting man, I'd," but after receiving a very stern look from grandma, he moved away and found another spot from which to view the finish.

JL CRAWFORD

Barbara and Petey were still standing next to each other, Barbara rooting for her sister and Petey rooting for his best buddy. Barbara was so nervous she had her hands hanging straight down at her side, her fingers stretched to their fullest. Petey was spell-bound by the fact that the race was so close, amazed that Helena and Johnny were so closely matched. Barbara turned to glance at his reaction and could only smile at the bewildered look on his face. His mouth was still agape and he couldn't utter even a word, his hands open-faced against each side of his mouth. With ten feet left, it seemed apparent to everyone that this might be the first tie in Ashburn sled-racing history. The judges had already decided that, in the event of a tie, the race would be run again, agreeing that, "Surely, there couldn't be two ties in a row."

Helena knew that victory was hers and so did Johnny think that victory was his. With only five feet to the finish line, they looked at each other. Johnny was first to offer Helena his smile, but it was almost as quickly met by Helena's smile at him. Just as they were about to cross the finish line, they reached out and took each other's hand. Raising them skyward, they crossed the finish line in a dead tie! The crowd let out a roar that shook the snow on the peaks of Daedalus and Colossus. Everyone was waiting to hear what the judges would decide.

When Helena and Johnny had finally brought their sleds to a halt and walked back to the finish line, they were each met with well-wishes and congratulations. Some people were convinced that Helena had won and still others were convinced that Johnny had won. There was talk about another race, the first 'do-over' in Ashburn history, and that was the decision the judges came to. Calling Johnny and Helena over to the awards table and after getting the crowd to quiet down, the judges announced that another race was to occur after a fifteen-minute break.

Looking at each other though, and once again holding hands, the two they had clenched in the tie between them, Helena and Johnny waited for the crowd to settle down once again. Helena was first to speak, thanking everyone for cheering so hard, telling them that it was the hardest race she had ever run, and what a good racer Johnny was. Johnny also thanked everyone for cheering as they did and complimented Helena on being the toughest racing competitor he had ever raced against. With the crowd waiting for them to go back to the top of Wilkins Hill and do it all over again, Helena then said, "Johnny and I have decided that winning isn't the most important thing. We don't want to run another race." "That's right," Johnny chimed in. "Helena and I have decided that what's most important is just having a good time and having fun while sledding." Looking out at the crowd of friends, family, and well-wishers, they added in unison, "And this was the best fun we have ever had! We're glad that it's a tie!"

The roar of the crowd was so loud that a mini-avalanche of snow came barreling down Daedalus and Colussus. Helena and Johnny walked hand in hand over to where grandma and grandpa and Johnny's parents were standing. Their parents and grandparents were so proud of each of them that they got the biggest hugs of all time. Barbara and Petey had hugged when the decision of a tie was made official, with Johnny and Helena each receiving a trophy, but it was just a short, kid-type hug that left both of them feeling weird. As they walked over to congratulate Helena and Johnny though, they had slipped their hands together, completely unaware of doing so.

Barbara was chanting Helena's name and Petey was yelling for Johnny. As they got closer, Johnny and Helena both took notice of the hand-holding between Barbara and Petey and, staring at their hands then, looking questioningly at their faces, Helena asked, "Do you guys have something to tell us?" Only then realizing what everyone was staring at and what Helena was asking them, did they drop their hands quickly, putting two feet of distance between them, each proclaiming, "Yuck, why did you grab my hand," making faces all the while. With his arm round grandma's shoulder, grandpa said, relieved, "Phew! I'm almost prepared to deal with Helena and her first love, but I'm not ready for Barbara; at least not anytime soon!"

Walking arm in arm, they followed Helena and Johnny into town, who were walking hand in hand. Johnny was asking Helena about something called 'muffin-melts,' to which she replied, "Oh, they're just one of many wonderful traditions that we have in our family . . . that you just might have to get used to!" Johnny looked over at her and, realizing what her words meant, gave her his best smile and squeezed her hand a little more firmly. Barbara and Petey brought up the rear, separated by at least twenty feet, making yucky faces at each other the entire way.

In town, the four kids were greeted with great cheers. Helena and Johnny were co-champions for the year to come, Barbara was the saucer champ, and Petey was the sled champ for his age bracket. All of the age-bracket champions were collected in a group, first-place ribbons were awarded and the town applauded all of them. For the younger ages, all of the kids were brought forward for recognition and to receive ribbons. Those who were not covered in muffin-melt tomato sauce got to wear their ribbons home. Most of the kids' ribbons were presented to their parents for the trip home such was the popularity of grandma's muffin-melts!

Chapter 15

THE CHILDREN ENJOYED the snow for the full month of February and half of March, but on the first day of spring, Mother Nature brought them temperatures in the seventies and the snow was disappearing as though it were even hotter. Julia and Carl had been staying on the side of the barn where Floyd had stayed previously, where the sun did not shine. The air temperature was rising daily though, and they knew that it would soon be time for them to serve the greater purpose. Grandpa and Mr. Cranford were anxious to get the first crop into the ground, certain that this season would be just like the season they had enjoyed two years before. Grandpa had been busying himself in the barn for weeks, probably sharpening his tools, re-shoeing Bernie, and getting the plows ready, but no one really knew for certain. Grandma was talking about how this year's garden would be every bit as good as two years ago, if not better. She was convinced that the placement of the garden crosses would bring about even more good fortune. While the girls were not anxious for the snow to melt, they had been waiting for the ground to soften so they could place Aly's and Floyd's garden crosses into softer ground.

On the last day of March, a Friday, it was Good Friday. The family had just finished a sumptuous dinner and was still sitting at the table, preparing to talk about Easter Sunday. Grandpa noticed a swirling of activity outside the window, recognizing it as the way the snowflakes would get their attention. Going over to the window, he looked outside to see what was afoot. Turning back to face grandma and the girls he said,

"Well, it's not a snowstorm, but it appears they might have something to say." "Open the window, Walter," grandma told him. "Let's see what the snow wants." Never before did she think she would hear herself say something like that! Grandpa opened the window and in flew millions of snowflakes, led by Julia and Carl.

When the snowflakes had settled, Julia and Carl each landed on grandma's nose, much to her surprise. "My, my," grandma started. "To what do I owe this great honor?" "Dear lady," Carl began. "It is indeed our honor to address you and your family this night, for we make ready to serve the greater purpose in only a few days, depending upon the weather that Mother Nature brings." "Yes, Carl is right. It is our honor to speak with you," Julia added. "We wish to thank you also, for showing us and proving to us that this land is the true land of the snow angels. There are not many snowflakes remaining and we must all decide where it is we wish to serve the greater purpose."

"You are certainly welcome to serve the greater purpose anywhere on our land, if you wish," grandma told them. "The rivers, streams, and creeks are all running full and fast," grandpa added, "But they can always use more water, if you prefer. I believe the fields and pastures are all very moist as well. We cannot thank you enough for falling here as heavily as you did and for staying here so long. We will always be grateful for the snow." Helena and Barbara just couldn't wait to get a word in edge wise, each raising their hand as though they were in school. Barbara jumped in first, thanking the snow for coming to Ashburn, for staying so long and for all of the fun that they had enjoyed. Helena also thanked Julia and Carl and asked that they say thank you to all of the snowflakes not present, telling them that it was their leadership that helped convince the snow to stay in Ashburn. She asked whether they knew if snow would return to Ashburn next year and the next, curious to know what they thought, but half-knowing what their answer might be.

"As you know, Helena," Julia replied. "The snow cannot decide where it will go, but we can decide where we choose to serve the greater purpose. As long as Mother Nature doesn't blow us too far in one direction, we can land where we wish. We chose to land here because you provided us with the sign that this is the land of the snow angels. After we came to be here and heard the prayers of your people, we knew we had made the right decision, but we cannot speak for the snow of next year." Grandma started to raise her hand to speak, then realized she didn't have to, but asked, "Snowflakes, do you think it will be a good idea if we place the snow angel shapes on the ground throughout our land as we did last season?"

Carl quickly joined back in, telling grandma, "Dear lady, it was those angel shapes that first attracted us to your land, even though we thought later that it might have been just a trick. Without them, we may have flown over your land and kept on, but we also heard the prayers of the people of your land. Whether you place the angel shapes upon the land or not, you must convince all people of this land to say the prayers for snow, for we will hear their prayers even if we do not see angel shapes." Looking at all of them, grandma reminded them, "What have we said about the power of prayer? We must convince all of the people of Ashburn that they must pray for the snow." "I don't think you'll have any problem with that again, mother," grandpa told her. "Just look at how wonderful the snow was this season," and everyone shook their head in agreement.

Grandpa stood to open the window so the snowflakes could go back outside, but Carl called out to him, "Kind sir, if we may, we wish to speak with you more about serving the greater purpose." Sitting back down, grandpa said, "Yes, of course, please go ahead." Carl told them again about serving the greater purpose and how they were all deciding what to do. He reminded them of the story the family told them about Aly and Floyd, thinking that was a very special thing to do. Growing impatient, Julia jumped in, saying, "Excuse me Carl, but sometimes you just have to come out say something. What we would like to ask you, and why we are speaking directly with you," she said to grandma, "is whether we may also serve the greater purpose in your special garden. We know that much snow has fallen, but we also know that land which is used for growing food can never have too much water and moisture." Cutting her off, Carl added, "Ah, yeah, that's exactly what I was going to say. Also, dear lady, we believe it was you who were instrumental in getting so many people of this land to say prayers for snow and for making us so welcome. For these reasons, we would consider it a great honor if we could be allowed to serve the greater purpose in the place where Aly and Floyd served."

Before grandma could even say a word, Helena and Barbara were jumping up and down with joy, each of them shouting, "Oh, yes, yes, yes, you may certainly join Aly and Floyd in grandma's garden. That is the best idea of all time, isn't it grandma?" Grandma didn't need any convincing at all. She, too, was ecstatic with the idea, telling them, "Just as you said snowflake, gardens can never get too much water. Father, what do you think?" Grandpa stood up and moved toward the door, replying, "I think it's a fantastic idea, snowflakes. If you'll excuse me, I need to run out and check on Bernie."

Baffled by grandpa's abrupt departure, grandma turned to the girls and, asking no one in particular said, "What gets into that man? What could possibly be wrong with that horse that he must go outside at just this moment?" Surprised every bit as much as grandma, the girls just shrugged their shoulders and replied, "Beats me, grandma." While grandpa was outside, the girls pointed out the window to where grandma's garden was. Remembering the garden crosses, Helena told them, "We are going to honor Aly and Floyd by placing their crosses at each end of the garden. That way, from whichever end we go into or come out of grandma's garden, we will always remember them." Julia and Carl flew from grandma's nose to Helena's and Barbara's, landing gently on each. Looking at them both, Carl and Julia told them, "They must have been very special snowflakes to decide to serve the greater purpose in that spot, and your grandma must be a very special person for them to make that decision."

Unbeknownst to any of them grandpa had come back inside and was listening to the conversation. Before anyone could reply to their comment about grandma, Floyd, and Aly being special, grandpa began, "Snowflakes, you are correct. This woman, my beloved wife and grandmother to these most wonderful angels, is a very special person indeed. Her garden brings forth the bounty that it does in response to the love and care that she extends it. Aly and Floyd knew the benefit of water and moisture to a great garden and convinced the remaining snow to serve the greater purpose in that special place, which resulted in a great bounty until the severe heat and winds of the summer dried it out. The snow of this season though, will bring us another bounty as it did two seasons past, and your decision to serve the greater purpose in that same special place will make it only better." Still holding his hands behind his back, grandpa said further, "I had a very good feeling about you, Carl and Julia, for you were the snowflakes responsible for keeping the snow in our land when many snowflakes wished to go elsewhere. Whether you decided to serve the greater purpose here, after having been here for so long, or if you went elsewhere, I was prepared to honor your memory in the same way that we did Aly and Floyd."

Slowly pulling his hands from behind his back, grandpa brought forth two more garden crosses, handing one each to Helena and Barbara. Not having seen them before, Carl and Julia had no idea what they were, but the girls were beside themselves with joy, calling out, "Garden crosses! They're garden crosses for Julia and Carl! Look, Carl, look, Julia," the girls said, excitedly waving the crosses in front of each snowflake. Still not completely understanding the garden crosses, Helena told them, "One cross has your name on it, Carl, and the other has Julia's name on it. Now that we have four garden crosses, we can put one on all four sides of

JL CRAWFORD

grandma's garden!" Yeah," Barbara chimed in. "And, now we can always remember Carl and Julia, along with Floyd and Aly!" The two snowflakes seemed as though they might melt away that very moment such was the warm feeling that permeated the house. Looking at the girls and then to grandma and grandpa, Carl and Julia thanked them profusely for what they called the 'greatest honor a snowflake could ever imagine.'

Still not finished though, grandpa walked over to where grandma was sitting, still holding one hand behind his back. Standing next to grandma, grandpa said to all, "There is one more thing that will make grandma's garden complete, with your approval, of course, dear." Already excited to the point of bursting, the girls couldn't imagine what else could be done to make this the most special garden of all time, but unable to control themselves any longer, they shouted, "What, grandpa? What else is there to do? Please tell us!" From behind his back, grandpa pulled yet another garden cross and handed it to grandma. Confused, Barbara asked, "Grandpa, what other snowflakes have we to honor other than Aly, Floyd, Carl, and Julia?"

Having turned the cross over to look at the engraving on the front, grandma pulled it tightly to her chest and, lowering her head into her hands, began to weep. Placing his hand on her shoulder, grandpa told her, "Now, now, mother. No time for tears. This is supposed to be a happy memory." Wiping the tears from her eyes, she turned the cross for Helena and Barbara to see what grandpa had made. On the front of the cross was engraved from top to bottom, "Grandma's Garden" and, from side to side was engraved "Eleanor and Samuel." Well, that was enough to get all three of them balling their eyes out, until they had the presence of mind to run to grandpa and surround him with the best hug of all time!

When everyone had recovered from grandpa's wonderful surprise, Helena and Barbara spent the next few minutes explaining to Julia and Carl who Eleanor and Samuel were. Upon hearing the story, the snowflakes asked to be excused, afraid their snowflake tears would have them melt before they got to fly to grandma's garden. They said they were going to tell all of the remaining snowflakes about how the snow would always be remembered in this most special of places even in years should snow not fall on Ashburn which, they agreed, was "highly unlikely!" Still half-blubbering and half-speaking, Barbara jokingly told them, "After all the trouble we have gone through to get the snow to fall on our land, it better snow here every year, forever and ever," which brought a big laugh from everyone!

After Carl and Julia had flown out the window to round up all of the other snowflakes, grandpa asked the girls and grandma to come over to the table. Telling them he had an idea about placing the garden crosses, he reached into his coat pocket, pulled out a folded piece of paper and spread it out before them. Reminding them that grandma's garden was a very long rectangular shape, he told them how he had come up with the idea for the last garden cross. It had come to him when he was upstairs looking out at the garden from the window. When he had dug the garden years before, he had purposely designed it so that they could see the full length and breadth of it from the second-floor window, with the vantage point from the bottom of the garden to the top. Turning the paper so that it was longer from top to bottom, he took a pencil from his pocket and began to draw how he envisioned the crosses being placed. He hoped his design would bring about the most special garden in all the land, creating a lasting memory for their four, favorite snowflakes, all future snowflakes, Helena and Barbara's parents, and of course, grandma. Working slowly and very carefully, grandpa brought forth his vision of grandma's garden.

At the very top edge of the garden, right in the center, would be Aly's garden cross, and at the very bottom edge of the garden, in the center also, would be Floyd's garden cross. About one-third of the way down, on the far left-side edge would be Julia's garden cross. Immediately to the right of Julia's cross, smack in the center of the garden would be grandma's garden cross. Holding it up, grandpa pointed out that he had made it bigger

JL CRAWFORD

than the others, so all would know that this special place was grandma's garden. To the right of grandma's cross, on the far right-side edge of the garden would be Carl's garden cross. With his drawing complete, the girls and grandma stared closely at grandpa's design. Looking a little bewildered, Barbara said, "Grandpa, it looks like it's just a big 'T' shape." "No," Helena jumped in. "It's more like a big '+' sign." Together, they asked, "What's so special about a 'T' or a '+' sign, grandpa?" Her eyes tearing again and close to sobbing, grandma pointed out to the girls that grandpa's design was neither a 'T' nor a '+' sign. Instead, if they looked more closely, they would see that his design was in the shape of the "cross," with grandma's garden cross the focal point of the garden!

ALY'S GARDEN

G
R
A
JULIA'S GARDEN   ELEANOR AND SAMUEL   CARL'S GARDEN
D
M
A
'S

G
A
R
D
E
N

FLOYD'S GARDEN

Seeing it for themselves finally, the girls rushed to hug grandpa. Surrounding him, they covered him with kisses on both cheeks, telling him once more that he was the best grandpa of all time. Holding Julia's garden cross, Barbara pulled away from her grandpa and, standing with her hands on both hips, announced to all of them, "I have the best idea, everyone! Maybe, before all of the snowflakes fly over to grandma's garden, we should go put all of the garden crosses in place! What do you think, Helena? Grandma? Grandpa?" No one could deny that she had the unbridled exuberance of youth and at this moment, it knew no bounds. As she was running upstairs to get her coat and mittens, grandma called to her, "Just a moment, Barbara. Come here and sit. Before we go outside and place the garden crosses, I would like your grandpa to tell us how he came by this great inspiration for garden crosses and the design for all of the crosses in my garden. Walter, would you care to share your wisdom with us?"

Coming in from the kitchen and joining them in front of the fire, grandpa seated Helena and Barbara on the floor in front of where grandma was sitting in her favorite chair. Bending down on one knee next to grandma, his arm round her shoulders, looking from grandma to Helena to Barbara, he answered, "Mother, it was from no great wisdom that the idea for the garden crosses and your garden design came to me. I must confess though, any good idea which should come my way *is* due to the great inspiration I receive every day, just by virtue of being married to and loving the most wonderful woman in the world and, the great fortune I have to share my life with the two most precious angels of all time!" They all enjoyed a warm, wonderful family hug, with grandma crying happily and Helena and Barbara beaming with adoration and love for their grandparents. Breaking the solemnity of the moment, Barbara stood and, looking back and forth at Helena, then to her grandpa, said, "Grandpa, don't you mean your two precious 'snow' angels," which brought about a huge laugh from all of them!

They placed the garden crosses in grandma's garden later that day and, upon looking down on the garden from the upstairs window, all agreed that the placement represented a wonderful enactment of the cross of Jesus. The next morning, Carl and Julia rounded up billions and billions of snowflakes, all of them arriving in what appeared to be another furious snowstorm, but when they swirled high above grandma's garden, the girls knew what was about to happen. Dancing and darting, twirling and spinning, they put on one last glorious light show, all of them reflected brilliantly in the sun's golden rays. Grandma and grandpa had come out on the porch with the girls and watched with them.

From across the field, grandpa could see Mr. Cranford come running, Samson and Duchess were running beside him. Arriving nearly out of breath, he told them, "I thought you were having a blizzard over here. Thought I'd come and help." Grandpa told him what was going on and he sat down on the step and watched the show, amazed at the beauty of the spectacle. Samson and Duchess were in the middle of all of the snow, jumping up and down, trying to catch as many snowflakes with their tongues as they could reach. Finally, the snow settled on grandma's garden, every inch of it covered in almost one foot of snow. Helena and Barbara were holding onto Samson and Duchess when Carl and Julia flew over and landed on the porch railing.

Wondering why the two snowflakes weren't with the others, Helena asked them, "Why aren't you with the rest of your friends? You don't want to melt on the railing." Answering for both of them, Julia said, "We were going to land on our very own garden crosses and melt there, but Carl thought it might be nice to melt on the big cross in the middle. Would that be okay for us to do?" Moving close to the railing, grandma told them, "Snowflakes, I would be honored to have you land on my garden cross and to melt there. The girls' parents would also be honored to have you serve the greater purpose there, and thank you so very much for gathering all of your friends and having them serve the greater purpose in our garden. This garden belongs to everyone and the snow will always be welcome!" And with that, Carl and Julia flew off to grandma's garden cross, landing on each cross piece, one above Eleanor's name and the other above Samuel's name.

Enthused with emotion and vividly moved by the lovely gesture of the two snowflakes, grandma walked toward the garden. Turning her back to the garden and facing the girls, she spread her arms and legs and fell flat on her back, excitedly flapping her arms and legs together, laughing and laughing. In between laughs, she could be heard to yell, "Helen Broadhurst loves the snow!" Grandpa burst into a laughing fit as did Mr. Cranford, never having witnessed grandma do something so crazy. Helena and Barbara ran to the garden, inspired by their grandma's silliness and plopped down on their backs alongside grandma, the three of them making the last snow angels of the year! Samson and Duchess jumped and leaped all around them, furiously trying to catch as many snowflakes as they could, but found it much easier just to lick the snowflakes from Helena and Barbara's faces!

Chapter 16

MILD TEMPERATURES ARRIVED within days and before anyone realized, all of the snow in Ashburn had melted. Helena and Barbara told grandma and grandpa that they must go throughout Ashburn and pick up the cloth snow angels that grandpa, Mr. Clements, and Reverend Hastings had placed. Having completely forgotten about them, they arranged to do so that evening after the sun went down. They didn't want people to see what they were doing anymore than they wanted anyone to see them putting them down last season. Mother Nature was busy painting the land with all of her lustrous colors, including pink and yellow petunias, yellow and white daffodils, pink and red cherry blossoms, blue and purple begonias, orange mums, and the greenest grasses imaginable. Many trees had new leaves the lightest shade of green as they drank of the moisture from the roots on their way to being dark green and strong, while just as many still had their first buds, with new ones popping open daily. Helena couldn't wait for the first buttercups to open up and Barbara let her know in no uncertain terms that, she had had her fair share of buttercups last year! Helena just laughed it off and told her, "We'll see. Buttercups are good for the spirit, Barbara!" Each morning the girls went to school with flowers in their hair and came home with handfuls of flowers for grandma.

As expected, because of the heavy snow, grandma's garden was soon bursting with the first vegetables of the season. Grandpa and Mr. Cranford had already put in their first crop, earlier than ever before.

They knew for sure that a second crop was guaranteed and were actually talking about the possibility of a third crop this year—the first time that would ever have happened! The ground was so moist and rich that the plow blade carved through it like a "hot knife through butter," grandpa had said one day when coming in from the fields. Cragun's Creek was filled to the top of its banks and word had it that the Rapidon River was flowing at an all-time high. The pond where most kids went swimming was still ice cold and the cool spring mornings weren't going to allow it to warm up anytime soon. The girls still wore light jackets to school each morning, but had them slung over their shoulders on the way home. Helena was always seen skipping gaily along, flowers behind each ear and in her hair.

Even though there was no snow remaining with whom to talk, the girls still pretended it was there, thanking Carl and Julia as though they were on the end of their nose. Barbara asked Helena one afternoon, "Do you think that Carl and Julia ever got to meet up with Aly and Floyd? I think they would have been the best of friends!" Helena responded, telling her, "Well, heaven is supposed to be a very big place, with room for animals and people. Why not room for snowflakes, too!"

Spring quickly turned into summer and the kids were out of school once more. Johnny Cranford was working full-time for his father and grandpa as the crops were coming in so fast and furious they couldn't keep up with them. Grandpa and Johnny's dad decided that it was time he got paid for all of his hard work and between them, said they had never had as hard a worker as Johnny. He was becoming very tall and quite strong, features not overlooked by Helena, who was still being teased daily by Barbara. Grandma's garden had been such a great success that she had filled every canning jar she owned and the full summer was still ahead of her. One day she asked Johnny Cranford to take the wagon into town to buy some more canning jars. He had never before taken a wagon into town all by his self and the great pride showed on his face. His father

　　　JL CRAWFORD

reminded him to be very careful, but grandpa said, "Aw, don't worry, Buddy, ol' Bernie here knows his way back and forth!"

Jumping onto the wagon seat from out of nowhere, Helena proclaimed, "Yeah, we'll be okay. Good old Bernie will take good care of both of us!" Red-faced and somewhat embarrassed, but very pleasantly so, Johnny put a soft reins to Bernie and off they went. Grandpa looked over at Buddy and said, "You know, if I didn't know better, I would have sworn that ol' Bernie looked over and gave me a wink!" As they watched them drive off towards town, they couldn't help but notice Helena scoot a little closer to Johnny, prompting grandpa to issue, "Oh brother!" When they witnessed Johnny put his arm round her shoulder, Mr. Cranford playfully poked Walter in the ribs and said, "That's my boy!"

Summer found Johnny turn fourteen, Helena thirteen, and Barbara eleven. Barbara had caught the eye of a new boy whose family had moved to Ashburn. He was twelve and, according to Barbara, much more mature than Petey! As a result, Petey Braun was seldom seen. Grandpa and Mr. Cranford had already brought in their second crop by the middle of July and the third crop of the year was already in the ground. The summer heat was quite normal this year, nothing like the blistering, dry temperatures of last year. The ground was still moist and quite fertile, so much that grandpa and Buddy were thinking about a fall crop as well. All of the farms in Ashburn were doing well and folks were talking about having enough food for two years to come.

Reverend Hastings reminded everyone of the importance of keeping the church food supplies plentiful and no sooner had he mentioned that one Sunday, then the church pantry was flooded with food supplies the very next day. Folks were thanking him because, as one woman said, "I don't have any more room in my pantry or my cellar, and my husband is bringing in more food every single day!" The girls swam in Cragun's Creek almost every day, only seeing Johnny at the end of the day or on Saturday, when grandpa and Mr. Cranford gave him the day off. He told

Helena that by the end of the summer he would have enough money saved up to buy his own horse and maybe, a gift for her, too!

Faster than anyone could remember, summer was over and school started up once more. Just as they had thought, grandpa and Buddy had harvested their third crop of the season and the fourth one was in the ground. Never before had they sowed and reaped the harvest of three crops in a single season, and this year had brought four! They were sure to remind Reverend Hastings of the fact and he was quick to tell all the parishioners to continue to say thanks for the snow of the past year and to pray for even more snow this year. Any time a bit of grumbling was heard, he would ask one of the farmers to stand and tell of the abundance of crops grown and that would settle things down. He also reminded them of the power of prayer and how it had delivered snow only to those areas where it was loved and wanted.

He regularly asked the few snow-grumblers, whose numbers lessened each week, "Did you have any snow on your porch last year? On your steps or on your roof? Was there any snow on the roads?" When nary a soul could answer in the affirmative, he simply recommended, in his very encouraging way, that everyone pray for snow in their own way, even where they did not want snow to fall. He told them all that he "had it on very good account," that the prayers they said were heard not just by Jesus, but by Mother Nature as well. When he asked if anyone could question his 'connection with a higher power,' not a single hand was raised!

By the first of October, the temperatures had dropped into the high thirties and were forecast by the Almanac to drop even lower. The clouds were forming high above Daedalus and Colossus and everyone's hopes for snow were even higher! Within days, the peaks of the two fierce mountains were covered in snow, but none had fallen yet in Ashburn. One evening, when a bitter mist was falling, grandpa came inside and proclaimed, "I think tonight just might be the night for the first snow.

There's lots of moisture in the air and it's plenty cold!" He went out to the barn and gathered up all of the cloth snow angels that had been stored flat on tables in his barn. Putting them in the back of the wagon, he made his way over to Buddy Cranford's house and asked him if he wanted to help him with a "special project." Always helpful and neighborly, Buddy said he would be glad to help, not even knowing what he was in store for.

They drove over to Harold Clements' house and on the way, grandpa told Buddy what they were going to do. Flabbergasted, all he could say over and over was, "Well, I'll be darned!" By midnight, Harold, Buddy, and grandpa had distributed close to one hundred snow angels throughout Ashburn, as conspicuously as they could, though each of them wondered what if the snow didn't fall. Almost as one, they all said, "The power of prayer, my friend!"

To everyone's delight, Ashburn awoke to more than two feet of snow everywhere, except for the porches, steps, roofs, and roads! "It's a miracle!" was heard over and over, wherever anyone went. Helena and Barbara made new snowflake friends and asked about snowflakes of old, whether anyone knew of the elder snowflake of years passed, or who had heard of the land of the snow angels. They were told by the new snowflakes that Mother Nature had told them of a land so-called, and they should look for it after crossing the highest peaks in the land.

Pretending not to know anything of what they were talking about, they feigned ignorance when the snowflakes told them they had seen what appeared to be hundreds of snow angels in this land as they flew over. Reminding the girls of the importance of telling the truth, grandma thought they should make a full disclosure about the cloth snow angels and let the snow of this season decide if Ashburn was where they wished to stay and serve the greater purpose. Telling grandma how wise she was, the girls gathered a group of snowflakes together. They began by falling backwards and making real snow angels and then told them the entire story from start to finish.

When the girls had finished telling them the story, the snow arose high into the sky as they had seen snow of past seasons do. Not knowing for certain just what the snowflakes were going to do, Barbara and Helena called out to them, "We love you snowflakes! All of the citizens of Ashburn love the snow." In a startling downward wave, the snow flew all around them, finally settling at their feet, covering the ground everywhere in sight and Helena and Barbara as well. Grandpa and grandma had come out onto the porch to watch and were laughing and laughing at the spectacle. A very fat snowflake landed on Helena's nose and when she heard him say, "Hello, Helena," she shook her head furiously, shaking off enough snow so she could finally see out of one eye. Her mouth wide open, she asked, "How do you know my name, snowflake?" No sooner had she asked that then all of the snowflakes burst into laughter! The fat snowflake hopped up and down a couple of times on her nose, then settled down.

After the rest of the snowflakes had quieted down as well, the fat snowflake introduced himself, saying, "Helena, my dear lady, I am Franz. I know your name as do all of the snowflakes here. We also know Barbara's name." This drew a frenzied, harried shake of Barbara's head, accompanied by the loudest sneeze, which blew snow in every direction. Grandma and grandpa had moved closer, not wanting to miss a bit of this show. Franz continued to tell them that the snowflakes also knew grandma and grandpa and all about the cloth 'snow angels' that were laid throughout the land to help guide the newly arriving snow to the land of the snow angels. "But how do you know all of this?" Helena asked in total surprise. Franz went on to tell them that many snowflakes had travelled round the globe this past winter and regaled Mother Nature and the new snow of this season with the stories they had heard from snowflakes named Carl and Julia. "Oh, you must come see," Barbara shouted as she jumped off the porch in the direction of grandma's garden. As she was so used to doing though, she landed face first in two feet of snow, which drew a laugh from every snowflake, Helena, and grandma and grandpa, too! Jumping up and down with glee, Barbara laughed it off and made her way to grandma's garden.

Just as Franz landed on her nose, Barbara pointed out the garden crosses of Carl and Julia for all of the snowflakes to see. Running next to those of Aly and Floyd, she told them all about how the snowflakes had decided to serve the greater purpose in grandma's garden. Even though the snowflakes had already decided that this was the land where they should stay and serve the greater purpose, this sight sealed the deal. Franz told the girls how special it was that they should honor and remember four snowflakes when trillions had visited this land. Helena quickly reminded Franz that Aly, Floyd, Carl, and Julia were not just 'any' four snowflakes, but were very special snowflakes in deed, and that was why they had decided to honor them with garden crosses. All of the snow in earshot rose up and flew in great circles around grandma's garden, swirling round and round, over and under the crosses, before finally settling down. One snowflake landed on Helena's nose, another on Barbara's, and yet another on grandpa's nose. Franz landed on grandma's nose. Looking at her then, turning so all of the snowflakes could hear, he said, "The snow loves these kind, wonderful people! The snow loves Ashburn . . . the real land of the snow angels!"

That year, snow fell on Ashburn even more than the year before, but only where people wanted it to fall, and never where people did not wish for it to fall. No children went hungry for the great bounty of the past season and Ashburn even had enough food to help neighboring lands in need. In years to come, Ashburn received snowfall amounts in record volumes. Communities that did not receive as much snow as they wished sent wagons to retrieve all they wanted and the citizens of Ashburn gladly shared what had fallen, always telling them, "You must love the snow and want the snow. The snow is your friend just as it is ours, and you must trust the snow!" At both ends of town, the town council had approved the placement of signs that read, "Welcome to Ashburn—The Land Where Snow is Loved and Wanted." No one ever found out who the miscreants were that scratched the words, "and the land of snow angels," but grandma and grandpa figured they just might have an idea!

The End

CPSIA information can be obtained
at www.ICGtesting.com
Printed in the USA
BVHW031315091219
566100BV00003B/6/P

9 781483 637341